THUNDER STICKS

It was a small camp. Only two tipis remained erect. The others smoldered atop charred lodge poles. Nearby brownish clumps lay strewn like so many discarded sacks. Cloud Dancer saw these were bodies. Dried blood stained bare backs and shoulders. Foreheads were split open where scalplocks had been cut away. A boy Cloud Dancer recognized as Rabbit Tail sat beside a slain woman, holding his left arm and fighting back tears.

"What manner of wound is this?" Cloud Dancer asked. A terrible swelling above the wrist was stained black with flecks of powder.

"It was the Kiowas," Rabbit Tail said. "With them rode a hairy face and another of the pale people. They pointed sticks at us that exploded like thunder. I tried to stop them; but the hairy face touched his fire stick to my arm, and I was thrown back."

"We must tend to the dead," Cloud Dancer said to the Suhtai who had ridden with him. "Then we will summon others. This deed must not go unpunished!"

THE
MEDICINE TRAIL

G. CLIFTON WISLER

ZEBRA BOOKS
KENSINGTON PUBLISHING CORP.

ZEBRA BOOKS

are published by

Kensington Publishing Corp.
475 Park Avenue South
New York, NY 10016

First printing: June, 1991

Printed in the United States of America

Chapter One

It was early. Darkness still bathed the half-sphere of his father's mud hut, and only the quiet breathing of his parents on the far side of the lodge broke the perfect silence. He yawned. Most days he would have burrowed deeper into the heavy buffalo hide and lost himself in sleep. But this day was different. He shook off the hide and hurriedly dressed himself.

That didn't take long. Boys who had not yet seen their eleventh winter wore only a deerskin breechclout and moccasins in the autumn. When the snowy breath of winter came, their mothers or aunts or sisters would provide leggings and shirts. Later a wife would tend to such things.

"Your mother still has many winters of sewing," Laughing Bear had announced the day before. "What girl would have you? It would take twenty buffalo hides! More. Your father doesn't have enough."

The words stung. The laughter of the other boys hurt even more.

"He will never be much," they all agreed. "He is just a dreamer."

5

It was what they called him now—Dreamer. The men wondered how it was possible, a son of Gray Wolf and Little Crane. His father had named him Little Wolf—after a grandfather who had led the People through many struggles. It was a chief's name, and great things were expected from the boy who carried it.

"It's a punishment," some said. "Man Above takes offense when a brave-heart name is given to one yet unproven."

Or perhaps it was Trickster, who was forever bringing trouble down on the People, who had shaped Little Wolf into a smallish thing, a boy doomed to lag behind the others and stare off into the distance, lost in his dreams.

Yes, Dreamer thought as he crawled through the short, narrow tunnel that led outside. *It must be Trickster. Who else could put so many twists and turns in a boy's path?*

Dreamer emerged from the lodge and stepped out into the crisp morning air. It was turning cool. The plum moon was already gone, and the leaves of the cottonwoods and willows were showing traces of amber and scarlet. The deer and buffalo were taking on their winter coats, and the men set out from the village often to hunt. Hides were needed to keep off the icy chill. Meat was being dried so as to be ready when the snows came.

Dreamer knew all this only too well. Laughing Bear and the other boys set out with their fathers and uncles in search of deer, and many times a boy returned boasting of his skill with the bow.

"This deer will feed my family!" Laughing Bear had declared proudly as he and his uncle, Avenging Crow, had dragged a carcass past Gray Wolf's lodge.

Dreamer had dropped his gaze toward the ground. Often he walked beside his father, hoping they would spy a deer or even a rabbit. But soon his mind filled with other things. He would stare at a hawk turning circles in the skies overhead or sit beside a stream and listen to the water's song as it bubbled over rocks.

"The hunt requires concentration," Gray Wolf had told his son. "Perhaps when you're older."

When I'm older, Dreamer thought. How often had he heard those words!

He crept through the camp, taking care not to alarm the camp dogs. Whenever he neared one, it would lift its nose and sniff the air. But dogs were used to boy scent and took little notice. Dreamer tried sniffing, too. He noted the burnt odor of old cook fires and the stale aroma of dew-dampened hides. He recognized the foul stench of the dog camp, too, and quickened his pace. The air was much sweeter at the river.

He stood beside the water for some time, staring toward the east as dawn painted the horizon yellow-red. Soon Sun would climb into the sky, and a new day would be born.

Perhaps this will be the day when I kill a deer, Dreamer thought. He turned to stare at the weapon stand where his boys' bow rested beside the larger one carried by his father. Could such a thin bow help a young arm lend enough power to a stone-tipped arrow that it might snatch the life of a deer?

"Man Above," Dreamer quietly prayed, "give me the true aim. Make my arm strong. Give me a warrior heart."

Dreamer jumped as he felt a heavy hand grasp his shoulder. For an instant he thought the all-knowing one

7

himself might be there. Instead the boy glanced up into the eyes of his uncle, Touches the Sky.

It was a long way to look. Two bows laid end to end would not much surpass the top of Touches the Sky's forelock. He towered over everyone, even the other men. Gray Wolf, his own brother, was shorter by an arm's length.

"Uncle?" Dreamer asked as he recaptured his wits.

"It's good to make prayers," Touches the Sky said, nodding somberly. "But not that way. Come greet the grandfathers with me."

Dreamer followed as his uncle walked along the river. They left the village and its surrounding fields behind. Finally Touches the Sky climbed a low hill overlooking the river and gazed eastward toward the rising sun.

"Stand here," Touches the Sky said as he motioned Dreamer to his side. "I will make a fire. Then we will pray."

Dreamer stood silently while his uncle piled tinder on the red earth and struck flint to create a spark. As the tinder began to glow, Touches the Sky blew on it. Soon a flame appeared, and Touches the Sky added small twigs. As the fire grew, he drew out a long pipe. Before lighting it, he offered tobacco to Mother Earth, Father Sky, and to the four cardinal directions. Then he lit the pipe and smoked briefly.

"Touch your lips to the pipe," Touches the Sky instructed, and Dreamer did so. The bitter taste of the tobacco made him cough, but his uncle only nodded and took back the pipe.

"Grandfathers," Touches the Sky bellowed, "thank you for this day. Thank you for the struggles it will bring. We know they will make our people strong.

Thank you for the rain that makes the plants grow. Thank you for the warmth of sacred sun. Bring us game that we may hunt our winter food. Give us power that we may understand what will come to be."

"Pray now," Touches the Sky said, handing the pipe to Dreamer.

"Grandfathers," the boy began. Then he paused. What should he say? Why would the spirits listen to the mutterings of a boy after hearing such words as Touches the Sky spoke?

"Speak," his uncle urged.

"Grandfathers, help me to grow tall," Dreamer prayed. He saw his uncle's frown and regretted the words. "Show me the sacred path," Dreamer added. This time Touches the Sky nodded. "Make me strong in the ways of Man Above."

The wind seemed to sing an answer, and the sun blazed brighter. The boy trembled as he felt something touch his bare back—something unseen and hitherto unknown. Dreamer gazed up reverently and watched as clouds slowly crept across the sky.

"It's well," Touches the Sky said as he touched the pipe to his nephew's lips and then his own. He smoked once for Mother Earth, again for Father Sky, and then for each of the sacred directions. Finally he put out the pipe and sat beside the fire, waiting for it to extinguish itself. Only when the last embers had died did the man turn toward Dreamer.

"You've done well," Touches the Sky declared. "Man Above may answer you. I saw the wind touch you, and you showed no fear. Others have."

"I don't understand, Uncle," the boy replied.

"There's time, Dreamer," Touches the Sky assured

9

him. "You're young. Understanding is a thing for old men. Time brings it. Now is the time for believing. And trusting. Believe in the spirit voices that will come to you, and trust what they tell you. Everything else will flow from that."

"Is that how it was for you?"

"As it is even now, Nephew. Now we must go to the river."

Dreamer nodded, and the two of them descended the hill and hurried back toward the village.

Each morning, as the sun broke over the village, the men gathered at the river for their morning swim.

"It's good to greet the day as we once greeted life," Gray Wolf had once explained. The water washed away sickness and made a man strong. As soon as a boy desired to come, he followed. Dreamer had come for a long time now, as had other boys. The younger ones grouped to one side and respectfully waited for their elders to splash into the water first. Only a boy who had counted coup on an enemy or had received a wound in battle was welcome among the warriors.

More than one boastful young hunter had daringly joined his father too soon. Some uncle or brother quickly splashed over and plunged the offender's head under the river. Afterward he was certain to be taunted and jeered, or perhaps dragged bare into camp for the women to see.

"See this one!" someone would shout. "He thinks himself a man!"

Dreamer kept warily clear of even the older boys. His bony brown shoulders bore no scars, nor even much flesh. No one would have mistaken him for a man. Sometimes he would gaze upon his father's scarred chest and thighs and remember the stories he had heard of hard fights against the Chippewa people to the north. And he would wonder if his time would ever come.

It was at such times that Laughing Bear would creep up and jump upon Dreamer's back, burying him in the muddy bottom and howling with triumph. Once the Bear had even sliced off a lock of Dreamer's hair.

"See how I've counted coup!" the larger boy had cried.

That morning Laughing Bear came as before, but Dreamer sensed it. He turned at the last minute. Laughing Bear plunged face first beneath the surface, and when he reappeared, sputtering, Dreamer dipped his head and rammed the Bear's middle.

"Umph!" Laughing Bear grunted as he helplessly sank in the river.

"Help him!" the other boys, who had fled from the expected battle, urged.

Dreamer scowled, then reached down, grabbed Laughing Bear's arms, and dragged the limp boy to the bank. As the Bear recovered his breath, he stared up with anything but gratitude.

Enemies are so easily made, Dreamer thought. *Friends only with great skill.*

He returned to the river, and for once the other boys seemed to crowd around him. Even so, he busied himself with washing and avoided the foolishness of the others.

"He's a strange one," Corn Boy remarked.

The others nodded. But where before their eyes had shown contempt, they now held a mixture of surprise and respect.

When Dreamer had washed away his weariness and made himself ready for another day, he left the river and dressed himself. Then he hurried to his father's lodge. His mother was busy building up the morning cook fire. He watched her stack bundles of tall grass collected across the river, then bring a coal from a nearby fire to ignite them. Then he added sticks and logs until the fire was ready for her cooking pot.

Little Crane was small and graceful, as her name implied. Dreamer never tired of watching his mother pound corn flour into a paste for baking. Her hair, black as a raven, was tied in twin braids which fell down her back. She wore a simple deerskin dress with blue beads sewn down the front. Halfway between the knee and ankle the dress stopped, showing off her delicate calves.

Her left arm was bare, and six red stripes painted there attested to the coups counted by her husband.

Yes, Dreamer thought, *Father is a brave heart. Will I ever be?*

His thoughts were interrupted by the camp crier, who started at the opening of the camp circle, facing the sun, and called out news of the People. A son was born to Stalk Woman. Two warriors of the Windpipe band had come in search of wives. Finally the crier recounted the laws of the camp and the commands of the camp chiefs. It was not yet winter, and so there were no new instructions. No enemies were near, so the war chiefs were silent.

Dreamer nodded as the crier walked south across the village circle to repeat his news. Gray Wolf, as a respected warrior, had an honored place near the opening of the circle. Far across, on the north, Laughing Bear

12

stared angrily as his mother examined his ribs. Per
the Bear's resentment stemmed from his origins. H
own father was dead. He now lived in the lodge of
Avenging Crow, an uncle, who saw to the needs of his
own wife and the widows of two dead brothers. There
were nine children as well. Even a great hunter would
be sore pressed to provide for so many, and Avenging
Crow often depended upon the generosity of others to
feed his large family.

"They have a hard time," Little Crane observed as
she shoveled coals from the fire with the shoulder blade
of a buffalo. She placed the glowing embers in an
earthen oven. As the oven warmed, she slid her
pounded corn cakes inside. Soon the aroma of baking
bread flooded the air.

By the time the cakes were ready, Gray Wolf had arrived. He broke the first of the cakes and offered some
to the fire, to Mother Earth and Father Sky. He then
thanked all for the bounty they had provided.

"Always we walk the true path," he concluded. Then
they hungrily ate.

"I hunt today," Gray Wolf explained after swallowing
the last of the corn cakes. "Will you go with me,
Naha'?"

"I have the fish traps to set," Dreamer reminded his
father. "And I have started a lance."

"Set the traps," Gray Wolf replied. "The lance can
wait. Touches the Sky has had a dream of many deer.
We'll hunt."

"Yes, Ne' hyo," Dreamer answered respectfully. "Us
alone?"

"Others, too. Avenging Crow has need of meat."

Dreamer sighed. He didn't welcome another encounter with Laughing Bear.

Dreamer did his best to avoid trouble that morning. He and Corn Boy fetched the traps — willow twigs woven into a thatch, with bait to attract the larger river fish. It was easy for a fish to enter the trap, but the door would close behind it. Smaller fish could slip between the twigs, but the large ones would be hauled out of the river ready for a waiting cook fire.

The two ten-year-olds knew the river well, and they were skillful at locating the traps in the best pools. It was a game of sorts, trying to catch the most fish. Once Dreamer had hauled out a trap with three monsters in it!

On their trips to the river, they sometimes spied on the girls busy gathering wood and roots in the nearby wood. Sometimes the boys would taunt these girls, but only the older boys were allowed to harass the women. Once Laughing Bear had shot an arrow into a water flask and been set upon by ten girls. They pricked his back with porcupine quills and tied him to a willow.

Afterward his uncle had scolded him for his actions.

"Uncle, I have seen others do the same thing," the Bear had complained.

"You are still a boy!" Avenging Crow had answered, dragging Laughing Bear to the lodge of his mother's father. There the grandfathers had told frightening tales of boys who had boasted too often.

As for Dreamer, it was enough to watch. The pranking time would come later.

After the traps were set, Dreamer and Corn Boy returned to the village. Along the way they dodged younger children at play, wrestling in the mud or throwing blunt arrows at each other. In the village, men sat be-

14

side their fires, smoking and gossiping. Older boys huddled near the grandfathers, learning to craft arrows and lances. Others worked willow and ash limbs into bows.

Most days Dreamer would have sat beside Touches the Sky, listening as his uncle spoke of visions or told old stories of the long-ago times. But Gray Wolf and Avenging Crow were standing with bows in hand, and Dreamer knew better than to keep his father waiting.

"Can I come?" Corn Boy asked as Laughing Bear hurried over.

"A boy should hunt with his father," Laughing Bear declared.

Corn Boy frowned. His father, Hawk Feather, had taken Corn Boy's three brothers on a long journey to visit his brother among the Hill People.

"You're welcome," Gray Wolf said, and Avenging Crow nodded. Laughing Bear glared as the two smaller boys hurried to fetch their bows and arrows.

It was Gray Wolf who led the way from the village. Avenging Crow walked on his left, and the boys fell in behind. Dreamer tried to slip in beside his father, but Laughing Bear pushed him away.

Dreamer thought to strike back, but he didn't. Instead he dropped back with Corn Boy. The hunters forded the river and spread out in a line as they entered the woods. Dreamer tried to concentrate on the task at hand, but he soon found the songs of the birds a distraction. The trees themselves seemed to come alive, singing an autumn hymn that touched the boy's spirit. When he looked up, Dreamer discovered the others far ahead.

Even so, he was the first to spy a deer. It was just a

fawn, but following, he came upon three larger animals drinking at a pond. The largest was a tall buck which seemed suddenly alarmed.

A large hand then clamped Dreamer's shoulder. He turned and saw Gray Wolf's stone face urge quiet.

For several minutes the hunters stood, silently praying to the deer spirits to make their aim true. Then Avenging Crow readied an arrow and fired. The shot missed, and the deer sprang into flight. Laughing Bear and Corn Boy loosed arrows, but the fleeing deer outdistanced each. Only Gray Wolf's shot found a target, for he had held back and waited for a deer to close the range. The arrow took a doe in the throat, and the Wolf was able to stalk the wounded animal and kill her with a second shot.

"Ayyyy!" the others cried when they saw what Gray Wolf had done.

"Come, brothers," the Wolf urged as he made the throat cut. "Share my kill."

As they butchered the carcass, Dreamer heard Laughing Bear grumbling.

"I might have killed a deer myself if Dreamer had not alerted them."

"It was my shot started the deer," Avenging Crow insisted.

"He should have stayed with us," Laughing Bear argued.

"It's not his way," Corn Boy whispered. "I saw. The spirits spoke to him."

"No, he's just a dreamer," Laughing Bear said, laughing. "One day he will be dreaming, and the Chippewa people will take his hair."

Gray Wolf scowled, and Dreamer ached inside. He

longed to prove his worth to his father—to everyone. But how could he explain that the birds and the trees had called to him? He didn't understand it himself.

Chapter Two

Dreamer had always been different, but never did he feel it so intensely as that afternoon. Laughing Bear scurried through the camp like a hungry dog, telling of how Dreamer had spoiled the hunt.

"Pay him no attention," Gray Wolf urged. "It's always the way with the boastful ones. They're forever blaming their failures on others."

"Father, what he's saying . . . it isn't true, is it?" Dreamer asked. "Did I warn the deer?"

"No more that the sun did," Gray Wolf declared, laughing. "You walk quietly, more spirit than boy. Had Laughing Bear come upon us, no animal could fail to have heard. But not you, Naha'."

"I fell behind, Ne' hyo."

"No, your path led you in a different direction."

"I didn't mean to stray."

"You didn't. When spirits call a man, he must follow."

"No one understands," Dreamer said, sighing.

"No one?" his father asked. "You're not the first. You walked with your uncle this morning."

"He told you?"

"I saw you come to the river together. I remember how it was with him. I tried to teach him the warrior

18

path, but he was forever setting off alone, staring at the sky, or speaking with the birds. It's a hard path, that one. A lonely one, I think. But what would the People be without Touches the Sky? He has the far-seeing eyes."

"He knows things."

"All things, Dreamer. I think you must go to him. Let him be your guide on the path you must travel."

Dreamer gazed sadly at his father. Gray Wolf had but one son. Surely Trickster was at work, sending a dreamer to walk at the side of such a famed warrior.

"We can hunt again tomorrow," Dreamer suggested.

"We have meat enough for now," Gray Wolf answered. "And you will be busy."

And so he was. Even before dawn broke that next morning, Gray Wolf was leading his son through the darkened camp to the lodge of Touches the Sky. Gray Wolf crawled through the door, then sat with his legs folded beneath him on the right side of the door. Dreamer settled in beside his father, and they waited patiently. Touches the Sky was sitting on a buffalo robe on the far side of a fire, warming himself. The tall man looked up as if to acknowledge his visitors, but he said nothing.

Dreamer felt strange. Many times he had walked with his uncle, but only rarely had he stepped into this lodge. It was a place of strong medicine, for Touches the Sky was famous as a healer. His cures had chased illness from the camp many times, and he often restored health to the infirm.

But Touches the Sky was much more than a medicine

chief. He understood the greatest mysteries of all. And although Dreamer didn't truly understand much of the tall man's magic, he knew its source. Touches the Sky was the keeper of the four sacred Arrows of the People — its greatest medicine.

Finally Touches the Sky looked up and motioned for them to come closer.

"My brother and his son are welcome," he said as Gray Wolf and Dreamer slowly crawled around the circular lodge until they had joined their guest on the buffalo robes. It might have been quicker to cross the center of the lodge, but that wasn't allowed. To come between a host and the fire invited misfortune for all.

"I killed a deer, Brother," Gray Wolf said as he sat. "Perhaps you will help us eat it."

"Little Crane's a good cook," Touches the Sky replied. "I will come tonight. But that's not why you've come."

"No," Gray Wolf admitted. "My son is troubled. His dreams are full of mysteries, even when he's awake. He seeks an understanding."

"Ah, that can only come from Man Above. But we will walk. I welcome company. I'm too often alone."

"You should take a woman," Dreamer advised. The words were met with two frowns, and the boy bowed his head in apology.

"Earthly ways are not for Arrow-keepers," Touches the Sky said somberly. "It's solitude that gives him power."

Dreamer nodded respectfully, but he didn't begin to understand. There were obviously many mysteries along the medicine trail.

For a time Gray Wolf and Touches the Sky sat and talked. They recounted old times when, as boys, they had hunted and fished together.

"Then the spirits came to me," Touches the Sky explained. He was speaking to his brother, but the words seemed aimed at Dreamer. "It's a hard path I walk. Often I think of the warrior road and wish it were mine. But a man doesn't choose such things."

"No," Gray Wolf agreed as he drew Dreamer close. "All he can do is seek to understand what he is. Soon my son must decide his path. Maybe you will walk with him today."

"Yes," Touches the Sky agreed. "We'll smoke on it."

Touches the Sky produced a pipe, and the brothers smoked. Then Gray Wolf withdrew as he had come. Dreamer started to follow, but his uncle stopped him.

"No, we go later," the tall man explained. "Soon we must greet the new day."

Dreamer nodded. After Touches the Sky dressed, he led the way along the river to the hill. And once again Dreamer stood at his uncle's side and made the morning prayers.

Afterward they sat together on the hillside and gazed out past the river as the sun rose in the eastern sky.

"Uncle, is it hard walking the sacred path?" Dreamer asked.

"Hard?" Touches the Sky asked, laughing. "Is it hard to breathe?"

"Sometimes," Dreamer said, frowning. "When Laughing Bear holds me under at the river, I think my lungs will burst."

"A good answer. Life is often difficult in the same way. Not because it is by nature, but because we try the impossible."

"Most things seem impossible to me."

"That will change. When you let the spirits guide you, they will show you the way, the sacred path."

"Will you teach me, Uncle?"

"Perhaps," Touches the Sky answered. "If the spirits call you."

"How will I know?"

"You will know," the tall man assured him. "And so will I."

Dreamer nodded, but he didn't understand. He suspected, though, that it was but one of the mysteries whose solution lay ahead.

"Now it's time to go to the river," Touches the Sky announced as he rose.

"And after?" Dreamer asked.

"You should join the other boys. Learn from them. The spirits can't teach you everything."

So Dreamer followed his uncle to the river. They joined the others in the stream, washing and splashing about. And for once Dreamer shared in the foolishness.

In the days that followed, Dreamer did his best to heed Touches the Sky's advice. He swam and wrestled and raced. Whenever Gray Wolf set off into the wood in search of game, Dreamer followed. Once he shot rabbits, but deer was always too elusive.

In the evenings, Dreamer sat among the grandfathers, listening to their stories of long-ago times. Sometimes Corn Boy or one of the others would come, but only Dreamer stayed until the last words were spoken.

One night, as he returned to his father's lodge, Little Crane drew him aside.

"Your father's fire is too quiet," she said. "He misses you. Stay with him more."

"I'll try, Nah' koa," Dreamer replied.

"Soon enough a boy takes his own path," she added. "A woman should have many sons. We are not blessed that way. I hoped we would have many summers yet, but I see now I must soon lose you."

"How?"

"You have the strangeness of all medicine men in your eyes. Your uncle sees it, and your father, too."

"And you?"

"Yes, little one. So I ask you to stay while it's still possible. You'll be alone soon enough."

Dreamer welcomed her embrace, but he could have told her he was alone already. Perhaps he had always been so.

Dreamer's introduction to the medicine ways came quite by accident. One morning, after setting the fish traps at the river, he and Corn Boy joined the younger boys at the bank. In the beginning, they formed monsters from the wet red clay. Strange figures took shape, and the young ones laughed and taunted their clay men. Then Corn Boy scooped mud and flung it at a monster. It missed and struck his cousin, Younger Elk. Younger Elk made his own mud ball and struck Corn Boy on the side of the head. Others joined in, and soon mud was flying everywhere. Boys darted into the village, seeking the shelter of lodges as protection from their attackers.

Dreamer stayed at the river and was struck often. He was troubled by an odd feeling and ignored the spattering clay. In time his gaze drifted to the village and settled on the lodge of his uncle, Touches the Sky. Its walls were adorned with hides painted with healing symbols, and even the youngest child knew to stay away. Nevertheless Younger Elk chased a smaller boy in that direction and threw a mud ball that should have spattered harmlessly on the little one's back. But the little boy turned, and the mud ball struck the Arrow Lodge instead.

"Stop!" the camp crier shouted, and the boys scurried away. Women left their work and huddled in awkward silence as Touches the Sky emerged, shaking an eagle-feather fan and gazing at the reddish splotch on the side of his lodge.

"This is bad," the medicine man announced. "What fool has brought misfortune upon himself?"

No one would admit to the act, but some of the younger ones pointed to Younger Elk.

"I'm sorry," the boy said, shrinking back from Touches the Sky's hard gaze. "I didn't mean it."

"This must be undone," Touches the Sky declared. "It's certain to bring misfortune. Once before the Arrow Lodge was struck, and soon after Thunderbird burned the boy with its fire lances."

"Yes," the grandfathers all murmured. "This boy must be purified."

"How is it done?" Dreamer asked as he stepped closer to his uncle.

"Bring the white sage from my medicine gourds," Touches the Sky answered. "But only after you have cleaned yourself. Go now to the river. And take this hide with you."

Dreamer accepted the stained hide and hurried to the river. He took great care to wash it gently. He also rid himself of every trace of mud. By the time he was back at the Arrow Lodge, Touches the Sky had built a small fire near the door.

"Bring the white sage," the medicine man repeated as Dreamer returned the cleansed hide.

Dreamer stepped inside, taking care to make his way around the right side of the lodge. He found the white sage and returned outside.

Touches the Sky then sprinkled sweet grass onto the flames so that a gray mist rose skyward. He stepped close so that the smoke could envelope him. Once he was satisfied the smoke had purified him, Touches the Sky motioned for Dreamer to do the same.

The boy stepped to the fire and waited patiently as his uncle fanned the smoke over his legs and trunk, even his head. The smoke stung Dreamer's eyes, and the boy fought the urge to cough as it burned his nostrils.

"You've done well," Touches the Sky finally announced as he motioned the boy back. "Bring Younger Elk."

When Dreamer returned with the other boy, Touches the Sky added the white sage to the fire. This smoke he used to purify Younger Elk. White smoke curled upward, enveloping the boy. All the while Touches the Sky chanted and shook a gourd rattle.

The whole village stood watching and waiting. When Touches the Sky was satisfied the boy was restored, and the danger from Thunderbird past, he announced he would go off in search of a dreaming.

"This boy is safe, but even so, I have fear in my heart. I must know what winter will bring to the People."

The others nodded. Women brought meat and bread

to the Arrow-keeper, and Avenging Crow atoned for his son's misdeed by bringing two fine deerskins to the Arrow Lodge.

"Is this how it will be for me, Father?" Dreamer asked Gray Wolf as they watched Touches the Sky prepare for his journey.

"Only your uncle can answer that question," the Wolf replied. "Come, a man shouldn't seek his dreaming alone. We must see a boy is chosen to go along."

"A boy?" Dreamer asked.

"Someone to bring water, to keep the fire lit, to watch for enemies," Gray Wolf explained. "We'll find someone."

As they approached the Arrow Lodge, Gray Wolf explained how he had once accompanied his grandfather on a dreaming. It required a brave heart to stand by a medicine man, for after all, the spirits dwelt there.

"You must take someone with you, Brother," Gray Wolf advised when they arrived.

"We'll find someone," Touches the Sky agreed.

"Take me, Uncle," Dreamer volunteered. "I know I'm small, but I wouldn't be afraid."

"No, you wouldn't," Touches the Sky agreed as he gripped his nephew's shoulders. "You never flinched from the smoke. Collect the food, Dreamer. You will have need of it. I will roll hides for us and ready my medicine bundles."

"Yes, Uncle," the boy said, respectfully lowering his eyes. He then gathered the required items and followed Touches the Sky toward the river.

They were gone three days. First came the walking.

26

After fording the river, Touches the Sky wound his way through the woodlands to a hill overlooking a distant valley. It was a long way, and Dreamer was hard-pressed to keep up with his uncle's long strides. Climbing the hill was no easier, and Touches the Sky allowed a rest only when they reached the summit.

Thereafter Dreamer busied himself with his duties. He would prepare food and water and see that his uncle partook of it. When the water skins were empty, Dreamer set off to a nearby spring and filled them. He also kept a watch for strangers, as they were farther beyond the village than was always safe. Sometimes raiding Chippewas would visit the woods, seeking out game or hoping to take captives.

Of course, Dreamer had brought no weapons. He wouldn't have been able to fend off any Chippewas, but he could warn his uncle. They could easily hide, for the Chippewas didn't know that country well.

Dreamer kept such concerns in mind, but mostly he sat beside his uncle, fed the fire, and watched. Touches the Sky painted his face and chest with medicine signs. He blew on an eagle-bone whistle or chanted. Sometimes he would shake a gourd rattle or dance around the fire.

The second day he took a knife and cut narrow strips of flesh from his forearms. The suffering would draw the spirits nearer. The sight of bright red blood flowing down his uncle's arms alarmed Dreamer, and he urged his uncle to eat and drink more often. But although Touches the Sky continued to accept the water, he refused the food.

"Starving will bring on the dreaming," Touches the Sky explained.

"But you're weak already," Dreamer protested.

"I will soon fall into a deep sleep, Nephew. Cover me if I grow cold, but don't wake me. I must find the dream."

"And if it doesn't come?"

"It will. I know that much."

It happened as Touches the Sky had foretold. He grew weak first and sat beside the fire. Then his eyes clouded, and he collapsed. Dreamer covered his uncle's bare shoulders and legs with skins and built up the fire. The medicine man's forehead was feverish, and the powerful shoulders now trembled.

"Man Above, send him his dream," the boy prayed as he stared at the setting sun. "Keep him well."

There was a strangeness to the air afterward, and that night Dreamer heard wolves howling in the distant hills. The woods were alive with other noises, too — unearthly stirrings and haunting calls. Dreamer felt his knees wobble, and he was cold in spite of the nearby fire and a heavy buffalo hide which he had wrapped tightly around himself.

The final morning, Touches the Sky awoke with the dawn. He, in turn, roused a weary Dreamer. Together they added fresh logs to the embers of the fire and greeted the rising sun reverently.

"Did the dream come, Uncle?" the boy asked afterward.

"Yes," Touches the Sky replied. "We will smoke the pipe and thank Man Above. Then we will prepare for the journey homeward."

"I heard many sounds last night. I felt odd."

"The spirits touched you. I suspected they would."

"Will I one day have dreams, too, Uncle?" Dreamer

asked. "Will I see into what awaits me?"

"Yes, and soon," Touches the Sky answered. "That much I saw in my dream."

"You saw me?"

"Grown tall and wise," the medicine man said, smiling broadly. "You will do many great things, Dreamer. Yours will be a remembered life, and your story will be told long after you have joined the great mystery."

"Father will be pleased," Dreamer said, glowing at the thought. "Ah, Laughing Bear won't taunt me now."

"You must not speak of this to anyone," Touches the Sky scolded. "I only told you so that you may accept your own dreams when they come."

"I dream now," the boy said. "Even when I'm awake."

"These dreams will be different, Nephew. Spirits will show you things. Great wisdom will be shared. And if your heart is true, and you keep to the sacred path, you will help the People on the difficult road which lies ahead."

"Is that what you saw?"

"Yes, dark days are coming. Some will die. And there will be a far journey. This is what I will tell the chiefs. But you must say nothing. It would be a bad thing for the People to worry."

"But surely we will warn them. We must protect the ones in danger."

"There is no stopping what will be," Touches the Sky argued. "Our task is to prepare ourselves for it."

"Yes, Uncle," Dreamer replied.

Touches the Sky drew the boy close and gripped his slender arms.

"It's well the People will have you to guide them," the Arrow-keeper declared. "You will be a light to them.

When we return I will speak to your father. Soon you will come to stay with me in the Arrow Lodge and learn my power."

"I'm honored, Uncle."

"It's not an easy way, especially for one so small. But no man chooses his way, Nephew. It's Man Above who sends you to me."

Chapter Three

After Dreamer returned to the village with Touches the Sky, everything changed. The people noticed the respect his uncle gave him. Now the grandfathers welcomed him nearer their fires, and the young men often invited him along on their mock raids and hunts.

He was still different from his age-mates, but now that was accepted.

"Touches the Sky told my father the spirits speak to you," Corn Boy said one morning as they swam together in the river. "What do they tell you?"

"Little that I understand," Dreamer explained. "But soon I hope my uncle will help me to hear better."

"He has great power, Touches the Sky," Corn Boy declared. "Once he made my cousins well when the winter fevers seized them. If anyone can help you see, Touches the Sky is the one."

"Yes," Dreamer agreed. "Soon he will invite me into his lodge, and I will begin to learn the healing ways."

"You will come to be a man of power and vision," Corn Boy said, gazing enviously. "When you do, you'll have no need of poor friends like me."

"Can anyone have too many friends?" Dreamer asked. "I won't forget that when all the others tormented me, Corn Boy thought me his brother."

Corn Boy cheered, and suddenly they were boys once more. They swam and laughed and wrestled — until it became time to tend the fish traps. Work always had to be taken seriously, and so it was. But later the river continued to flow, and so they resumed their play.

In the days that followed, Dreamer accompanied Touches the Sky on his morning walk to the hills. The two would sometimes gather medicine roots in the wood, too, or sit beside the fire and search the dancing flames for understanding.

"Is it time yet for me to join you?" Dreamer asked again and again.

"When the time comes, you won't need to ask," Touches the Sky answered each time. "For now, learn what you may from your father. Even a medicine man can hunt food."

And so Dreamer scurried off to locate Gray Wolf.

No one noticed the changes in a son as much as his father. So it was with Gray Wolf. The warrior missed the company of his son, though, and often he organized hunts even when meat remained from the last kill.

"There are always others eager to eat who have no men to hunt for them," Gray Wolf told his son. "A man who would belong to his people must show generosity toward the old ones, the families with many children."

"When I go to join my uncle, you should bring another boy into your lodge, Ne' hyo," Dreamer suggested. "There are many poor boys who would be proud to have such an honored place. And Nah' koa will be lonely."

"I, too," Gray Wolf confessed.

"I never thought to leave my father's side," the boy explained.

"A man doesn't decide where his path will lead him."

"Maybe your new son will be a better hunter, Ne' hyo."

"But not a better son," Gray Wolf said, gripping his son by the shoulders. "As for hunting, I can still teach you a trick."

"We'll go tomorrow," Dreamer said, gazing up into his father's moist eyes.

"After the fish traps are set. Invite Corn Boy. He has a brave heart, and Hawk Feather will welcome the meat."

So it was that Gray Wolf and the two boys left the village that next morning. After fording the river, they wove their way through the woods, all the time alert for sign of game. Oddly, though, even in the thickets where deer generally passed midday, no deer appeared. Nor was there sign in the sandy ground.

"Something is wrong," Gray Wolf murmured. "Come. And be silent."

Dreamer and Corn Boy did as instructed, and Gray Wolf led them to a nearby hill. As they made their way up the ridge, they noted birds scattering below.

"Ne' hyo?" Dreamer whispered.

"Quiet," Gray Wolf admonished. "Stay low."

The three would-be hunters hid themselves behind a pile of boulders. Through narrow openings between the rocks, Dreamer studied the slope beneath. For a long time he saw nothing. Finally his vigilance was rewarded, though.

Dreamer counted seven figures. Clearly they were

foreign. Their tall, slender bodies were painted with unknown symbols, and their hair was worn long across the center of the head, but shaven on the side as far as the ear.

"Chippewas," Gray Wolf explained.

"A raiding party?" Dreamer asked.

"Too few," his father observed. "Scouts perhaps. They appear to be searching."

"For game?" Corn Boy asked.

"Game isn't so hard to find," Gray Wolf answered. "Whatever they search for, it's odd they should look here. This has long been our country, and they risk war coming here."

"What will we do?" Dreamer asked.

"Watch," Gray Wolf explained. "Listen. Warn of any danger."

The Chippewas appeared anything but threatening. They carried only hunting arrows, and there weren't, after all, many of them. Nevertheless, Dreamer sensed there was danger from those men, and he'd learned to trust his feelings.

Suddenly one of the Chippewas shouted, and the others ran to his side. It was impossible to see more than movement in the thick woods, but men were shouting and thrashing about. Then it was quiet again.

"Whatever it was they were looking for, I think they've found it," Dreamer told his father.

"What makes you say so?" Gray Wolf asked.

"My heart tells me," the boy explained.

"What does it tell you, Naha'?"

"That something has died," Dreamer said solemnly. "I can't be certain, but that's my feeling."

"Then, it may well be so," Gray Wolf said, frowning.

"We must make sure. Come."

The Chippewas seemed satisfied to turn back toward their own country, and Gray Wolf waited until he could count seven men on the northward track before he dared explore the woods below. Dreamer knew, were his father alone, he would take on any risk. But with boys along, Gray Wolf became cautious.

When they did descend the ridge, Dreamer found his feet guiding him past the track and into a dense tangle of cedars. He spied sign now—moccasin tracks and crumbs of dried corncakes. Later there were traces of red on thorny briers, and he knew the land had fought the Chippewas and punished them for the intrusion.

The smell now guided Dreamer's movements. The air had grown stale, and what wind there was tasted pungent. It was the odor of death. But where he might have greeted it with understanding had a deer or rabbit been slain, he knew this was death of another kind.

He walked only a little farther before coming upon the body of a slight-shouldered young man. Three Chippewa arrows protruded from his belly, and his face was washed with blood from where the forelock had been taken. The only other marks were a knife wound behind the left thigh and several scratches on the arms from where he had grappled with his attacker.

"It's one of the Hill People," Gray Wolf announced as he knelt beside the body.

Dreamer felt his chest tighten. The Hill People were his father's band. The dead young man might well be a cousin.

"Strange that he should be so far from his village," Dreamer noted. The Hill People made their camp a day's walk westward.

"To come so far alone . . . it is odd," Gray Wolf said, passing his bow to Dreamer and then lifting the slain young man onto his shoulder.

"I can help," Corn Boy offered, but Gray Wolf refused.

"He's of my father's band," the Wolf explained. "It's for me to do."

And so Gray Wolf bore the corpse back to the village. Corn Boy and Dreamer walked alongside, keeping their eyes and ears alert for traces of others. The appearance of Chippewas was alarming and nearly as confusing as the mysterious body they had discovered. Dreamer deemed that enough surprise for any day.

But when they returned, they found still another shock. Gathered at the riverbank were twenty young men from the Hill band. With them were Avenging Crow, Moon Hunter, Many Lances, and others of the warriors. And to one side, towering over the young Hill warriors, stood Touches the Sky.

"Ayyyy!" one of the Hill warriors trilled as he recognized Gray Wolf's deadly bundle.

"Red Porcupine has come back to us," a second said, helping Gray Wolf ease the body onto the ground.

"He was my brother," a third young man said, staring hatefully northward.

"He was sent ahead to scout the Chippewa camp," the leader of the Hill warriors explained. "We warned him to be careful, but it's not the way of the young. He was rash, and they've killed him."

"Where?" the brother asked. "When?"

"This very day," Gray Wolf answered. "Not far. There was a party of Chippewas searching for him. He might have been spotted spying their camp."

"Now he is dead," the leader lamented, "and can tell us nothing."

The assembled men nodded sadly. Avenging Crow provided a buffalo hide in which to wrap the body, and men set off to attend to its purification.

"Why was he scouting the Chippewas?" Gray Wolf asked, and the others of the River band murmured their suspicions.

"Three days past, Chippewas stole his sister," the Hill warrior's leader, who was called Charging Bull, explained. "We rescued the girl, but she was shamed. Such a thing must be punished. We don't wish the Chippewas coming to our country again."

"We see them sometimes," Gray Wolf muttered, "but never have they dared to raid us. We're strong, and they are far away."

"Not so far as once," Charging Bull declared. "We've seen much sign of them in the wood. If Red Porcupine found their camp, it must be close. He was with us this morning."

The crowd muttered its disapproval. Chippewas close by? They had never gotten along with the People. Now they were stealing women!

"We came here," Charging Bull said solemnly, "because the River People guard Mahuts, the sacred Arrows. We seek the Arrows' advice. What must we do? If it's to be war with the Chippewas, we will need help. All the People must act as one."

"We are scattered," Gray Wolf argued. "It will take time to gather, and a big camp in winter is dangerous. There would never be enough food for all. Better to act when the green grass moons come, and our corn is in the ground."

37

"Will the Chippewas wait?" Charging Bull asked.

"We must ask Mahuts," Touches the Sky announced. "First, tend to the dead one. You must mourn the three days and undergo purification. I'll make ready the sweat lodge. After, we will ask the Arrows."

"The Chippewas will have time to scout our villages," the Bull warned.

"And if we act in haste and offend Mahuts, their power is lost to us," Touches the Sky replied angrily. "It must be done in the old way. Don't fear. We're many, and Man Above has always favored us."

"I only know the enemy is near," Charging Bull warned. "And one of us is dead already."

"You should have sought the power of Mahuts before," Touches the Sky scolded. "But there is time yet. Come, Dreamer, help me make ready."

Dreamer turned to his father, but Gray Wolf motioned the boy toward his uncle.

"Am I to live with you now?" Dreamer asked.

"Not yet," the tall man responded. "But soon. For now you will help me make ready the Arrows."

Dreamer quickened his pace. His spirits soared. All his life he had heard of the medicine Arrows, the most sacred possession of the People. Their power and wisdom was legendary, and many brave-heart deeds were attributed by the grandfathers to their intervention.

They entered the Arrow Lodge slowly, reverently. Touches the Sky made his way around the wall to his bed. There, dangling from a buckskin strip, was the Arrow bundle.

"Yes, Mahuts are inside," Touches the Sky told his young companion. "Here they are kept safe, even as Sweet Medicine said long ago that it must be."

Dreamer felt his flesh grow cold. There, on the far side of his uncle's lodge, was the strongest of all medicine, brought to the People in a time before the oldest grandfathers by the great culture hero, Sweet Medicine. He, too, had been a strange one, so the story went. When he acted contrary to his elders, he was sent away. When he returned long afterward, he told of many wondrous adventures. And he brought four stone-pointed Arrows of great power with him.

From Sweet Medicine came strange prophecies. One day a great four-legged beast would come to take on great burdens. He would carry the warriors across the hills as wind carried the birds, and man would rise above all other creatures. More daunting was the warning of the pale, earth-colored people who would come from across the great water. These strange ones would bring great calamity.

"Sweet Medicine brought us terrible news," the grandfathers said, "but he offered us protection, too. The sacred Arrows will keep us safe so long as they are respected and honored, used for good and not for selfish ends."

All this Dreamer knew, but he now felt it more than ever, sitting in the lodge with them so near. He knew, too, that their power was preserved by their keeper, his uncle.

"An Arrow-keeper's first obligation is always to Mahuts," Gray Wolf had explained when Dreamer had once asked why his uncle took no woman to his lodge. "In denying himself, he makes the Arrows strong. Prosperity has come to the People through the sacrifices of my brother, and I honor him above all other men."

"What can I do?" Dreamer asked as Touches the Sky

inspected the Arrows.

"Watch," the medicine man explained. "Listen."

"Should I prepare food for you?"

"Yes, and bring water."

Dreamer set off to his father's lodge. Little Crane offered bread and meat, and Dreamer took them to the Arrow Lodge. Afterward he filled the water skins. Finally he built up the fire and sat at his uncle's side.

"Listen carefully," Touches the Sky urged. "Do you hear anything?"

"Only the noises outside," Dreamer answered.

"No, listen with the inner ear. Listen to your heart. Does it tell you anything?"

"Nothing," Dreamer replied.

"Close your eyes. Listen harder. What do you sense? How do you feel?"

Dreamer started to repeat his answer, but he froze. He did sense something. A chill rose from deep within him and spread throughout his body. He felt a terrible hollowness, and he cried out.

"Yes, they speak to you, too," Touches the Sky observed. "Do you remember my dreaming?"

"Yes," the boy answered.

"All that has come to be this day I saw. One death. Much sadness. And more."

"What?"

"More death," Touches the Sky explained. "Women, children, bodies falling like leaves dropping from an oak. Many friends I saw climb Hanging Road to the other side. And my heart ached."

"What will you do, Uncle?"

"I will make prayers, and I will bleed myself. I will search for power to turn the lances that would spill my people's blood. And I will ask Mahuts to show me what to do."

"Show me a way to help."

"You will watch over me, Nephew. And when I faint, you will bathe my forehead and cool my fever so that I may reawaken with new vision."

"What of the Hill warriors?" Dreamer asked.

"First I will make ready the sweat lodge. They will be three days mourning Red Porcupine, and another undergoing purification. Four days. I will have my dream in two."

"Yes, Uncle," Dreamer said, warming as Touches the Sky confidently clasped his hand.

That afternoon Dreamer helped Touches the Sky prepare the sweat lodge for the purification ritual. The sweating would force the sorrow and hatred from the hearts of the warriors and allow them to come before Mahuts unburdened.

Afterward Touches the Sky entered his lodge. Dreamer followed solemnly and waited while his uncle stripped himself bare. Touches the Sky chanted and sprinkled dust on the fire, turning the yellow flame blue and green and scarlet. Then he took a knife and cut his chest, his thighs, his arms. Bright red blood trickled across his brown flesh until it appeared to cover Touches the Sky from throat to toe.

"Man Above, hear my prayers," Touches the Sky pleaded. And later he prayed to Mahuts, seeking their power.

Dreamer remained at his uncle's side throughout those two days of starving and bleeding and praying. He forced water down the feverish man's throat, and when Touches the Sky fainted, Dreamer bathed the medicine man's tormented body and fought off the raging fever.

Finally Touches the Sky regained his senses. Dreamer read a new brightness in his uncle's eyes, and he respectfully knelt in wonder.

"The Arrows have told me what I must do," Touches the Sky explained. "Perhaps we can turn the lances, Nephew."

"I worried you would not awaken," Dreamer confessed as he gripped Touches the Sky's cool hands. "I'll bring more water. You must wash the blood away and treat the cuts."

"I'll show you how it's done," Touches the Sky said, wrapping a weary arm around the boy's still-shuddering shoulders. "And when the big-wheel moon appears in the sky, and winter gives birth to the grass and the trees again, you will have your place here at my side. Then I will teach you the great mysteries."

Dreamer nodded. Three moons more would be eaten before he would take to his uncle's lodge. Once he would have shown his disappointment, but he had grown to trust Touches the Sky's wisdom. The delay had purpose, as all things did. Dreamer would practice patience.

Chapter Four

After Charging Bull and his companions emerged from the sweat lodge, they walked to the river and cooled themselves. Then, dressed in their finest robes, with eagle feathers tied in their hair, they came to the Arrow Lodge.

"I bring a pipe," Charging Bull announced. "I would smoke and speak to the Arrows."

"Bid them enter, Nephew," Touches the Sky told Dreamer, and the boy stepped outside and instructed the warriors to file in. Three did so. Dreamer then returned to his place at his uncle's side.

He felt invisible. The men spoke back and forth as they passed the pipe, but no one paid any attention to the boy who fed the fire and brought fresh tobacco to the Arrow-keeper.

Finally Touches the Sky emptied the pipe's ashes in a small pile beside the fire and gazed solemnly into Charging Bull's eyes.

"You would speak to Mahuts. Have you brought a present?" the tall man asked.

"Yes, we bring these eagle feathers," Charging Bull answered as he took three feathers from a buckskin bag.

"This is good," Touches the Sky said as he tied the feathers to the Arrow bundle. "The tail feathers of White Eagle hold great power. Wisdom will come of our talk."

"Yes, that's good," Charging Bull agreed. He then spoke to Mahuts of the proposed raid against the Chippewas, of the need to avenge Red Porcupine.

"The Arrows feel your pain," Touches the Sky assured the Bull. "But this thing you talk of will cause no good. Blood will flow across the land like a river, and the People will know great suffering."

The warriors dropped their heads in respect. Wrinkles furrowed Charging Bull's forehead.

"What will we do?" the Bull asked.

"The Arrows urge a parlay. Meet with these Chippewas and make peace. Wrong has been done, and it must be made right. Hear their words, and tell them yours. Plant the first seeds of understanding so that peace can grow between us."

"Can there be peace?" Charging Bull asked, fighting back his anger.

"If we work hard to cultivate it," Touches the Sky explained. "Since you came to us, I have had a dream. In it I saw only terror and death. The cries of the women were like wolves howling at the moon. Little children climbed Hanging Road, and all the People tasted the bitter roots of despair.

"If you take the warrior trail, we will know these places no longer. We will walk strange lands, and we will feel the teeth of the wild creatures on our bones. This good red earth that has given us corn and melons will be ours no longer. Is this what you want?"

"No, Uncle, we want only what's right," Charging

Bull answered. "We know the power of your dreams, and we will do as Mahuts advise. Our blood is warm for war, but we don't see what will grow from it as you do."

The others nodded their agreement.

"I will carry a pipe to the Chippewas myself," Charging Bull continued. "We will speak with them at the river, and there will be presents and feasting. We would have you with us during the talking, for even our enemies know the power of Touches the Sky. Your words will carry weight with them."

"I will come," Touches the Sky promised. "Go now to our enemies. Bring them close that we may breed kinship."

Charging Bull took his pipe and motioned the others to leave. The three young men then greeted their companions with the grim news. Afterward Charging Bull headed for the Chippewa camps while the others prepared a feasting.

"What will *we* do, Uncle?" Dreamer asked as the others hurried to their duties.

"We'll gather the healing roots," Touches the Sky replied. "I'll show you what to collect. Then you will go to the wood and dig them. Only four each trip, though. If you dig more, their power will die. Understand?"

"Yes, Uncle," Dreamer answered.

"Then come and learn."

So it was that while Charging Bull was off on the long walk to the Chippewa villages on the plain beyond the wood, Dreamer received his first lessons in the healing craft. First, Touches the Sky would introduce him to a root. Then the medicine man would explain which plant to search out and how to dig the root. Just as each root had its own magic, each had its own ritual. One might be pulled from the ground while another required digging from the side closest to the sun. Always there was a song or a prayer to be performed before taking the root.

"Mother Earth gives us much," Touches the Sky explained, "and she asks little. Always respect. And reverence. As we value the life of the People, so we must honor the medicine which will restore health or ease suffering."

Dreamer was surprised at the ease with which he learned the complicated ceremonies. He was, after all, the boy who had needed days to learn the stringing of the bow.

"Man Above guides your thoughts," Touches the Sky declared. "You are finding your path, Nephew."

Certainly it seemed so. Once the roots were collected and arranged in baskets of woven cornstalks, Touches the Sky led Dreamer into the woods once more.

"Now we search for herbs," Touches the Sky explained. "And paint. From clay and ashes, we make red and black. The other colors are more difficult."

Dreamer didn't come along to learn this time. No, he was merely there to carry Touches the Sky's medicine bag. He knew without asking that there were more mysteries to the herbs, and that Touches the Sky would save this instruction for later.

"These are the true mysteries," his uncle told Dreamer. "What will cure in small quantity will send a man on the long sleep if used too often."

Indeed, Dreamer was puzzled at the odd way Mother Earth went about her work. Often the most dazzling blossoms held the deadliest fruit. And weren't the sweetest fruits and berries protected by the thorniest plants?

"That's the way of the world," Touches the Sky explained. "Always there is harmony between life and death, pleasure and pain. Don't we experience suffering before we receive true understanding?"

Dreamer nodded. Certainly his own life attested to that.

Four days after Charging Bull departed the river, he returned with a band of Chippewa warriors. Their faces weren't painted for war, and they carried only hunting bows. Still, there was no mistaking the hardness of their calves or the power in their shoulders. They wore fine robes and beaded shirts, and their leader, who called himself Stone Hatchet, held fire in his eyes.

The Chippewas brought a woman, Yellow Doe, who had been captured from the Windpipe People, to translate. Aside from that one girl, the party was made up of men. Dreamer thought it a bad sign. Trading parties always brought women to assure their guests of peaceful intent. But then these Chippewas surely feared ambush, too. Hadn't they killed a man of the Hill People? Blood always cried for revenge.

Dreamer wasn't invited to the first meeting of the Chippewas and the Hill People. Charging Bull and his companions built the council fire, and it was they who offered their enemies presents and urged the taking up of the pipe. Afterward the Bull summoned Touches the Sky.

"Bring my small medicine bag, Dreamer," the medicine man instructed as he tied up his hair and slid a painted shirt over his slender shoulders. You will sit at

47

my side, but say nothing. Nothing! Do only what I say. You understand?"

"Yes, Uncle," Dreamer answered respectfully.

And so the boy accompanied the Arrow-keeper man to the river. They forded the stream and joined the council, which had grown to include many of the River People. Gray Wolf and Avenging Crow were there, as were other of the warrior chiefs. Many of the grand-fathers had come to offer their counsel. But it was mostly Stone Hatchet who spoke. Yellow Doe trans-lated.

"He says this man who was killed came to our camps with murder in his heart," the woman explained. "He carried no pipe, and he didn't offer to trade for the woman. Instead he waited for the hunters to leave. He took back the woman and sent her on her way. This would have been enough."

Yellow Doe paused a moment before continuing, and Dreamer read the anger in her eyes. This woman, who had been one of the People, held no affection for her kin.

"This Hill man was hungry for blood," Yellow Doe said, repeating not her chief's words but speaking from her own heart. It was unheard of for a woman to talk in such a fashion, and the men stirred uneasily. "My own son, Deer Foot, was killed," she said. "Stone Hatchet's brother, Bent Bow. Badger Heart. Three boys of ten snows. For each of them an arrow was sent into the heart of this bad one."

"The woman was his sister," Charging Bull declared angrily. "She was taken from his father's lodge."

"As I was long ago," Yellow Doe answered.

Stone Hatchet rose from his place and rebuked

the woman. Then he addressed the council. Yellow Doe swallowed her feelings and translated.

"Our hearts are heavy with sorrow," she said somberly. "We come to speak of pain. You give us presents and talk of peace, but my brother is dead. I say if you wish peace, go from this place and be seen no more by my people."

Now Gray Wolf rose.

"You're strangers here," the Wolf spoke, turning first to the Chippewas and then to the Hill warriors. "This is our country. We, the River People, have lived here since the first snow. You, our brothers, bring your trouble to our camp. You, our old enemies, bring your warriors into our wood. Why? Do you hunger for death as this other man did?"

Yellow Doe translated, and Stone Hatchet responded.

"This wood we have known, too," the Chippewa chief argued. "The grandfathers tell of how we fished this river. Even so, we have left you in peace, for Man Above has been good to us, and there has always been enough.

"Now your warriors come and kill my brother. A boy no older than that one who sits at the tall one's side. I ask you. If your brother was killed, would you not seek justice?"

"And if your sister was taken, would you not feel wronged?" Charging Bull answered angrily. "Your people came to our camps first. This is your doing!"

Yellow Doe passed on the words, and Stone Hatchet's face sweated with rage.

"Enough of blood and death!" Touches the Sky then cried, rising to his full height and hushing the others. "I

49

have seen both in my dreams. Sons and brothers, wives and daughters, all will die if the bad hearts decide. It's for us to make good our peace, brothers. Wolf does not hunt wolf! Badger does not eat his own kind! Spotted eagles may eat the dead, but never their own kin. Come, are we not more alike than different? Bad things have happened, but the pipe can make them right again. Let's smoke."

Yellow Doe passed on the words. Such talk of death spoken by a respected one, a man of vision, held weight. Even the Chippewas nodded respectfully. Stone Hatchet's answer was brief.

"He says three have died," Yellow Doe explained. "Can they be forgotten?"

"One of our own people is dead," Charging Bull answered. "And a woman was shamed."

Stone Hatchet barked a reply, and Yellow Doe interpreted.

"He says it's not enough," she said. "You, tall one, judge it for yourself."

"He's right," Touches the Sky agreed. "But what would make your heart right? The death of a boy? Would you have us offer up one of our own so that you might kill him? Would the pain in his mother's heart make right your own loss?"

Stone Hatchet's eyes fell upon Dreamer, and the boy grew cold. Was that his uncle's intention, to offer up a boy's life?

Stone Hatchet adjusted his feet and folded his arms against his chest. Then he spoke, and Yellow Doe again translated.

"We'll smoke," she explained. "I ask no blood be spilled. Even so, a debt is owed, and it should be paid.

50

Send back to us the woman who was taken. She will feel no shame in our camp. Send also a boy to take my brother's place in my father's lodge. These things are only right. They will not take away the sadness, but they will make right the peace."

"It is so," Touches the Sky agreed. He took a wondrous painted pipe from its doeskin cover then and filled its bowl with red willow bark and tobacco. Then, facing the fire, he touched the stem to the sky and said, "Man Above, smoke." He turned the stem toward the ground and said, "Mother Earth, smoke." Likewise he addressed each of the directions and finally raised and lowered the pipe four times.

"In this way I promise to keep my agreements," Touches the Sky explained. "I make no war on the Chippewas, and I cast from my heart all anger."

He passed the pipe along to Gray Wolf, who repeated the pledge on behalf of the River People.

"The woman will be brought to your camp," Charging Bull said, fighting back the bitterness that flooded his face. "A boy of ten snows will bring her to you."

The pipe rose and fell four times, and Dreamer warmed with relief.

Stone Hatchet took up the pipe and spoke as well.

"There shall be peace among our peoples," Yellow Doe said.

Then the pipe made its way around the council fire. Those who wished to smoke did so. Afterward there was much feasting and dancing.

Dreamer joined his father, and they danced to a stirring drumbeat. Dreamer himself joined in the singing, and there were corncakes and fresh venison steaks to eat when he finished. Among the River People gladness spread like smoke on the wind, for war had been averted. The Hill folk were more reserved, for theirs would be the sacrifice.

As for the Chippewas, they kept to themselves. They were strangers, and they didn't speak their hosts' words. Touches the Sky urged his people to welcome new friends, but the scars left by years of fighting cut deeply into many memories.

"I fear I have failed," Touches the Sky lamented when Dreamer led the way back to the Arrow Lodge.

"You've made the peace," Dreamer argued. "No one else could have done it."

"My heart warns otherwise," Touches the Sky said, sighing. "Bring your father to me. We must talk."

Dreamer hurried off to do as bid. Gray Wolf was with the other warriors across the river, so Dreamer again forded the stream.

"Touches the Sky asks you to come, Ne' hyo," Dreamer said when he arrived. "He's worried."

"I, too," Gray Wolf confessed. "It's best we go."

They splashed their way through the shallows and walked solemnly to the Arrow Lodge. Inside, Touches the Sky was praying to Mahuts, seeking their power and guidance.

"Brother, you sent for me," Gray Wolf said as he sat beside the door.

"My heart is heavy," Touches the Sky explained. "We have smoked and talked, but I see no peace. Send men to watch the wood."

"Are we to fight?" Gray Wolf asked in surprise.

"We've promised not to," Touches the Sky answered, "and so we will not. But not all oaths are kept. It's well the People be warned."

"Yes," Gray Wolf agreed. "I'll send Avenging Crow to follow the Hill People. I will take a party into the wood myself. We can hunt—and watch."

Dreamer heard these words, and the gladness that had filled his heart when the pipe was passed left him. He read instead the dread on his uncle's forehead and the concern in his father's eyes.

Two days hence Avenging Crow returned with grim news.

"Charging Bull did as was required," the Crow told Touches the Sky. "He sent a boy and the woman to the Chippewas. The woman was dead, though, and the boy was feverish."

"It's bad that men with bad hearts have come to our village," Touches the Sky said, frowning. "Charging Bull has twisted his promise and made us a great enemy."

"Will the Chippewas attack us now?" Dreamer asked.

"Yes, they will come," Touches the Sky declared. "They hold anger for the Hill People, but it is our village they know best."

"We'll seek out their war party and ambush them," Avenging Crow boasted.

"No, we can't fight them," Touches the Sky objected. "We've vowed to Man Above, and so we must keep the peace."

"But they won't keep their pledge," Avenging Crow argued. "You say it yourself."

"The Chippewas have their own medicine," Touches the Sky explained. "They can go against ours. But we can not violate our own oath."

"And if their warriors come?"

"Then we must make ready," the Arrow-keeper said

53

sorrowfully. "But ours must not be the first blow."

"Then, many will die."

"So the spirits say it must be," Touches the Sky explained. "My dreams will come to pass, and the People will know grave times. Dreamer, bring your father to me. And send for the criers."

"Yes, Uncle," the boy said, hurrying on his way.

Dreamer brought Gray Wolf first, and the two brothers discussed what preparations might be made. Next the criers came. Touches the Sky explained the danger, and the criers gathered with the chiefs to make plans.

"What must I do, Uncle?" Dreamer asked.

"Help me to ready my medicines," Touches the Sky said, drawing the boy close. "Put aside your fears and trust in my vision. You will remain safe so long as you are at my side."

"My mother and father?"

"They, too, will escape the Chippewa lances."

But as Dreamer asked of other friends, Touches the Sky remained mute.

"Will so many die?" the boy asked.

"Blood will wash our village like a flood," Touches the Sky said, trembling. "And we will know the bite of hunger and cold."

"Shall I warn my friends, Uncle?"

"That's for the criers to do, Nephew. Stay with me now. I ache for company, and when the dying starts, you will help with the healing."

"Yes, Uncle," Dreamer said solemnly.

Chapter Five

For the first time in Dreamer's short life, the People made preparations for war. No one carried the pipe about, organizing the young men into raiding bands, but the signs of trouble were to be seen just the same. Scouts left daily to watch the approaches to the village, and women worked frantically to sew hair shirts or smoke meat. Even boys as young as Dreamer crafted arrows for their fathers and brothers.

Dreamer himself was too busy to notice the fear in the eyes of his elders. Touches the Sky sent him out to collect roots each morning. Afterward there would be flowers to ground into paint or charms to make. Beaver teeth or eagle claws added to a beaded bracelet offered protection against the approaching peril, and few of the younger men carried such.

Despite all the preparations, Dreamer didn't become alarmed until the criers took up their twilight admonitions.

"Brother warriors, keep bow and lance at your side this night," the criers began. "Sisters, bid the little ones keep their moccasins upon their feet lest they flee barefoot from harm's path. Cover yourselves with blankets, for the nights grow cold. Keep clothing ready against the need."

Other precautions were also taken. Two stones' throwing from the village, a rock wall was built. Food and clothing were buried nearby, and all were told that should raiders come, the women and children must hurry to that place.

"And where shall I go, Ne' hyo?" Dreamer asked. "I'm no longer a child, but I haven't taken my manhood instruction."

"Stay with Touches the Sky," Gray Wolf advised. "He will need help."

The criers worried about surprise, and one of them was forever awake. By night they tied camp dogs in the wood and along the river, knowing their yelping would alert the village. Boys built up fires and tended them by night so that no one might creep up on the lodges unseen.

Dreamer gazed around him, noticing the many preparations. He should have felt confident that the People would be safe. Touches the Sky's eyes warned otherwise, though. The boy worried.

There proved to be good cause. In spite of the dogs and the fires and the scouts, the Chippewas crossed the river and approached the village. Dreamer lay on a buffalo hide in his father's lodge, dozing lightly, when a scream woke him. He threw off the hide and hurried to rouse his mother and father.

"The enemy!" he shouted without really being certain of the fact. In his heart, though, he knew danger was near. Gray Wolf read the urgency in the boy's eyes and pulled on his clothes. Dreamer had his father's lance and bow ready, so that when Gray Wolf crawled out of the lodge, he was able to arm himself and prepare for what followed.

Dreamer next saw to his mother's safety. He helped Little Crane gather food and what few possessions the two of them might carry. Then they crawled outside and fled toward the stone wall. Behind them shouts and screams testified that the Chippewas had taken the village unawares, and Dreamer's heart ached for those who would suffer for it.

A body of young men was forming to protect the helpless ones, and some of them called on Dreamer to join as he passed.

"I must help my uncle," the boy told them.

"He's going to hide with the women," Laughing Bear taunted. "He's too little to fight anyway."

Dreamer turned but an instant and glared at his old enemy. There was no time for private quarrels, though, and he turned back to attend to his duties. Once Little Crane was among the other women at the stone wall, Dreamer hurried back toward the village.

All was confusion there. Already the Chippewas were setting lodges afire. Men, many of them nearly bare, tried to fight off the raiders. The Chippewas, with their naked chests painted with clan totems, and their heads shaved save for the very top, took on the appearance of demons. They fought savagely, and their lances cut down many good men.

The first one to approach Dreamer was a slender young man in his late teens. No scalps dangled from his lance, nor were there war markings alongside the beaver painted on his chest. Even so, he was a head

57

and a half taller, and the flint point of his lance danced deadly in the faint glow of the burning lodges.

Dreamer grabbed a discarded bow and notched an arrow as the Chippewa approached. The wild eyes and terrible shriek of the raider might have shaken another, but Dreamer remained calm. Often he had missed deer, and sometimes rabbits, but his hand was steady that night. He sent an arrow into the Chippewa's thigh, and the young man cried out in pain.

Dreamer started to notch a second arrow, but he caught sight of several children fleeing raiders near the medicine lodge, and he hurried over that way.

"So, Nephew, you come to fight," Touches the Sky said as he dragged a buffalo hide from the Arrow Lodge. "You would be of more use here."

"Tell me what I can do, Uncle," Dreamer pleaded.

"Take these medicines to your mother and return. We have much to do."

"Yes, Uncle," Dreamer said, taking the heavy bundle and dragging it along. It was difficult at first, for the medicines weighed as much as the boy. Later, as fatigue set in, it became impossible.

"Let me help," Corn Boy called as he raced over from the river. "Together we can carry it."

"Yes," Dreamer agreed, and they struggled to get the bundle to safety. Again they passed the young fighters, but no taunts came now. Two of them lay facedown in the cornfield, and the others struggled with a band of Chippewas.

"Perhaps we should stay and help fight," Corn Boy said when they reached the rock wall.

"I must go back," Dreamer answered as he rested

58

the bundle beside Little Crane. "Nah' koa, watch these things," he added.

"Take care, little one," she urged.

Dreamer then flew back toward the village. Corn Boy was at his heels.

The two boys made two other trips to the stone wall, dragging the precious medicine bags and painted hides from the lodge. Only Mahuts remained, and Touches the Sky alone could touch them.

"Come, Uncle," Dreamer pleaded when he returned a final time. Half the camp was burning now, and those warriors who continued to fight were withdrawing toward the cornfields.

"All is safe?" the medicine man asked.

"Yes, Uncle, all except Mahuts. And you."

"Then watch the power Man Above gives the People," Touches the Sky said as he withdrew the Arrow bundle and tied it to his lance. As he waved it in the air and sang an ancient warrior song, the River men raised a horrible cry. Their line stiffened, and they surged against the Chippewas.

It was too late to save the village, but the determined charge forced the Chippewas to abandon many captives. And it filled the discouraged people with new hope.

"Ayyyy!" Gray Wolf cried as he struck down a Chippewa and advanced on Stone Hatchet. Hawk Feather struck down a second, and Many Lances pierced a third. The Chippewas fought back, though, and the band who had attacked the young men at the stone wall now added their weight.

Dreamer watched with alarm as Stone Hatchet

drew out an ax and broke Gray Wolf's lance. But the Wolf then drove the broken shaft past a flailing arm and pierced the Chippewa chief's belly. Blood flowed from where the point penetrated flesh, and the Chippewa sank to his knees. A final thrust, and Stone Hatchet was dead.

Dreamer hoped that would set the enemy to flight, but the Chippewas screamed in fury and battled back. Many Lances was the first of the People to fall. Then Hawk Feather went down. Only Gray Wolf of the chiefs remained, and he urged his companions on. But the Chippewas were too many, and even the Wolf could not hold on forever.

"Brother, it's time to go," Touches the Sky cried, and Gray Wolf at last stepped back.

"You've won this day," Gray Wolf shouted, "but this is not the end. We don't come like snakes in the night. No, we stand as men under the morning sun."

"You are a dead people!" one of the Chippewas replied. "Your women will tend our fires, and your children will hunt at our sides. Where are your chiefs? Dead. Stay and fight us. We welcome your scalps to our council fires."

It was not mere boasting. Dreamer read the truth in his father's eyes. It was written on the bloodstained ground, etched in the bleeding sides and scarred legs of the surviving warriors.

"Come, my son," Gray Wolf said wearily as he turned his back on the enemy. "It's time to tend to the dead."

"And help the living," Touches the Sky added.

"Yes, there's that," the Wolf agreed.

Actually, there was a great deal of helping to do. Some of the men erected a skin lodge in one corner of the stone wall, and Touches the Sky began administering to the wounded. There were many. For some there were but prayers to sing and powders to ease the pain.

"He started the long journey up Hanging Road," Touches the Sky would announce, and some loved one would begin the wailing.

For others there was more hope. Children had been thrown down by the raiders, and many had broken limbs. These were wrapped in moist deer hide or braced between sticks. Touches the Sky displayed great tenderness as he worked with the young ones, and he labored to quiet their fears and cast away their pain.

The warriors bore graver wounds. All had some injuries, and many were gashed horribly. Dreamer found himself wrapping wounds or shaving roots into medicines. Touches the Sky soon had to but point for the boy to understand what was needed.

After a time Dreamer paid little heed to the faces of the men who came before him. He didn't wish to know how many of his friends had lost their fathers. Even now he could hear Corn Boy calling, "Who has seen Hawk Feather? Are my brothers nearby?"

"They are all of them dead," Touches the Sky whispered. "Maybe you would go to him and offer comfort, Nephew. He's your friend."

"There's no comfort to be found this night," Dreamer replied. Touches the Sky nodded sadly, and the boy remained.

Later, as the sun painted the eastern horizon scarlet, he did seek out his friend. Corn Boy was standing in the midst of the burned village, gazing down at his father's lifeless body.

"Even the sky is bleeding this day," Corn Boy said, pointing to the fiery sunrise.

"Yes, it's a bad time for us," Dreamer agreed.

"For you?" Corn Boy asked. "You will become a great healer. Everyone says it. I have no father. My brothers are dead. The enemy has taken my mother. Before the winter snows end, hawks will pick at my bones."

"No, you will grow tall," Dreamer declared. "Many children were lost in the raid. There are women who will hunger for their dead sons, and men who will need boys to take hunting."

"I wish only to hunt the Chippewas," Corn Boy growled.

"Yes, my father also hungers for revenge. But first we must mourn the dead. Then Touches the Sky will ask the Arrows. They will guide us as always."

"I wonder if any medicine is strong enough to save us."

"We have been a great people. We shall be again."

"I wonder," Corn Boy mumbled. "I wonder."

Others, too, despaired of the future. Once daylight revealed the ruin of the village, and the survivors learned how few their numbers were, a new wail rose.

"If the Chippewas return, we will all of us die," one woman said.

"No, our people will survive," Gray Wolf argued. "Come. We must attend the dead. Then we will begin the mourning."

"And afterward?" the woman asked.

"We must seek a new place to make our home," Touches the Sky announced. "This river is death to us now."

"Aren't we fighting the Chippewas?" Avenging Crow shouted. "They must be near. We can strike back."

"We?" Gray Wolf asked. "There are but a handful of men who can walk. We've shot our arrows. The enemy is too strong. Our duty lies here, with the defenseless ones."

Avenging Crow turned and read the fearful faces of his companions. Few were eager to renew the fighting, and Touches the Sky reminded all of the obligation to mourn the fallen.

"The Chippewas, too, have dead to tend," Touches the Sky pointed out. "You will busy yourselves three days, praying and singing while I climb the hills and seek a vision. Afterward I will see what we must do."

"Your medicine has led us to this!" Avenging Crow said, pointing to the ruined encampment.

"No, Charging Bull's deceit brought this," Gray Wolf argued. "And so the Hill People must help us."

"Will we go there?" Dreamer asked.

"We'll wait for Touches the Sky to tell us what he sees," Gray Wolf answered. "Then we'll know which road to take."

While the others set about observing the rituals of the dead, Dreamer prepared to accompany Touches the Sky into the hills to the west of the river. Once they would have journeyed into the wood, but that was

63

now Chippewa land. Smoke from the enemy camps could be seen clearly, and it would be death to go there.

"Be careful," Gray Wolf urged nevertheless. "These Chippewas are prowling wolves. Their blood is up, and they hunger to resume the hunt."

"Man Above will guide my steps," Touches the Sky replied. "And Dreamer will see to my needs."

"I'll be safe, Ne' hyo," Dreamer added. "Maybe while I'm gone, you can take Corn Boy into your heart. He's alone now."

"No longer," Gray Wolf promised. "You have been his brother a long time. When the mourning time is over, I will take him as my son."

Dreamer managed to smile in spite of the grim surroundings. Then Touches the Sky motioned that it was time to leave, and the boy followed his uncle westward.

Twice before, Dreamer had tended Touches the Sky during a starving, but this time it was different. Once they reached the hills, Touches the Sky located a clearing atop a low ridge and turned toward the sun.

"This is the place," the Arrow-keeper explained. He took a pouch from Dreamer and spread white sage across the ground. Then with his head facing east, he lay facedown. He remained there, without so much as a skin to cover him, for four days.

Dreamer built a small fire nearby and kept a pipe ready. Three times each day Touches the Sky would smoke and pray for a vision. He would drink some water, but he disdained all food.

"This is sacred *wu'wun*," Touches the Sky explained.

"The starving. If Man Above wills it, He will send Maiyun into my dreams, to tell me what must be done. To show the way."

Dreamer nodded. He understood little about Maiyun, but had heard stories of how this spirit came to men in the form of wild creatures. His father knew Maiyun as a wolf. Others knew Maiyun as a fox or an eagle. It was not the form that mattered most. No, it was the message Maiyun brought that marked the starving as a success.

The fourth evening, Touches the Sky stirred uneasily. Dreamer watched as his uncle rolled and thrashed. Often he cried out in his torment. Overhead the sky was lit with yellow flashes of lightning, and the echoing thunder shook the earth.

"Surely Maiyun is here," Dreamer told himself. And he looked on in awe as the dream continued.

When the wild movements stopped, and Touches the Sky grew quiet, Dreamer built up the fire and lay down beside it. By the time he awoke, the sun was rising in the east, and his uncle was preparing for the return journey.

"Maiyun came," Dreamer said as he dressed himself.

"Yes, Nephew, I have seen the future."

"What will become of us?"

"We'll rejoin our people, and I will speak to the chiefs. Then the criers will tell the People."

Dreamer frowned with disappointment, but Touches the Sky drew him close.

"Find us some food, Nephew. I'm hungry," the medicine man said as he gripped the boy's shoulder. "One day soon you will have the far-seeing sight yourself. Then you'll understand a vision isn't news to be whispered from boy to boy or jabbered about by old women. What I have seen can only be shared after much smoking and prayer."

"Yes, Uncle," Dreamer replied.

"This much I will say. I have seen you walking with four legs in a distant land. When the last of your days are upon you, little ones will look at you as a great man, and even the grandfathers will whisper your name with respect. Your trail will be a rocky one, Nephew, but greatness awaits you there."

"Maiyun has shown you all this?"

"That and much more," Touches the Sky answered. "Now we must eat some. Then we walk."

Dreamer offered his uncle a corncake and some dried venison. Touches the Sky ate slowly while Dreamer collected the medicine bags and rolled his sleeping hide. Finally they started down the hill. By late morning they were back among the People.

In their absence five others had died, and Touches the Sky attended to them first. He next treated fevers and inspected wounds. When the last of the cures was finished, he summoned Gray Wolf and the other chiefs. They built a council fire and smoked a pipe. Finally they summoned criers, who in turn shared the decisions with the People.

"Make yourselves ready for a long journey," the criers announced. "Collect the dogs. They must pull the weak on litters. Messengers are going to the Windpipes in search of their help. Soon we will leave this place of death and find a better life."

"We're leaving this good country to the Chippewas," Avenging Crow grumbled. "If ten men would follow me, I would punish these raiders."

"There aren't that many fools left among us," Low Fox said. "They are many and we are few. We should follow Touches the Sky. His medicine is strong."

"He failed to save us from the raiders," Laughing Bear said, stepping to his uncle's side.

"Was it his duty to post the scouts?" Low Fox asked. "Where was Avenging Crow when the raiders crept through the woods?"

"Enough!" Gray Wolf shouted. "Have we so few enemies that we can now fight among ourselves? Come, brothers, we are one people. Put aside what has been. Look to tomorrow."

That night the People sang and danced around the tall fire. Many children orphaned by the Chippewas were taken in by new families. Warriors took new wives. Old men gave their brave-heart names to boys who had proven themselves in battle. And the stories stretched on deep into the darkness.

On the morrow the People began the long trek westward. Except for some of the old ones, who chose to stay and die, all walked together. There were songs and prayers, remembering and forgetting. Dreamer walked beside his new brother, Corn Boy, and hoped all Touches the Sky had seen for him might come true. Hope, after all, was a balm for the pain and sorrow that tormented life.

Chapter Six

They were the River People no longer. As they made their way westward across the wooded hills, fording streams and avoiding enemies, they became a ragged band of stragglers. They stopped first at the Windpipe village and later camped among the Hill band. But those bands had their own worries, and soon the journey was renewed.

In the beginning others called them the homeless ones, or the wanderers. Later, it became easier to call them Hof no wa — the Poor People. As the winter snows at last began to fall, it seemed to Dreamer the name was an apt one. Where before the band had been rich in buffalo hides and their lodges had kept off the worst chills of the hard-face moons, now the young ones shivered in their sleep. The surviving warriors fought to supply fresh meat while the women tried to manage the makeshift camps. As for the old ones, they simply walked off to die in solitude.

When Dreamer was not fishing the streams or hunting small game, he would accompany Touches the Sky through the camp, aiding the medicine man and learning what he could of the healing art. At night the boy clawed the frozen earth and cried out as memories flooded his mind.

"Here, this will help," Touches the Sky finally said, rousing his nephew from a troubled sleep.

"What is it, Uncle?" Dreamer asked.

"Bitterroot," Touches the Sky explained as he tied it in the boy's hair. "It will ward off the ghosts that bother you."

"Maybe we should dig more of it," Dreamer said, listening to the sounds of others thrashing about.

"Yes, many are troubled," Touches the Sky agreed. "We'll do it."

Two winters came and went before the Ho'f no wa band stopped its slow trek westward. They didn't come alone. The Chippewas were but one tribe encroaching on the People's old territory. The Windpipe and Pelt bands soon found themselves, too, swept from the old familiar valleys and into the safety of the foreign woodlands.

It was in this world that Dreamer took his first manhood steps. There wasn't, of course, any one day when he realized he was no longer a boy. No, it happened gradually. First, Touches the Sky took Corn Boy, Younger Elk, and Dreamer aside and spoke of obligations.

"A man never forgets his duties," the medicine man explained. "He brings food into the camp, and he always remembers the old ones and the poor who have no one to bring them meat. He always cuts them a good piece when there is enough.

"He respects his chiefs. When a decision is made, he doesn't speak against it. He may not choose to follow a man he feels is wrong, but he never becomes quarrel-some.

"Finally, he is careful around women. Never would he take an unmarried woman away. If he desires a wife, he brings presents to the girl's father and speaks of the matter. He doesn't pass time with married women, as this is a cause of discontent. Don't offer your attention, and shun that of a woman."

"Yes, Uncle," the three boys said together.

"Make yourselves strong, for the People should regain their old power," Touches the Sky continued. "Learn to hunt like Hawk, listen like Badger, and run like Deer. Then you will stand tall and proud as a man of the People."

Dreamer decided that was easier to say than to do. He was but a boy of twelve snows, and his shoulders appeared too frail to bear the burdens already thrust upon them. Even so, he was determined to try his best. He always chose the biggest opponent when wrestling pairs squared off, and he challenged the fastest to race. In the beginning he often lost, but he gained the respect of his companions. And soon, growing stronger, he began to triumph regularly.

Now that the People were forever on the move, it wasn't possible to plant corn and melons as before. Small patches were cultivated sometimes, but the old days of dwelling in a permanent village had changed. More and more the People relied on game for their food, and so the hunt was all-important.

For a long time Dreamer had stalked deer in the woodlands, occasionally felling one with a well-aimed arrow. The fresh meat and hide were always welcome, as were the other parts. Little Crane found a use for everything. The sinew became thread, and horns made handles for knives or cooking implements. Deer ribs were fashioned into breastplates to protect warriors from enemy arrows, and shoulder blades made excellent digging tools.

Yes, Deer was useful. But as they wandered westward, the People came to rely heavily on Bull Buffalo as well. The great hairy beasts abounded in the woods, and they often blackened whole stretches of prairie in their multitudes. A buffalo would feed the whole camp, and buffalo hides offered warmth against the fiercest winds.

Dreamer heard tales of how the People once ran a small herd over a cliff back in the river country of his birth, but there were few cliffs in this new land. Instead warriors would dig a pit and cover it with brush. Then they would creep up behind the buffalo and beat their bows against trees, scream, and stir the beast into motion. If they were skillful, they could force the buffalo to run toward the pit. Once it stepped onto the brush covering, it would fall into the pit where it was easy prey for the warriors' arrows.

Some brave men tried to stalk buffalo as they did deer, but the sharpest arrow often failed to pierce the buffalo's tough hide. Three men once killed a calf with their lances, but no one was foolish enough to challenge a bull with a lance. The monster would trample the man with little trouble.

The best time for hunting buffalo was in winter, when deep snows would hamper the escape of the bulky beasts. It was the choice time for taking hides, too, as they were heaviest when there was greatest need. But the same snows that slowed the buffalo hindered its hunters and often exposed them to peril.

Nevertheless, when Avenging Crow brought word there was a herd near camp, Dreamer immediately turned to Touches the Sky.

"Uncle, I've never been on a buffalo hunt," the young man said. "I'm taller now, and even Gray Wolf admits I'm a boy no longer. It's time I went."

"It's the mark of a man," Touches the Sky noted. "But there's danger. And we have much to do. There's fever among the People, and I have medicine to make."

"There are the buffalo prayers, too," Dreamer noted. "If we prepare the medicine today, I could still go. No one will leave before tomorrow."

"This hunt isn't like a deer stalk, Nephew. You'll have preparations to make. A man takes the buffalo trail in his finest dress. Do you own a war shirt?"

"Little Crane will make me one."

"So quickly?" Touches the Sky asked, an amused look crossing his lips. "Remember, she has to sew for her new sons, too. Corn Boy and Younger Elk have needs."

"Yes," Dreamer said, sighing. "But if I always stay behind, how will I ever be a man?"

"Then, maybe you should go," Touches the Sky said, lifting Dreamer's chin. "Come, we'll make arrangements."

Dreamer stiffened his back and fought to keep the excitement off his face. He wasn't entirely successful. Clearly Dreamer wasn't the only young man excited about the coming hunt. All over the camp boys hung near their fathers, hoping they would be pronounced old enough. And although Dreamer no longer dwelled in his father's lodge, he sought the approval of Gray Wolf for the undertaking.

"Yours is not a warrior's trail," Gray Wolf observed. "Does my brother have no use for you?"

"I will tend to my duties before leaving, Ne' hyo."

"We don't kill Bull Buffalo for honor, Dreamer. We need the food he gives us to keep off the pains of hunger, and his coat warms us through the long nights of winter."

"I know," Dreamer said, nodding solemnly. "I also know the prayers to speak, and I understand meat must be set aside for the spirits. If I kill a bull, I will give a shoulder to the helpless ones."

"Come then," Gray Wolf said, waving Dreamer along. They walked to the earthen lodge that was the Wolf's current home. Outside the door was a weapon stand. Gray Wolf took down his bow and handed it to the young man.

"String the bow, my son," Gray Wolf instructed.

Dreamer took the bow and studied his father's solemn face. That bow was carved from an ancient ash of unequaled strength, and few men alive possessed the power to bend it.

"Man Above, help me," Dreamer prayed as he braced the lower tip against his leg and touched his fingers to the opposite tip. The bowstring lay only inches below, but he would have to bend the bow in order to move it into place.

"No, don't fight it," Gray Wolf barked as Dreamer

73

leaned his body into the bow. "Twist yourself so that it springs down."

"Yes, Ne' hyo," Dreamer answered, trying it that way. The bow moved but slightly, a finger's length perhaps. But as he continued, it moved more—and more. Finally Dreamer slid the knotted string into place, and the bow was strung.

"Ayyyy!" Corn Boy howled. "Now it's my turn."

"Wait," Gray Wolf instructed, and the boys did just that. Their father crawled inside and returned with a new, shorter bow cut of willow. Corn Boy, using Dreamer's technique, easily strung the new bow.

"You, too?" Gray Wolf asked when Younger Elk reached for the bow. Again the Wolf searched the lodge. He returned with yet another willow bow, and Younger Elk strung it on the third try.

"A man must have a good bow," Gray Wolf observed. "You have your own arrows. Bring them with you to the council tonight."

"Yes, Ne' hyo," the three young men said as one.

"Go to Touches the Sky now," Gray Wolf added. "It's not fitting for a father to show his sons the rest."

Dreamer turned and walked toward the Arrow Lodge. The others followed.

Dreamer worried they wouldn't be welcome. Hadn't Touches the Sky complained there was too much to do? And there were things needing his attention. The boys found the tall man waiting for them, though.

"It's time you were men," Touches the Sky announced. "Come in and learn."

Dreamer followed his uncle into the lodge. Corn Boy and Younger Elk trailed a few paces behind. The others had never been inside the Arrow Lodge, and they were awestruck at first.

"Look here," Touches the Sky growled as he touched the small hairs on Dreamer's chin. "Have you ever seen a man wear hair on his face?"

"No, Uncle," Corn Boy said, frowning. "Do you cut them off with a knife?"

"No," Touches the Sky said, laughing. He then produced two small slivers of bone joined at one end. The medicine man held them halfway down the sides and placed the tips around a chin hair. Then he pressed the bone slivers until they clamped down on the hair. With a yank, he plucked the hair.

"Oww!" Dreamer shrieked.

"You will do the others," Touches the Sky explained. "Chin, cheeks, above the lip. Others will grow in later, and you must pluck them as well. Between the brows, too."

"There are so many," Dreamer complained.

"Be happy you're not hairy like old Bear Claws. He was three days plucking hairs!"

"Laughing Bear's uncle," Corn Boy whispered, grinning.

Dreamer fought the urge to laugh at the notion of Laughing Bear plucking hairs. That boy had no tolerance for pain.

"When you finish, go to the sweat lodge," Touches the Sky said as he prepared to leave. "Take your father. Gray Wolf will teach you the rite. Once you are purified, you must braid your hair. Come back then. I will have charms to keep you safe."

"And then?" Dreamer asked.

"We'll make ready your clothes. A man must walk proudly when he first joins the council. Tomorrow, before you leave, I will paint your faces in the fashion of our family. Ever afterward, you will do this yourself."

"Yes, Uncle," they said as Touches the Sky left the lodge.

The grandfathers often spoke of terrible tortures devised by enemies to test the courage of young warriors. Dreamer judged them unnecessary. This hair-plucking would do. He actually couldn't pluck but five or six at a time before passing the cruel implement along to Corn Boy. He, in turn, would pass them on to Younger Elk. In this way the boys spent the early afternoon, removing the accursed hairs from their faces.

When they left the Arrow Lodge, their chins and eyebrows were speckled with bubbles of blood, and some of the younger boys laughed at the sight. Their elders only nodded knowingly.

Dreamer located Gray Wolf at the edge of camp, talking quietly with Avenging Crow. The two warrior chiefs grew quiet when the boys approached. Both took note of the hairless chins and greeted the young men warmly.

"Touches the Sky says we must enter the sweat lodge, Ne' hyo," Corn Boy explained. "You will tell us what must be done?"

"Come," Gray Wolf replied. "It's proper to wash the past from your heart before hunting buffalo. I'll go there myself. It's fitting a boy should take his first sweat at his father's side."

"Ayyyy!" the young men howled.

76

The sweat lodge occupied a low hill beyond the camp circle. When Dreamer, Gray Wolf and the others arrived, it was already crowded with men undergoing the purification rite. Touches the Sky was there, making the prayers and preparing the men with white sage.

"Free your heart of trouble and pain," he whispered to Dreamer. "Let the heat cast away the old and renew your spirit."

Gray Wolf stripped to his breechclout, and the boys did likewise. The heat from the sweat lodge had melted the snow there, but the wintry chill remained. Moreover, Dreamer felt awkward and self-conscious, standing there with his boyish shoulders amid the scarred and muscled men.

The ceremony continued. Other prayers were spoken, and the pipe ritual was performed. Inside, the men sat in a circle around hot rocks. From time to time they sprinkled water over the rocks and drank in the flood of steam. They spoke sacred words and passed a pipe. Dreamer touched his lips to the pipe, following Gray Wolf's example. Others drew in the smoke deeply.

The steam did seem to cleanse the soul. Dreamer felt his mind leave his body and wander the land. He was a hawk soaring over the rivers. He was a wolf, hunting in the deep of night.

Gray Wolf jarred him awake.

"Drink," the Wolf said, and Dreamer sipped water from a gourd. "It's easy to drift."

"Yes, Ne' hyo," Dreamer whispered.

They remained but a while longer. Then Gray Wolf

led the way out of the sweat lodge. The warriors rubbed themselves dry and wrapped up in robes before returning to their lodges.

That evening, after sharing a dinner of roasted venison and stewed turnips prepared by Little Crane, the three young men followed Gray Wolf and Touches the Sky to the council. There the men made a place for them close to a towering fire.

First, Touches the Sky prepared the pipe.

"Man Above, smoke," he said as he lifted the pipe stem skyward. "Mother Earth, smoke," he added as he dipped the stem toward the ground. Likewise he passed the pipe to each of the cardinal directions.

"Tomorrow we seek strength from Bull Buffalo," Gray Wolf announced, taking the pipe and smoking. "Who will follow me on this hunt?"

Avenging Crow stood and took the pipe.

"I will go," he declared.

Moon Hunter took it next.

"I will go," he said in turn.

And so the pipe passed around the circle, from one warrior to another until it was Dreamer's turn.

"I will go," he called out proudly.

"Ayyyy!" the older men howled.

And it was the same when Corn Boy and Younger Elk took their turns.

Next, Touches the Sky invoked the buffalo spirits. He spoke of how, in the beginning of the world, Buffalo had come to the land. It was a wondrous story, and Dreamer warmed at the exciting thoughts that surged through him. Touches the Sky quietly prayed for success on the hunt as

78

he told of the People's terrible needs.

Afterward the pipe again made its way around the circle. An old warrior named Walks in the Morning smoked, then told the story of his first hunt. That was in a time long past, when the People still had their village by the river. It was winter then, too, and the children were cold.

"I followed my father, Moon Dancer, through the deep snows," the old man recounted. "It was cold, and Buffalo's breath boiled from his nostrils. I carried my lance in my small hands, for I was no bigger than these boys here tonight. Moon Dancer approached from one side, and I came from the other. Buffalo snorted and stomped, and I prepared for his charge. He could not move, though, for he was trapped in the snow. We stepped closer, softly singing the buffalo song:

'Bull Buffalo, we hunt in reverence.
Lend us your power and strength.'

"Moon Dancer plunged his lance into Buffalo's side, and I did likewise. Blood washed the snow, and Buffalo gave up his life. That day I became a warrior of the People."

"Ayyyy!" his companions shouted.

"Now, who will tie another onto this story?" Gray Wolf asked, and Avenging Crow accepted the pipe. The Crow also told of his first hunt, although it was in summer, and the buffalo made its charge. Even so, Avenging Crow escaped to the safety of a thicket while Buffalo grunted his challenge from a clearing.

Other stories followed until Touches the Sky announced it was time to begin the dancing. The grandfathers took up their drumming, and others sang ancient songs that emboldened the hunters. Warriors paired off and danced about in mock combat. One would place his hands atop his head to imitate a buffalo, and the other would challenge the beast with bow or lance.

"Come, join us," Gray Wolf urged the boys, and they, too, paired off. Corn Boy and Younger Elk turned circles around each other, yelping or grunting as the role required. Dreamer found himself facing Laughing Bear.

The Bear was painted with earth colors, and he wore a bear's head bonnet. He balanced a lance lightly in his hand and stared into Dreamer's weary eyes.

Dreamer placed his hands on his head and stomped the ground. Laughing Bear grinned and steadied himself. The Bear made a thrust with the lance, and Dreamer felt the stone point tear through his shirt and slice the tender flesh near his ribs.

"Again," Laughing Bear urged. "Perhaps I will make you a hunter after all."

Dreamer felt blood drip down his side. His hands dropped down, and he gazed at his old enemy with quiet confidence.

"You can make me nothing," Dreamer declared. "Man Above chooses my path. Consider well if you choose to turn my power against you."

Laughing Bear started to renew his attack, then paused. He read the fire in Dreamer's eyes, and his hands began to tremble.

"What's this?" Avenging Crow shouted as he took note of the blood on Dreamer's shirt.

"No one may shed blood in the buffalo dance!" Walks in the Morning cried. "This is a bad sign."

"Go to Touches the Sky," Avenging Crow commanded. "He may give you a charm to protect you from Bull Buffalo's anger."

"I need no charm," Laughing Bear whispered to Dreamer as he followed Avenging Crow toward the medicine man.

No charm can protect a man from himself, Dreamer thought as he resumed the dance, praying misfortune would not again find the People. There had already been enough pain for twenty winters.

Chapter Seven

After making the dawn prayers and cleansing themselves, the hunters set out from the camp. For once the sun spread its morning warmth across a clear, unclouded sky, and the snow-clad landscape glimmered white-gold.

Dreamer, Corn Boy, and Younger Elk followed Gray Wolf as he led a small band of hunters toward the right flank of the milling buffalo herd. Avenging Crow swung his party to the left. Many Lances spread his companions into a thin line and held the center.

"This is the way we approach the enemy," Gray Wolf explained as he wove his way between the trees on a hillside overlooking the buffalo. "See how much we are like the horns of Bull Buffalo. As we drive the buffalo before us, they will flounder in the snow. Then we will kill what we need for winter food."

"And for coats," Younger Elk added.

"Those will be welcome," Gray Wolf agreed, "but we must never waste Bull Buffalo's flesh just to take his hide. We kill only what we can eat. There will be hides enough."

Younger Elk frowned, and Dreamer nodded. Once that would have been true, but already the hard-face winds were coming, and so many of the little ones needed hide coats. The People would again know hardship.

"There," Gray Wolf whispered as he pointed to the three buffalo standing with their noses to the wind, sniffing out approaching enemies. Dreamer took note of them. Gray Wolf then waved his band into an uneven line and motioned toward the herd.

Dreamer had only taken three steps when Many Lances shouted a war cry. The others in the center howled and waved bows. Instantly the buffalo surged into motion. The snows made flight difficult, but the huge beasts nevertheless plodded onward.

Then it was the flankers' turn. Whooping and beating his bow against his thigh, Gray Wolf charged the herd. Dreamer lent his own voice to the cry, as did the others. Avenging Crow's band echoed the noise from the opposite side, and the confused buffalo began to bunch in the center. With noisy hunters approaching from three sides, the animals turned toward the one remaining direction. And that was their undoing.

Even as Gray Wolf was driving an arrow into a straggling cow, the first of the bulls was stumbling through a snowdrift and on over a steep embankment. Another and another of the hairy beasts followed. Cries of triumph marked the death of those giants, and Dreamer regretted not being closer. He was occupied chasing a buffalo cow.

Corn Boy and Younger Elk pursued the animal, too, but Dreamer ran on the wind that day. He seemed to dance across the snowy hillside until he was but three bows' length from the struggling calf. Then, praying for forgiveness for killing his brother creature, Dreamer

83

loosed an arrow into the calf's side. The point pierced the brown hide behind the shoulder and drove straight into the heart.

"Ayyyy!" Corn Boy cried. "Brother, you have the true aim this day!"

Younger Elk offered a second cry of agreement, and the boys rushed to count coup on the dead calf.

It was later, as they started to drag the calf out to the skinners, that Dreamer sensed something was wrong.

"Come," the boy urged as he turned toward the nearby wood. "Hurry. There's danger."

"Where?" Younger Elk exclaimed.

Corn Boy, though, followed his friend, and the Elk hurried to join them. They scarcely reached the trees when the ground began to tremble. Staring back toward the plain, they saw to their dismay a rolling white cloud of snow dust climbing skyward.

"The buffalo!" Corn Boy cried in alarm.

"They've turned," Younger Elk observed.

Indeed, they had stopped their charge at the cliff and turned back on their tormentors. Dreamer felt his insides grow cold as he searched for signs of Gray Wolf and the others. The Wolf, though, knew well the ways of Bull Buffalo, and he had managed to take refuge in a rock-strewn ravine.

Dreamer could see Many Lances and his band, too. They were on the far ridge, waving their bows and honoring the skill of Bull Buffalo. Half the herd escaped in that wild charge. The hunters had to content themselves with stragglers and the beasts that had flown over the rim and fallen dead in the ravine below.

As the air began to clear, Dreamer resumed the labor of dragging the calf. Gray Wolf strode over, assured himself the boys were well, and set off after a wounded cow. Many Lances announced all his hunters were unhurt, and those men with sons among the flankers rejoiced no harm had come to the boys.

Even so, Dreamer's heart remained heavy with foreboding. No one had heard from the other flanking party, and he feared the worst. Finally, though, Avenging Crow appeared with a band of followers, and the hunters whooped in celebration.

"Brothers, have you seen my nephew?" the Crow shouted.

"He was at your side but a moment ago," Many Lances replied. "He followed you up the ridge."

"No, Laughing Bear was chasing a calf," Moon Hunter argued. "I saw him, and I thought, Here is a boy in danger!"

Men and boys spread out in search of the missing young man, but though they located slain bulls, cows, and calves, they found no trace of Laughing Bear. Dreamer's feet carried him beyond the others into a stand of willows. There, trampled by a thousand buffalo hooves, lay strips of torn buckskin. Underneath was what remained of Laughing Bear.

"Ayyyy!" Dreamer shouted as he knelt beside his old enemy. The bruised and battered mouth no longer uttered cruel taunts. The eyes which had only that morning flashed defiantly were clouded with death. As for the rest, it was broken and mashed beyond belief.

"This was once Laughing Bear, of the Poor Band, a boy of the People," Dreamer whispered as he gazed up at the morning sun. "He has set his feet on Hanging Road now."

Dreamer was singing the medicine prayers when the

others arrived. They stood by respectfully as the young man finished. Then Avenging Crow took charge of the body, and the other hunters turned back to prepare the slain buffalo for the women who were even now approaching to start the skinning.

Laughing Bear's death rested heavily on Dreamer, and his mind clouded with odd visions. His sleep was troubled, and Touches the Sky insisted he renew himself in the sweat lodge. Afterward he remained unsettled, though, and Touches the Sky bound the boy's hair with bitterroot and tied an elk tooth charm behind one ear.

When Dreamer continued to cry out in his sleep, Touches the Sky erected a skin lodge on a distant hillside and took the young man there.

"You have a question in your heart," the Arrowkeeper noted. "What is it?"

"Am I the cause of his death, Uncle?"

"How could that be?" Touches the Sky asked. "He was no friend, but you didn't will him dead."

"There were times when I would have welcomed it."

"As when he pricked your skin with his lance? Yes, I remember that, and I know the grandfathers say it brought the boy misfortune. But Laughing Bear chose to disdain warnings and reject the medicine I offered him. Surely he had stepped from the sacred path, and such a man is doomed to find ill-fortune."

"He and I were born the same summer."

"As were others, Nephew. He's not the first to die. Corn Boy's brothers were even younger when the Chippewas killed them. A man doesn't choose the length of his trail. He walks it in the sacred manner and accepts what comes to be."

"It's hard, Uncle."

"Yes," Touches the Sky agreed. "And our path is steeper. A man who would see tomorrow's perils and safeguard the People will also suffer more when misfortune comes. Since the Chippewas have come to cast us from our river, my hair has grown white as snow, and my heart is heavy as stone. But I told you our way isn't easy."

"No. Sometimes I wish I were like the others, Uncle. Is it wrong to hunt and fish with Corn Boy, to gaze at the maidens and dream of the day when one of them will join me in my lodge?"

"It's a boy's way," Touches the Sky said, smiling. "I, too, had dreams of that life, but my medicine forbid me women."

"And me?"

"You'll find your own answers."

"So many questions, Uncle. Will I ever find the answers?"

"Soon," Touches the Sky said, drawing the boy closer. "But the medicine trail will always seem a strange path to the others, even as it was when Sweet Medicine first left the People in search of his visions. Maybe he, too, wished to follow a different path. But where would the People be without his sacred gifts?"

"Tell me about him, Uncle."

"Yes, it's time," Touches the Sky agreed. "Let's build up the fire. It's a long tale."

And so they added thick oak logs to the willow twigs and watched as a red glow circulated through the small shelter. Dreamer sat with his legs folded beneath him, waiting for his uncle to begin the story. But before speaking Touches the Sky drew out a pipe and smoked.

Only then did the medicine man begin to talk of Sweet Medicine, the great culture hero of the People.

"Before Sweet Medicine came, there were no bands among the People," Touches the Sky explained. "Also, we had no laws and no chiefs. The warrior societies, also, were unknown to us, and we didn't enjoy the wisdom of Mahuts, the sacred Arrows. All these things grew from Sweet Medicine's visions.

"Even as a small boy, the People knew here was a strange one. In his tenth summer, a terrible hunger came upon the People. It was then he made up the hoop game, which children still play. No one knew of it then, though, and they gathered to watch as Sweet Medicine flung his sticks at the buffalo-calf hoop. As it rolled by, he flung his stick. Three throws failed to find the hole in the center. The fourth did, and the hoop became a buffalo calf pierced by an arrow. Sweet Medicine pulled out the arrow and bid the People come and cut a piece of meat to chase the hunger from their bellies.

"So it was great things were expected of this boy. As he grew, he, like yourself, was invited to go with the men to hunt Bull Buffalo. Sweet Medicine, though, had no father to follow, and so he went off ahead of the other men. His path led him to the buffalo, and he made the sacred prayers, strung his bow, and killed a bull calf. As he was skinning this calf, an old man came upon him.

"Even as the old ones do today, those who are not strong will help carry meat back to the village or join in the skinning. So it was this old man came and offered to skin the calf. Sweet Medicine was already cutting away the hide, though. Even so, he offered this old one a share of the meat.

" 'Thank you,' the old one answered, 'but it's this hide I most admire. I need a hide like this.' But this was Sweet Medicine's first kill, and he desired to keep the hide. 'Here's a share of the meat,' the young one said, 'but I want the hide for myself.' 'Give me the hide,' the old man insisted. 'I'm bigger and can take it from you!' Such words made Sweet Medicine angry, and he raised up a stone and struck the old man, knocking him down.

"This was a bad thing, and Sweet Medicine knew it. He took his hide and meat back to the village, and his grandmother cooked some for them to eat. Then a party of men gathered and sought out Sweet Medicine to punish him. 'Grandmother, don't lie to them,' Sweet Medicine said. 'But when they come in, throw water on the fire and make smoke so I may escape.' The men entered, but Sweet Medicine disappeared when the smoke rose from the fire. Angry now, the men set out to find Sweet Medicine.

"He was no longer welcome among the People, so he fled. One of the men cried out that he was on a nearby ridge, and many saw him there. They ran after him, but he vanished. When he next appeared, his body was painted, he wore feathers on his head, and he held a stringless bow."

"This is the dress of the Fox Society," Dreamer noted. "My father dressed in this way to meet the Chippewas."

"Yes," Touches the Sky said, nodding. "But no one knew that then. Soon Sweet Medicine disappeared once more. The men ran on, and when they spotted him on the next ridge, he carried an elk horn and a crooked spear wrapped in otter skin with three eagle feathers tied to it. This became the symbol of the Elk Society."

"Yes, Uncle," Dreamer responded. "And next?"

"Sweet Medicine disappeared, but on the next ridge he stood wearing feathers and red paint, as do the Red Shields today. But again before the men could catch him, he disappeared. On the fourth ridge he stood with a rawhide rope hanging from the side of his belt, carrying a round rattle decorated with feathers. Now the Crazy Dog Soldiers adopt this dress.

"Finally, on a fifth ridge he stood wearing a buffalo robe, holding a pipe, with one eagle feather stuck through a braided lock of his hair, such as chiefs now wear. After that he vanished from sight. The men could not find him on the next ridge or the next. He was gone, and four snows came and went before the People saw him again."

"Where did he go?" Dreamer asked.

"Long and far, Nephew," Touches the Sky explained. "When he finally returned, he told of many strange things. He had journeyed past the place where Sun dies to the heart of the world. Here, in this sacred place, Noahvose, where hills dark with timber rise from the great emptiness of the flatlands, he came upon a big lodge. Grandmothers sat on one side, and Grandfathers sat on the other. They were not people, though. They were the all-knowing ones, and they bid Sweet Medicine learn from them.

"They called him Grandson, and they showed him four sacred Arrows which became the great power of the People. Two were for hunting. The others were for war. The Grandfathers taught him the Arrow ceremonies, showed how they could be renewed, and what to do when their power and wisdom was needed.

"Next Sweet Medicine was taught how the People should choose forty-four chiefs and split into bands for hunting. He learned, too, of the warrior societies he was to create. Finally, when he had learned all these things, he returned to the People.

"The first to see him were small ones gathering berries. Since Sweet Medicine had left, the People had known great want. There was rarely enough to eat, and Bull Buffalo had turned away from the hunters. Sweet Medicine bid these children come close. He carried the sacred Arrows in their medicine bundle, and with its magic he changed their berries into buffalo meat. 'Take this food to the People and say that Sweet Medicine has returned,' he told them, and the little ones hurried to share the news.

"That next day an eagle flew over the camp, and the People watched in wonder. A second eagle appeared the next day, and a third came after that. Afterward, the wolves and coyotes made a great noise in the hills, and all the camp dogs took up the cry. When a fourth eagle came with dawn, some young men followed it to the hill where the children had been. There stood Sweet Medicine with the sacred bundle.

" 'Go back to the People and tell them to prepare a lodge for me,' Sweet Medicine instructed. 'I'm bringing with me great power that is given to all the People!'

"A lodge was made ready, and the young men returned to welcome Sweet Medicine back to his people. He came, singing and crying out as he walked. Then he set the Arrows in their honored place and began instructing the People in the new ways he had learned. The People now had law, and the hunts were successful.

In war their power was great, and enemies trembled before them."

"All that's now changed," Dreamer said, frowning.

"Yes, the People have lost their way," Touches the Sky observed. "When Sweet Medicine was old and near his death, he warned of many things, Nephew. Some have come to pass. Others remain beyond my eyes. Perhaps you'll remember them and use your wisdom to guide the People."

"I'll try, Uncle," Dreamer promised.

"Sweet Medicine spoke of a light-colored people who will come among us. Their ways are all-powerful. They cut their hair short and speak in unknown tongues. They will not walk the sacred path, but will turn the rivers and cut the sacred earth where they go. We must not follow the example of these strangers, for that will lead to death and disaster.

"Bull Buffalo will disappear. Another creature will take his place—one with a smooth hide, a long tail, and split hooves. The People will learn to eat its flesh, but it won't make them strong like Bull Buffalo did.

"Another creature will come before that, though. This will be a wonderful animal, and the People will carry themselves on his back. He will have round hooves, a shaggy neck, and a tail which will flow down almost to the ground. Now the far hills are only a blue vision, beyond walking. But this animal will take us there.

"Sweet Medicine left us for a holy place atop Bear Lodge Mountain, a high place with steep slopes on all sides. He said as he left that these things would come to pass, and the People would forget the old ways. Perhaps this is so, for even now we are changing. I fear for these things to happen, Nephew, and I fear the arrival of these strangers with the light skin. Even so, they come to my dreams sometimes. I ache at the thought of days when there are no buffalo to hunt, no brave deeds for the young men to perform. What will make us strong and wise?"

"Maybe these times are far away, Uncle."

"Maybe," Touches the Sky agreed "I pray they are. Already we have lost our old home beside the river. We've buried too many children. Great warriors have fallen long before the first white streaks have painted their hair. It's a sad time."

"We can stay here on this hill," Dreamer suggested. "I can gather food, and you can invite a dream. Your visions can direct the People back on the sacred path, and—"

"No, that's no longer for me to do," Touches the Sky declared. "Once Man Above gave me power, and I turned the bad medicine away from the People. I'm growing old now, though, and the spirits speak in whispers I can barely hear. Soon my eyes will see only today and not tomorrow."

"What will we do then, Uncle?" Dreamer asked.

"I will find my rest, Nephew," Touches the Sky explained as he gripped Dreamer's slender shoulders. "And you will seek the vision that will carry the People on into tomorrow."

"No, Uncle," Dreamer argued. "I'm still a boy. I don't know anything."

"What I can teach you, I will," Touches the Sky promised. "We will renew the Arrows, hoping their power may hold off Sweet Medicine's visions. And I will show you the mysteries I hold closest to my heart.

93

Then will come a time when you will walk alone. And finally, when all recognize the greatness that is in you, your turn will come to keep the sacred Arrows."

"You've seen all this, Uncle?"

"That and more," Touches the Sky answered. "When your days come to an end, no one will remember the old man who shares this night with you. But they will sing of you so long as there are brave hearts."

Dreamer felt a fire spread through his chest, and he sat straighter and taller than before. His walnut eyes sparkled as they recognized the confidence flowing from his uncle into his shoulders.

Before he had worried he would never prove worthy of that confidence. Now he set aside that concern. If he had learned anything, it was to trust Touches the Sky's visions.

Chapter Eight

Winter snows melted away into memory, and spring brought a sweetness to the land. As for the People, Touches the Sky's visions led them ever westward. Gone now were the tall pine forests and red pipestone they were accustomed to. Instead they drifted to Muddy River — a raging stream wider than any remembered by the grandfathers. Here, among their new allies, the Mandans and Rees, they constructed villages and planted crops.

Dreamer passed his fifteenth summer at Muddy River. He was growing at last — not yet tall, but long of leg at least. He was coming to be a man now, and he rarely ate at his father's fire. More often he, Corn Boy, and Younger Elk would set off on hunts. Sometimes they would visit the Mandan camps or watch the maidens dig tubers along the river.

Mostly, though, he accompanied Touches the Sky, helping him with the medicine cures and seeing to his needs. For the days were now weighing heavily on the Arrow-keeper, and his white hair was not the only testament to the fact. Touches the Sky walked with a staff. Old wounds and bitter memories plagued his sleep. The years and hardships twisted his limbs and bent him over with their burdens.

"Soon it will be your day," he told Dreamer often.

"No, Uncle, that's still a blue vision. We have many days together."

"I've taught you what I know," Touches the Sky insisted. "It's for Man Above to do the rest."

"But I know so little," the young man complained.

"We all of us are born," Touches the Sky replied. "As we walk the sacred path, we learn. I did. You will also."

Dreamer wondered.

The green-grass moon of midsummer was overhead the night the stars called him. Perhaps it was just a whisper carried by the wind. Or maybe it was the echo of a Mandan flute upriver. Whatever sound first enticed him from his uncle's lodge, it was the stars above that led him from the camp.

Long ago Touches the Sky had pointed out the figures of the old ones up in the heavens. There were stories of Eagle and the great Bear Lodge. The seven Star Boys continued to play up there, too. But it was Traveling Star that drew Dreamer's attention.

"Where are you going, little one?" he asked. "Will you never stop? Are you like the People, destined to flee one enemy after another until the light-skinned ones of Sweet Medicine's prophecy arrive to bring on your end?"

He sang a brief medicine chant, hoping that would clear his mind and allow him to see more clearly. Afterward he only saw more stars. Then a great weariness took possession of him, and he lay in the buffalo grass and drifted into a heavy sleep.

At first he saw only darkness. Then his mind opened upon a rough, ravine-scarred land he'd never seen. He flew on Eagle's wings, soaring over broad valleys black-ened by Bull Buffalo's herds. He saw the strange wooded hills Touches the Sky had spoken of, the Black Mountains — and other marvels besides. Many brown-skinned peoples made their summer camps in the hills and valleys he saw, but none resembled the light-skinned terrors of prophecy. Their dress and speech were foreign, but they hunted Bull Buffalo, Deer, and Brother Elk for food and clothing. Their weapons were bow and lance. Dreamer felt only kinship for them.

The dream next took him along a shallow, reddish-colored river. Here, past a camp of skin lodges, lived bands of tall men who wore their hair long across the crowns of their heads and shaved above the ears, even as the hated Chippewas did. But it wasn't their hair that flooded Dreamer's mind. No, it wasn't the people at all.

At first Dreamer saw only a flash of buckskin racing through the yellow seas of buffalo grass. The dream took him closer, though, and he saw clearly a huge head trailing shaggy hair attached to a long, muscular trunk. The creature had four legs. Its tail was long, and its hooves were round!

This revelation shook Dreamer awake. He sat up, shivering with cold fear and shaking from chin to toe.

"My dreams," he muttered. "Man Above has let me see with the far sight."

He caught his breath and studied the sky overhead. The stars had turned, and he knew much of the night had passed. Collecting his wits, he struggled to his feet and started for the Arrow Lodge.

When he reached the village, he moved quietly past the sleeping camp dogs and crawled inside the door of the Arrow Lodge. The fire inside burned brightly, and

Dreamer saw his uncle was sitting beside the flames, awaiting his return.

"You've had a dream," Touches the Sky announced. "Sit and tell me what you've seen."

"Much, Uncle," Dreamer replied.

"How did it come to you?"

"I heard a song," Dreamer explained. "I followed it outside, and the stars seemed to summon me. I walked for a time. Then I grew sleepy, so I lay in the grass. The dream came to me out there, past the river."

"Tell me what you remember."

"I flew above the earth. I saw broad valleys, and the Black Mountains you told me of. The place where Sweet Medicine learned from the Grandfathers. I saw many strange peoples. And beside a reddish river I saw the four-legged animal with the hairy neck and round hooves."

"Ah," Touches the Sky said, sighing. "Was it cold there or warm?"

"Warm," Dreamer said without really knowing why.

"Then, it lies south. Describe the people there."

Dreamer did so, and Touches the Sky frowned.

"These are the ones the Mandans know as the tall enemy. Rees call them Kiowa. They are fearsome hunters and great raiders. We must be wary of them."

"These animals were near their camp," Dreamer explained.

"This is a creature that will ease the burdens of life," Touches the Sky declared. "Long have I hungered to see it myself, even though it hurries the coming of the light-skinned ones. If I were younger, I would hunt these four-legged animals myself. But my time for adventures is past."

"I saw them in my dream, Uncle. It's for me to go. I'll take a pipe and form a raiding party."

"No, this is a thing you must do alone," Touches the Sky argued. "You saw no one else in your vision?"

"No," Dreamer admitted.

"You must go alone. Don't fear, though. I will make medicine to help you, and Man Above will guide your journey."

"Yes, Uncle," Dreamer agreed. "When must I start?"

"We'll smoke, and we'll pray. Then you must take a long sweat to purify yourself. Finally I will paint you with my own magic, and you will go. Five days this will take. You must leave on the sixth."

And so it was. Touches the Sky shared the smoking and praying. Gray Wolf, Corn Boy, and Younger Elk joined in the purification ritual.

"I'm proud my son goes to find his vision," Gray Wolf declared afterward. And Dreamer saw the envy painting the eyes of Corn Boy and Younger Elk.

The night before he was to leave, there was much feasting and dancing in the camp. Many Lances brought a fine painted bow, and Avenging Crow provided a quiver of arrows. Little Crane offered a soft buckskin shirt. Corn Boy and Younger Elk provided new moccasins.

Touches the Sky bid his nephew offer up prayers for these many benefactors and say his farewells. Then the two of them climbed the hills above Muddy River and made medicine.

First, Touches the Sky cut back Dreamer's hair above the ears in the style of his enemies so that the young man would not stand out. Then he tied two feathers in his hair — one the tail feather of white-faced eagle and the other that of the horned owl.

"Eagle will help you see far, Nephew," Touches the Sky explained. "Owl will help you to see in darkness."

There were other charms, too. The deer's foot would lend its swiftness; and the elk's tooth, its sacred protection. Lastly the old man painted Dreamer's chest red and his face a ghostly blue. With crushed buffalo-horn powder, Touches the Sky drew lightning bolts and horn symbols. Lastly the old man invoked the blessings of Wolf and Bear by tying a claw of each creature in the young man's hair.

"Rest well, Nephew," Touches the Sky finally said as he rolled out a buffalo hide for the boy. "I will tend the fire and sing for you. Tomorrow you are born a second time. Nothing that has been can ever be the same afterward."

"No," Dreamer confessed. "I feel it, too."

Dreamer stayed only long enough to make the dawn prayers. Then he dressed himself and clasped his uncle's wrists in a final farewell.

"Thank you for guiding my steps onto the sacred path, Uncle," Dreamer said as he turned to leave.

"Only Man Above can guide you now, Nephew," Touches the Sky said sadly. "May He watch over you."

Dreamer nodded somberly. Then he started the long walk south into the unknown. His first steps were reluctant ones, for he felt empty leaving so much of himself behind. But he remembered the stories of Sweet Medicine and knew the medicine trail must always be a lonely road, with many dangers and much uncertainty. And he gave thanks for the struggle he faced. It would make him strong.

* * *

The sun rose and fell many times before Dreamer reached the land of the Kiowas. The cherry-ripening moon of late summer was fast approaching by then. He had been too long alone, and he ached to swim and fish Muddy River again with his friends. Soon it would be time to hunt deer. And afterward, the autumn buffalo hunt would begin.

"Man Above, am I always to be alone?" Dreamer cried.

As if in answer, Thunderbird shook its wings, and the sky overhead darkened. Lightning flashes lit the late afternoon, and soon rain arrived in torrents.

Dreamer managed to find shelter along a small stream in a stand of willows. There he shivered in his buffalo robe and waited for the storm to pass. Strange that he should feel such a chill when a short time before he had burned in the summer heat. He gazed skyward and wondered what sort of ill chance had led him so far from his people. It must be Trickster who was even now tormenting him with this rain! But if the storm hadn't come, he would have continued walking along the stream as before. And now he came to understand what danger that would have brought.

Just ahead feet splashed through the shallows. Voices joined in angry argument. Through the mists Dreamer identified several slender young men crossing the stream. Even with their wet hair pasted against their heads, their flesh bare, and the light dim, he recognized them as the Kiowas from his dream.

Their camp lay just ahead, and Dreamer kept to the willows. A mixture of fear and relief flooded his insides, for at least he had reached his destination. His chance at greatness was near. Of course now was the time of the greatest peril, too.

"Man Above, you've shielded me from harm again," Dreamer whispered as he watched the Kiowa boys dress themselves and continue into their camp. He then wove his way through the underbrush until he was close enough to smell venison cooking on a nearby fire.

Hunger gnawed at him. He couldn't recall when he had last tasted fresh meat. The fear of revealing his presence had left him gaunt. Raw tubers and berries could not sustain one forever.

Dreamer started toward the camp, thinking to snatch a bit of meat from an unguarded fire, when he spied the first of the hairy-necked creatures. There were others, too. He counted six. A small boy watched over them in spite of the fearful crash of thunder echoing from across the stream.

A fresh cloudburst had the boy hugging himself against the cold. Soon misery overcame his determination to stay, and he fled toward a nearby mud hut.

Now, cloaked in fog, with his sounds swallowed by thunderclaps, Dreamer stepped to the fire and tore himself a piece of soggy meat. He then continued past the Kiowa lodges to where the four-legged creatures grazed.

The Kiowas had tied the beasts' forelegs with rawhide straps to prevent their escape, but Dreamer made short work of those. His knife blade neatly sliced the hide strips, and the animals were free.

Next Dreamer moved among them, whispering medicine prayers and inviting them to return north to Muddy River with him. The animals stirred uneasily at his first words, and they avoided his touch. By and by they accepted his scent, and when he climbed atop the powerful buckskin that had blazed through his dreams, the animal sprang into action.

"Ayyyy!" Dreamer howled as he drove the other animals before him. Not even thunder drowned that cry, and weary Kiowa boys dashed out of their huts to seek the source of that foreign sound. They were already too late to save their medicine creatures, though. The buckskin was five stone throws from the encampment, and its brother creatures, free of restraint, flew along on both sides.

Dreamer knew the Kiowas would follow. Perhaps they had other animals. Certainly they were better riders, for Dreamer barely managed to hang on to the buckskin's flowing hair as it rode the wind northward. And so when the storm finally passed, and the animals wearied of the pace, he herded his prizes down a ravine enclosed on one side by a rock slide and made camp.

He chewed the rest of the venison that night while staring at the stars overhead. No fresh visions visited his dreams, but he knew his trials were only now beginning. Riding the new wind racers, as he thought of them, he could cover a week's ground in a single day. Even so, he was a long way from friends, and there were Kiowa camps between him and Muddy River.

"Man Above," he prayed, "guide me back to the People."

And in so saying, he climbed atop the buckskin and resumed his flight.

The animals enjoyed their race across the scarred landscape. Less so Dreamer. His thighs were rubbed raw by the buckskin's rough hide, and his back and bottom were nearly numb. When he spied the first of the pursuing Kiowas, he saw they sat in a sort of U-shaped seat made of deer ribs and buffalo hide. He envied them both their saddles and the halter by which they controlled their animals' movements. Dreamer coaxed the buckskin to turn by pulling its hair or slapping its rump. Neither was very successful.

There were two Kiowa riders. The first was a tall man with his face painted for war. He carried lance and bow tied behind him on his animal's back. In his hand he waved a fierce war ax.

The second rider was the same slight-shouldered boy who had been watching the animals. Dreamer read a determined stare in the youngster's gaze and feared he would never give up the chase. An older man might grow weary and give way. That young one would continue so long as he breathed. Dreamer decided to evade the first rider and fight the second.

That wasn't so easy. The man was skillful, and he almost cut over and thwarted Dreamer's attack. The ground there was broken by a crumbling ravine, though, and the Kiowa's horse stepped in a hole, strained a tendon, and shed its rider.

As for the boy, he wasn't half so small as had first appeared. In truth he was a hair taller and considerably heavier than Dreamer. The two rushed at each other, screaming wildly, and collided with a crash. Both boys rolled off their surprised mounts and wrestled in the muddy ravine below. The Kiowa managed to slash Dreamer's left shin with a knife, and he clamped onto Dreamer's left wrist with daggerlike teeth. Dreamer countered by slamming an elbow against the Kiowa's forehead and kicking him hard in the belly — twice.

The Kiowa recovered and struck out again with his

knife. Dreamer dodged the blow, then turned the knife back against its owner. The blade slid neatly between two ribs and tore into the boy's vitals. There was a rush of air as a lung was pierced, and blood bubbled on the young man's lips. The Kiowa fell back, muttering his death chant as darkness closed upon his eyes.

Dreamer now tore off his shirt and wrapped it around his bloody leg. He then limped to the buckskin and mounted the poor beast. Driving the Kiowa boy's animal ahead of him, Dreamer continued the flight. Shortly he collected the other creatures and galloped away northward.

Twice more Kiowa riders approached, but none ever closed the distance. Once a flooded stream stopped them. The second time a thunderstorm broke out, and Dreamer was able to escape in the mists.

He returned to the People as summer ebbed. The seven animals he brought with him stirred all manner of curiosity, and each was encircled and examined by man and boy alike.

"This is Horse," Touches the Sky announced. "He comes to us even as Sweet Medicine foretold in the time when the grandfathers were still young. These animals will give our people wings to carry us across the land. Even Bull Buffalo will tremble at our approach!"

"Ayyyy!" the warriors cried.

"Welcome home, Nephew," Touches the Sky said as Dreamer climbed down into his uncle's powerful arms. "You've done a brave heart thing this day. I recognize a battle scar on your leg. Come. I'll make medicine. See my nephew, brothers! He's met the enemy and returned to us!"

"Ayyyy!" the men howled.

"I've had many adventures," Dreamer declared. "Uncle, I would tell you of them."

"No, that's for later," Touches the Sky argued. "Now is the time for mending and resting. Later we will talk of your quest."

Chapter Nine

So it was that Horse first came to the People. Ever afterward, as the story of Dreamer's quest was related, old men would tell of the boy's battle scar, of the dream that carried him into Kiowa country, and of the great council held to celebrate the young warrior's return.

Dreamer would always remember that night. His leg remained stiff from the buckskin binding Touches the Sky had applied, and he limped to the gathering. Corn Boy and Younger Elk led along the seven captured animals, for the celebration was as much for them as for Dreamer.

"Here is the hairy-necked beast whose coming Sweet Medicine foretold long ago," Touches the Sky reminded the other men.

"Ayyyy!" they shouted.

"And here is Dreamer, my nephew, who brings greatness to the People!" the medicine man added.

"Ayyyy!" the men cried even louder.

"Tell of it now, Naha'," Gray Wolf urged, and Dreamer stood before the fire, gazing at the attentive eyes of his elders. Then he told of the dream and the great adventure in the lands to the south.

Once the tale was shared, there was much feasting and

dancing. Afterward Dreamer led each horse out in turn.

"This is a good horse, Ne' hyo," he told Gray Wolf. "He will carry you swift and sure across Mother Earth."

He repeated the gesture, giving the second horse to Touches the Sky. Then he gave ponies to his adopted brothers, Corn Boy and Younger Elk. He kept the buckskin for himself. The last two he brought to Many Lances and Avenging Crow, who with Gray Wolf were chiefs of the band.

"Generosity is the mark of a man of the People," Avenging Crow noted as he accepted the gift.

"All this Man Above has sent us," Dreamer replied. "It's only right that those who will lead the young men should stand tallest among the People."

"Today I lead," the Crow said, nodding with approval. "But soon you will show the way. You follow your uncle on the medicine trail, and you see the road our feet must travel."

Dreamer glowed. It meant his counsel carried weight.

It was three days later when the Fox criers appeared at the Arrow Lodge.

"Dreamer, come!" they called.

Touches the Sky, who himself carried the stringless bow of the Foxes, guided his nephew into the arms of the criers. Dreamer tried to remain calm as the men clasped his arms and hurried him toward their council fire. He had seen other young men called to join the warrior societies, and he had heard the grandfathers tell of their own initiations. He had an idea of what would happen, but he nevertheless trembled with anticipation. For once he joined the Foxes' council, he would no longer be a boy.

They hurried out past the camp to where a tall fire burned beside Muddy River. Sacred totems hung on lances there, and skins were painted in symbols telling of brave fights from the past. The criers were challenged as they prepared to enter the circle, but they gave satisfactory answers to each question. Once inside the council circle, Dreamer noted places were marked out around the fire. All save one were occupied. It was to this empty spot that Dreamer was led and made to sit.

The Fox leaders, Gray Wolf and Avenging Crow, started a pipe around, and the men smoked. Then old men stood and told of brave deeds they had performed in their youth. Others recounted the deeds of relatives or friends who had since climbed Hanging Road. Finally Gray Wolf spoke of his son's recent quest to the south and the present he had made to the People of Horse.

"This boy is among us," Avenging Crow announced. "Dreamer he's been called, but he's a boy no longer. He should carry a man's name."

"Yes!" the others agreed. "Who would give him a name?"

An old man called Silent Walker, a great hunter, rose.

"I've heard this one talk of his dream," Silent Walker said, turning to gaze upon Dreamer's face. "In this dream he flew over Mother Earth and saw much that came to be. His name will now be Cloud Dancer, for he walks with Eagle and Hawk."

"It's a good name," Gray Wolf agreed. "I'm proud that my son should carry it. In honor of his new name and his manhood, I would give presents to my brothers."

The Wolf then stood and walked among the others, handing them hides or moccasins, knives and arrows. Mostly he gave to the old ones or men who had taken in nieces and nephews after the Chippewa war.

"Cloud Dancer," Avenging Crow said, "look around

you. Here we are all Foxes. Swift Fox is the cleverest of hunters. He runs fast so as always to catch his enemies, and he takes care to guard the defenseless ones. Fox Warriors always lead the way into battle. Foxes never abandon the weak to the enemy. Only the bravest carry the stringless bow! You have gone far into enemy country and brought back many horses. Long will this be remembered. Your heart is already that of Swift Fox. Come, join our circle."

"Ayyyy!" the others yelled.

"I'm done great honor," Cloud Dancer replied. He was shaking badly, but he did manage to stand and face the Fox Warriors. "I'll share your dangers and endeavor to stand as tall and proud as my father and uncle have before me."

"I am a Fox!" the others shouted. "Mine is the hard road."

"I am a Fox," Cloud Dancer repeated. "Mine is the hard road."

The others howled, and a drummer struck up a beat. Soon men rose and began dancing. Cloud Dancer was taken aside and given the sacred symbol of the society — the stringless bow. His face was painted, and his buckskin shirt was replaced by a soft garment of elk hide with the shapes of seven horses beaded on the front. Finally, a notched eagle feather was braided in his hair.

As he joined in the dancing and sang the warrior songs, he felt suddenly taller, stronger. His heart flooded with confidence as he searched the other faces for signs of doubt or suspicion. He saw none. Gone were the old taunts of Laughing Bear and the other boys. Of all the Foxes, Cloud Dancer was the youngest. It had been his destiny to bring Horse to the People. Now he was marked as a man who would lead others, who would show the way.

When the embers of the council fire lost their glow, and weariness overtook the Foxes, they disbanded their gathering. Cloud Dancer returned to the camp with his uncle. Along the way he paused to speak to his friends. He told Little Crane, his mother, the name he had taken, and he accepted the warm congratulations of Corn Boy and Younger Elk.

"Soon your turn will come," he told them.

"Yes, you'll lead us south in search of more horses," Corn Boy said. "Then we, too, will be welcomed as men."

It was later, after he removed his clothing and settled between two buffalo hides across the lodge from Touches the Sky, that Cloud Dancer spoke to his uncle of his new feelings.

"I'm proud to carry a brave name," the young man admitted. "But now the others expect so much. I worry I won't be worthy of their trust."

"You'll be what Man Above determines," Touches the Sky answered. "This will happen no matter what you choose or I advise. Already your dreams guide your path."

"Will it always be like that, Uncle?"

"Always," Touches the Sky answered. "As it's been with me. Our names are much the same. We both are closer to the sky spirits than others. We see and hear things. It's our destiny to sacrifice our own comforts for the well-being of the People. It's a hard trail we walk."

"You'll teach me what I must do, though."

"I've shared with you the healing cures, Nephew. I've taught you the ceremonies and prayers. Only the mysteries of the Arrows remain mine alone,

111

and they, too, may one day be yours."

"You'll keep them many winters yet. And I will be at your side, helping with the medicine, collecting roots—"

"No, you're a man now," Touches the Sky pronounced. "Tomorrow we make the dawn prayers together the last time. You'll erect your own lodge and busy yourself on young-man hunts and horse raids. You will seek dreams and follow their wisdom."

"I can't do these things alone," Cloud Dancer argued.

"Man Above will guide you, and there will be many men eager to follow your medicine."

"Have you seen this, Uncle?"

"For a long time," Touches the Sky answered sadly. "Even as Sweet Medicine told of Horse coming, I've known you would be the one to bring it. And I knew when you returned, you would be a boy no longer. It's a good thing, Nephew. Life is a tall climb, and you have reached the first summit. Gray Wolf and I have led you there. Now comes the time when you must lead others."

"I'm frightened by that thought," Cloud Dancer confessed.

"Don't be. Man Above would not have guided your steps so far if he intended you to falter."

"But there's Trickster, too," Cloud Dancer pointed out. "He's there, too, eager to turn a man's pride against him."

"Your eyes are bright, Nephew. They can see where Trickster may put his snares. Trust your dreams. And never forget the medicine prayers I've taught you."

"I won't, Uncle."

Cloud Dancer promised himself always to remember his uncle's words. He tried, too, to recall the confident gaze in the old man's eyes, especially when his own doubts grew.

The other young men shared no such doubts. When his dreams told of large horse herds on the rivers to the south, Cloud Dancer led small bands of warriors on raids. And as the People's herds grew, his dreams told of hunting Bull Buffalo on horseback. Never before was the autumn hunt so successful!

"Man Above," Cloud Dancer spoke as he greeted the dawn. "You've brought us hard fights to make us strong. Now you give us Horse so we can hunt meat and hides to keep us through winter's hardships."

By the following spring Cloud Dancer had reached his full height. Where once his slender shoulders and thin legs had marked him frail, new muscle and hard riding had broadened and hardened him. Never again would anyone judge him small or weak.

"There goes Cloud Dancer," the grandfathers often said respectfully. "I remember how he always listened to my stories of the old ways. Even then I knew he would know greatness."

Others simply remembered him as the boy who brought Horse to the People.

His sixteenth spring saw a greater than ever bond forged with Corn Boy and Younger Elk, too. These adopted brothers, who now shared a lodge, were always to be seen together. Their hunts always brought meat to the camp, and their raids never failed to swell the horse herd.

It was only natural Cloud Dancer would sponsor his brothers to the Foxes. The gift of many horses won acceptance for both. Younger Elk received the manhood name Horse Chaser, for he was swiftest and most daring of all the raiders. As for Corn Boy, he had chosen as his mount a pure-white stallion. He would thus carry the name White Horse.

"It's a fine way to mark yourself to an enemy," Cloud Dancer complained.

"Brother, I'm a Fox," White Horse replied. "My road is hard."

Yes, Cloud Dancer thought. But he feared Trickster often made it even more perilous.

Chapter Ten

As summers were born, passed, and died in the hard-face winds of winter, Cloud Dancer often led the young men on horse raids against the Kiowas. Each autumn there was the buffalo hunt to busy a man. And when enemies traveled Muddy River to attack the People, Cloud Dancer painted his face, took up the stringless bow, and followed Avenging Crow and Gray Wolf on the war trail.

By their twentieth spring, Cloud Dancer and White Horse were famous among the People for their courage in hard fights, and for the pranks they played on the females of the tribe. The two young men were forever hiding along the river, ready to attack the water gatherers. And many times they raided the root collectors in the woodland.

"Ah, it's time those two took wives," the grandfathers grumbled. "Young men with no families to look after are always getting into mischief."

Cloud Dancer, though, waited for his medicine to send him to the river with a flute. He remembered old Touches the Sky, whose medicine forbid him the company of women. And so long as Cloud Dancer took no wife, White Horse was determined to do likewise. As for

Horse Chaser, he had long since presented Many Lances with three horses and taken the chief's niece, Moon Willow, for a wife.

"Your brother walks the world in harmony," Gray Wolf told his older sons. "See what contentment can bring a man?"

When they were alone, White Horse laughed. "I only know the Willow has made Horse Chaser fat," he observed. "And he rarely races his horse or joins raids."

"Why would he?" Cloud Dancer asked. "He's traded for a wife. His lodge is warm. Soon he'll have sons to show the sacred way."

There was a hint of regret in Cloud Dancer's words. He himself enjoyed the company of women. Often Avenging Crow would invite him and White Horse to share food. The Crow's daughter, Little Horn Woman, cooked good fry bread, and she made no secret of her admiration for her father's young guests.

"I would welcome you for a son," Avenging Crow spoke more than once.

"She's a fine woman," Cloud Dancer answered each time. "But my dreams have not told me to invite a woman to my lodge yet. I will wait until Man Above directs me."

"Man Above has many obligations," Avenging Crow muttered. "Perhaps he's too busy to send a dream to you. Many young men come to speak with my daughter. She will marry before winter comes again."

"I've learned to trust my dreams, Uncle," Cloud Dancer said, addressing Avenging Crow as a respected elder. "I can only follow them in such matters. It's sometimes hard, but I know it's best."

"Perhaps," Avenging Crow admitted. "I'm sorry for it, though."

Sometimes I am myself, Cloud Dancer thought. *But I've never traveled the easy road.*

"Little Horn Woman's a good cook, Brother," White Horse pointed out. "And her face is pretty. Her older sisters and cousins have made good wives and borne many children. Our father has said it would be a pleasing match."

"Ne' hyo would like us to stay with his band," Cloud Dancer observed. "But I don't think it's what will happen. Sweet Medicine was sent away from his family. My power has come from long walking, from places far from Muddy River. I fear my path leads me elsewhere."

"Then mine will take me away, too," White Horse declared. "I don't have dreams, Brother. I only know the urge to follow."

"And if my dreams say I must walk my path alone?"

"They won't," White Horse said confidently. "My heart tells me that much. No, our sons will hunt Bull Buffalo together. They'll guard our ponies side by side. When the time comes to raid the Kiowas, they will be there together."

"It's a warming thought, Brother," Cloud Dancer said.

"Yes," White Horse agreed.

Three nights later a vision did come to Cloud Dancer's dreams. It wasn't the one Avenging Crow would have hoped for, nor was it the sort to offer warmth and comfort.

In the beginning Cloud Dancer saw only white smoke drifting along Muddy River. He himself was above that, singing a medicine cure for the People as he floated above the village. Down below children whispered death chants, and old warriors bared their chests and cut strips of flesh from their arms.

117

Then, from the south, a single rider approached. He sat atop a black horse, this shade of a man, and he carried a bow of dark walnut wood. From a beaded quiver he drew arrows with black flint points. The shafts were dark as midnight, and vulture feathers steadied their flight.

"I'm Death," the shade sang as he loosed his deadly arrows into the lodges of the People. "I come to carry away the People. Give me the weak, the young, the old. I hunger for them."

Cloud Dancer awoke trembling. He muttered the ghostly chant and shook the sweat streaming down his bare chest from his body.

"Brother, what have you seen?" White Horse cried as he crawled over from the far side of the lodge. "What has your dream told you?"

"Death," Cloud Dancer answered. "Coming from Kiowa country up Muddy River. Riding fast."

"What will we do?"

"Ask the Arrows," Cloud Dancer announced. "And seek another dream."

"Can the Arrows protect us from Death?" White Horse asked.

"Nothing can," the Dancer said, staring at his brother with tormented eyes. "Not from this. But they can tell us what to do."

Even before entering the Arrow Lodge and sharing his dream with Touches the Sky, Cloud Dancer knew another journey awaited him.

"You've seen the danger, Nephew," Touches the Sky observed. "Now the Arrows know of it, too. Some dangers may be faced. We would stand and fight the Kiowas, but this rider is a darkness from which we must flee."

"Where?" Cloud Dancer asked.

"Once I would have gone into the hills and sought a dream to guide our journey. I'm old now, and I don't see such things as I did once. It's for you to do."

"You'll go with me?"

"Yes, I can still feed a fire," the old man said, laughing grimly. "And when the dream comes, I'll help you find its truth."

They left after making the dawn prayers that next morning. Cloud Dancer enjoyed sharing the ritual, and he noticed his uncle's step was quicker thereafter. They rode out of the village upriver past the Mandan encampment before turning westward into the hills. Touches the Sky found a clearing high atop one hill, and they made camp there.

Cloud Dancer had experienced many dreams, but never before had he fasted and bled himself to invite a vision. Touches the Sky helped him by making prayers, invoking spirits, and beating a medicine drum. Even so, three days and two nights passed before the dream came.

It began with the shade, and Cloud Dancer sweated fiercely as it fired its deadly arrows into the People. Friends and relatives alike were struck down. Faces became peppered with ugly white blemishes, and bodies burned with fever. Soon whole bands climbed Hanging Road together.

All this Cloud Dancer knew, and that part of him that was aware cried for help.

"Man Above, I've seen the future. How can we save the People?"

Now the white smoke crept across the village, chasing Death from Muddy River. Cloud Dancer watched as two riders led the People. Horses pulled long poles laden with possessions. Those who had no pony to ride walked along behind. All the encampment took flight.

Ahead Bull Buffalo appeared, stomping his forefeet and urging the People to follow him onto the plain. Images of riders charging thundering herds along distant streams and rivers now flooded Cloud Dancer's mind. The People discarded their old huts of mud and straw. New lodges of buffalo hides—tall pointed shelters— formed circles on the plain. No longer would the People camp beside their corn and melon fields. Now Bull Buffalo would provide for them!

Cloud Dancer awoke in a cold sweat. Touches the Sky sat beside the fire, chanting and sprinkling powder on the embers.

"Uncle, I've seen it all!" Cloud Dancer shouted as he sat up. "Man Above has shown me our path."

The young man then described the vision, and Touches the Sky listened silently.

"We'll take the People west, into the lands where the sun dies," Cloud Dancer said, shuddering as a cool wind sent shivers down his spine. "Bull Buffalo will provide for us, and we'll follow his journey across the plain."

"There's power in your dreams, Nephew," Touches the Sky declared. "You see with wisdom. I'll not go with you again. Invite a boy to go and keep your fire. In this way he can learn the sacred path."

"I have no nephew," Cloud Dancer argued. "And there's much I still don't understand."

"No, you see what's in your dreams," Touches the Sky said, gripping the younger man's shoulders. "It's good for the People. Soon my time will pass, and you will keep Mahuts, too. I'm happy, knowing they will reside with a righteous man. So long as they do, the People will know prosperity."

"What of the pale people Sweet Medicine warned of?" Cloud Dancer asked. "Can the Arrows shield us from their medicine?"

"They could," Touches the Sky said, sighing. "But they won't be in our hands forever, Nephew. Bad men may use them for their own purposes, and the People will suffer."

"We must prevent that, Uncle."

"No man lives long," Touches the Sky said, gazing into the star-clouded heavens. "Even Sweet Medicine traveled Hanging Road. We can only warn those who will come. And they won't always have ears for wisdom. I've seen that. Sweet Medicine saw it. When you, too, are old, you will see it, too."

Cloud Dancer nodded, but he couldn't accept such prophecy. The shade would come to Muddy River, but the People would be gone. When the next danger appeared, he would lead the People away from it, too. What other purpose could his life have? Yes, he would always shield the People from harm.

Few men and almost none of the women welcomed Cloud Dancer's news. They listened to the young man's grim prophecy in awestruck silence. Some trembled at the notion of white sores and fierce fevers. Women pulled their children close, and men gazed sourly at the stunned faces of their sons.

"This will not happen!" Cloud Dancer vowed. "Man Above has shown me a road away from this dark rider. We will carry our camp on poles dragged by horses. These old huts of mud and sticks will be ours no longer. We'll sew new lodges of buffalo skins. No longer will we plant corn along the rivers. Instead Horse will take us on

Bull Buffalo's trail. We'll fill our bellies with his meat, and his hides will clothe our bodies and make our homes."

"Will we have no warm places when winter comes?" an old man asked.

"Must we build so many lodges?" another cried.

"Our lodge will be of skins supported by tall poles," Cloud Dancer explained. "When we move, we will pull it along with us. In this manner we can follow Bull Buffalo's movements. We'll have dung to fuel our fires, meat to eat, and hides to wear."

"This is good country," Avenging Crow argued. "These new places are far away, and I don't know them. We've fought enemies before to keep our land."

"I would fight the Kiowas," Cloud Dancer declared. "Or any other enemy that was flesh. But who can fight a shade? Who would watch the children die? My heart's not that strong. Is yours?"

Avenging Crow had no answer. He had buried young relatives, and the memory of those times overwhelmed his love for Muddy River and the rich country there.

"I'll follow you," the Crow promised. "Your dreams brought us Horse. They've led you to Bull Buffalo when the scouts could not find his sign. I trust your visions."

"As I do," Touches the Sky added. "Cloud Dancer spoke with the Arrows, and they urged him to follow his dreams. Can we do no less?"

"No," the People murmured.

And so the People collected their horses and packed up their camp. Messengers were sent to warn the other bands, and soon a great migration began.

"Dreams," a party of Mandans remarked when they came to investigate the departure of their neighbors. "They can tell much, but can one so young see clearly?"

122

Even as the last of the People rode away from Muddy River, one party of Mandans was coming to take possession of the deserted camp.

So it was that the People abandoned the old ways. No longer were they planters of corn. No more would they live in mud huts. Now they became known as the Desert People, those who moved with Bull Buffalo on the empty lands past Muddy River. They learned to make the pointed lodges supported by tall pine poles cut in the dark hills to the west. From deer and buffalo ribs they made improved saddles to ease the burden of their ponies on long rides. Cloud Dancer watched it all with approving eyes, for the horse herds continued to grow, and the People prospered.

In their wanderings, the People sometimes encountered new tribes of strange talkers whose manners and customs were most puzzling. Most such peoples were avoided. Some, like the Dakotas and Lakotas, people of the north, became friends. Others raided horses and became enemies.

Cloud Dancer's dreams sometimes warned of encounters with new bands, and he often sensed which could be treated peacefully. One dream puzzled him, though. In it he saw a strange buffalo-calf hat and a people who resembled his own in most manners. Still, their dress was peculiar, and he couldn't understand their words.

No sooner did he awake from this dream than White Horse announced a party of young men were galloping toward the camp with word of approaching strangers. Soon a band of Foxes was mounted and armed. They rode out to challenge the newcomers.

Cloud Dancer recognized them immediately from his dream. The men wore a flap of deerskin in front instead of a breechclout, and their leggings were tight above the knee and loose below. The arms and shoulders of the women were bare except for a strap passed over the left shoulder. The men rolled their hair tightly, but the women wore theirs loose in the familiar way.

Avenging Crow led the Foxes that day, and he was prepared to fight. But when he challenged the strangers, their reply startled him.

Cloud Dancer didn't know the words, but others among the party seemed to grasp their meaning. In the same way, some of the older strangers appeared to understand Avenging Crow's speech. Nevertheless, warriors on both sides strung their bows, and many waved lances and hurled insults.

"Stop!" Beaded Moccasin cried. He was an old man of sixty snows, but once he'd been a great fighter. His words carried weight, and the younger warriors lowered their weapons.

"What is it, Grandfather?" White Horse asked.

"I know these people," Beaded Moccasin explained. He then called out to them in their own talk, and they, too, put aside their arms. "These are the Suhtai, the left-behind band," the old man said. "My father was of their band. We've been apart many snows, but now they've rejoined us."

"Yes, it's them," Touches the Sky agreed. "Come, cousins, we also are of the People. I am Touches the Sky, who guards the sacred Arrows."

Beaded Moccasin translated the words, and the strangers shouted enthusiastically. They, too, carried a sacred bundle. In it was the sacred Buffalo Hat brought to the People long ago by Erect Horns, the other great culture hero.

124

"The Hat and Arrows are together again!" Touches the Sky shouted. "Now truly the People will be blessed."

That night there was much feasting. Old people from all ten bands visited each other, sharing near-forgotten stories of the Suhtai who had split off from the People long ago.

"Now Man Above has brought us back together," Touches the Sky told Cloud Dancer. "We're stronger than ever."

For three days and nights the celebration went on. Never was there so much food cooked or eaten. Young men raced horses or wrestled. Boys from many bands swam the nearby stream together, and women traded moccasins or robes.

Cloud Dancer kept to himself, for his dreams were troubled and confused. He saw the great camp swell with its new circle, but he felt more and more like a man apart — cut off from his world. Finally a woman appeared in his vision. She wore a deerskin dress died white, with beaded buffaloes sewn down the front. Her face was thin and solemn, but her eyes were bright and intelligent.

"A healer should have help," she whispered. "Many cures require a woman."

When Cloud Dancer awoke, he saw White Horse staring at him, a great grin upon his face.

"I think we'll have wives after all, Brother," the Horse said. "In your sleep you spoke. It will be a Suhtai woman, I think."

"Perhaps," Cloud Dancer replied. "Nothing is decided."

Clearly White Horse didn't believe that. There was good reason. Never in memory had so many young men and women been betrothed as at that reunion with the Suhtai.

Even after the dream, Cloud Dancer remained in his lodge. He was uneasy about visiting the strangers' camp, and he wasn't at all certain how to go about courting anyone, much less a girl he had never met.

But his dreams held power, and what they foretold came to pass. He was summoned to visit a sick child, and while he was preparing the cure, the girl from his vision appeared with medicine of her own.

"This boy is my cousin's new brother," she explained as she entered the lodge. "My father, Little Raven, has sent me to help with the cure. He says the medicine man has come alone. A healer should have help. Many cures require a woman."

"What are you called?" Cloud Dancer asked as he set aside his rattle and studied her eyes.

"I'm called Raven's Wing," she answered. "I'm Suhtai, but my father is of the Hill People. I know your words. And I've learned the healing craft."

"Then, help me," Cloud Dancer urged. "Sing while I paint his face and take away the fever."

They worked together, casting aside the dark spirits that had tormented the child. The powdered buffalo horn restored the boy's health, and the chants invoked the attentions of the kindly spirits. Finally the boy opened his eyes and smiled up at his healers.

"He's well," Cloud Dancer announced. He then left the lodge, followed by Raven's Wing. The family of the sick boy sang out their approval, and the father invited both to share a meal.

"Yes, when the boy is strong enough to invite us himself," Cloud Dancer replied.

126

"Yes," Raven's Wing agreed. "I must return to my father's lodge."

"You have no husband?" Cloud Dancer asked.

"I only have sixteen summers," she explained. "I look older."

"I'm not so much older myself," he told her. "I have no wife. Perhaps I may find a flute and visit your lodge."

"Father will welcome your visit, Cloud Dancer."

"You know of me?"

"Even among the Hill People the story's told of how you brought Horse to the People. I expected to find you an old man. The dreaming must have come to you very young."

"Always," he told her.

"And did you see me in a dream, too?"

"Yes," he said, nodding and smiling shyly. "I heard your words."

"Does this dream mean anything?" she asked.

"That you'll be my wife," he announced. "I know there must be courting, and I will speak to your father. But I also know we will be together. I feel that much, here," he added, touching his heart.

"I, too," she declared, touching his hand lightly.

Chapter Eleven

Cloud Dancer was well acquainted with the courtship rituals of the People, but he worried these Suhtai strangers might have their own ways. So it was that he went to Touches the Sky for advice.

"Uncle, I've met a girl who I wish for my wife," Cloud Dancer explained. "She's a Suhtai woman, Raven's Wing, and I wish you would talk to her father for me."

"Does the girl welcome your attentions?" Touches the Sky asked.

"She says she does," Cloud Dancer replied. "But I don't know her well. Even so, I saw her face in my dreams, and I know she's the one who I should invite to my lodge."

"I'll speak to her father," Touches the Sky promised. "We'll talk of presents and choose a time. There must be a courtship, though. Honor demands that. Do you have a flute?"

"No, Uncle."

"Then, I will make you one. Its medicine will be strong, and the music will draw you together. Walk with her beside the stream and talk of things."

"Things?" Cloud Dancer asked.

"The sky. Her people. She's the daughter of a healer. Talk about medicine cures. After you do this four times, bring a robe to her lodge. Invite her to share it with you. There must be only talk now, but afterward we can make the betrothal."

"I have many horses to offer her father."

"I've spoken with Little Raven. He's a good man, and a fair one. He won't ask more than is proper, and I expect him to welcome you for a son. This girl will know the ways of the medicine trail, and she'll understand the strange manner in which you must often act. She can help you with the cures, too. Many roots are best prepared by a woman."

"She said that."

"Now, you understand what must be done. I will go and talk to Little Raven."

They met again the next afternoon. Touches the Sky handed his nephew the promised flute — a fine instrument of polished willow, with many finger holes to vary the melody.

"Little Raven welcomes your attentions," the old man said, smiling faintly. "He says it's good for the Suhtai to mix with the other bands, and he would agree to the match. Three moons must pass before you may take the girl, though. His honor requires that time. Usually it would be a year; but many young people are marrying, and no one wishes to wait for winter."

"I'll go to her tonight."

"Tomorrow, Nephew. Don't be impatient. And make ready four good ponies. She's prized among the girls of her band."

"And worth four horses," Cloud Dancer readily agreed.

In the days that followed, the young man put the flute to good use. He would stand beside the stream and wait for the women to fetch water. Whenever Raven's Wing

129

passed, he would play the flute for her. Sometimes she would step over and share his robe for a time. Other times they would make a game of chasing each other through the reeds.

In the evenings, Cloud Dancer would walk to her father's lodge and sit with his robe open, inviting her company. Raven's Wing would tend to her duties, then step over and join him. They would sit together as the night darkened the horizon and talk of buffalo hunts and curing herbs. Sometimes he would take her hands and stroke them lightly, but that was all the physical contact permitted. Raven's Wing wore a chastity rope, and she wouldn't allow him liberties. To press his affections would bring swift retribution from her family.

The courtship intensified as summer arrived. Whenever there was dancing and feasting, Cloud Dancer joined Raven's Wing. The two were rarely one without the other except for the four days each month when she took to the women's lodge, and those times when he joined the other young men on hunts.

Cloud Dancer was not the only young man to court a Suhtai woman. Indeed, forty betrothals were celebrated that summer. He was happiest when White Horse announced he and Red Robe Woman had pledged their affections.

"It's a good thing, Brother," Cloud Dancer declared. "When we join our wives' people, we'll still ride together."

"As we will always," White Horse vowed. "Didn't I say as much to you? How would our sons grow tall together if it were otherwise?"

Cloud Dancer nodded. And while he worried White Horse might have acted out of haste, he knew it was more likely Man Above had chosen it to be that way. When the

Dancer saw his brother and Red Robe Woman, he cast aside his doubts. Their eyes were linked in a magical bond that could only have been love.

Many marriage feasts highlighted that summer, but none equaled the celebration hosted by Little Raven. The medicine man had many sons, but just the one daughter, and he held nothing back. The guests received fine presents, and many a poor Suhtai boy received his first horse in Raven's Wing's honor.

Cloud Dancer gave up four of his own horses, but still he thought Little Raven had lost in the exchange.

"A man with only one daughter can afford to be generous," Little Raven proclaimed. "And never has a father had a better child. Be worthy of her, son, and only good will flow of your joining."

"I will," Cloud Dancer vowed.

When the last of the marriage feasts concluded, the People broke apart into their many bands, for soon it would be time for the autumn buffalo hunts. Sadly Cloud Dancer bid his father and mother farewell. He said good-bye to Horse Chaser, too, and to Touches the Sky, who had so often showed him the way.

"Now you're truly a man, Nephew," the old medicine man said as he gripped Cloud Dancer's wrists. "Learn from this new wife, and make many sons. The People have need of strength, and your blood can only be the strongest."

"Uncle, we'll see each other again," Cloud Dancer vowed.

"Yes, Nephew," Touches the Sky agreed. "But not for a time. Lead well, and practice the sacred manner in all you do."

"I will, Uncle."

Next dawn the Poor People departed the camp they had shared with the Suhtai. Cloud Dancer and White Horse joined the young Suhtai hunters and set off northward toward Bull Buffalo's range. It was time to hunt.

Those were difficult days. Cloud Dancer missed the company of his old friends, of his family. He was a stranger among the Suhtai councils. Their speech and manners were foreign, and he felt himself a boy again, taking his first steps. If not for White Horse's company, he might have turned crazy.

After a time, the Suhtai recognized Cloud Dancer's merits, and he found himself accepted. They were new to Horse's ways, and they welcomed his suggestions and bettered their equipage. As for the hunt, their prayers and dances were less different than their words. When it was time to run the buffalo, the others made way for Cloud Dancer and White Horse. By now the two young men were as natural on horseback as when afoot, and they skillfully nudged the herd toward the waiting lances of the others.

It was after the hunt concluded that Cloud Dancer most distinguished himself among his new relatives, though. No one had killed more bulls, and he quietly made his way among the old and the young, offering them hump roasts or shoulders. Where there was need, he provided hides for winter coats.

"Here's a man of the People," Little Raven proclaimed, and the others howled their agreement.

"Husband, you've made me proud of my choice," Raven's Wing added when they lay together later that night. "Before, I saw the healing manner of your touch and the respect with which you walked Mother Earth. Now I see your heart knows generosity. You will make a good father."

132

"I hope to be one," he answered.

"Soon," she promised as she drew him to her.

The hard-face days of winter came and went. As horse-fattening moon was born, Raven's Wing's face took on a mother's glow. Cloud Dancer had known of the coming birth, for it was hard not to notice his wife's swelling belly. He looked upon the coming child with rare anticipation, for it seemed Man Above was rewarding him for keeping to the medicine trail. And he tended to Raven's Wing's every wish.

Finally she bid him occupy himself elsewhere.

"My mother and my aunts will see to my needs," she grumbled. "Go to the hills and make prayers. Or lead the young men on a horse raid."

White Horse, too, suggested leaving camp for a time.

"You're becoming a grandmother," the Horse declared. "This child will be born. I'm no medicine man, but I know that much. We'll go into the hills and seek a dream. Then maybe we'll hunt deer."

"Yes, Brother," Cloud Dancer finally agreed. "A dream would be good. I would know this child's destiny. But I can't be far when he's so close to coming into the world."

So they rode but a short distance from camp and climbed into the low hills. There Cloud Dancer prayed for a vision, danced beside a fire, and cut strips of flesh to induce fever. Three days he danced. And as before, on the third night the vision came.

He wasn't surprised to see Wolf, for that was his father's guiding spirit. Nor was it unexpected Raven should speak of great days to come, for the child's mother was certain to influence the little one's destiny. But

133

the dream soon flooded with swallows — eleven of them turning circles in the morning sky.

"Soon a son will walk the world at your side," the birds sang. "Teach him respect for the old ways, and guide him as he grows tall."

This part of the dream was bright and warm. Afterward White Horse was to tell him that. But then the dream darkened, and terror intruded.

"Mind my path and yours do not join," a chilling voice spoke. From out of a gray storm rode the shade that Cloud Dancer knew could only be Death. The specter carried his walnut bow and deadly arrows, but he didn't shoot them this time. No, instead he waved the bow and warned of danger.

"Take care the darkness does not descend," the phantom urged. "Hanging Road is full of people with no ears to hear my warnings."

The shade moved aside, then pointed with a skeleton hand at the parade of children climbing a black ribbon toward the sky. Their faces were spotted, and their bodies were swollen and distorted. Wailing women followed, and faceless warriors cried in agony until they, too, started the long climb.

It was then that White Horse roused him from his sleep. Cloud Dancer stood beside the fire, his hands reddening from where he had placed them near the embers, trying to chase the chill that was taking possession of him.

"What horrors did you see, Brother?" the Horse cried. "Your manner changed, and you shook like a medicine rattle."

"I saw my son," Cloud Dancer said, mustering a smile.

"And the other?"

"The death of a people," he explained. "Little ones, old

people, warriors and young women. . . ."

"It's a warning," White Horse observed.

"Certainly," Cloud Dancer agreed. "But of what?"

Once he would have sought an answer from Touches the Sky, but that wasn't possible now. The Arrow-keeper was with the Poor People, and he would only have sent the Dancer to search his own heart for the truth.

White Horse suggested asking for another vision, but Cloud Dancer ached to return to Raven's Wing.

"My son seeks the light," the Dancer explained. "The truth of this other dream will come to me."

"Search for it," White Horse pleaded. "I wouldn't welcome Death to this camp."

They took to their beds then. Next morning, after making the dawn prayers and eating, White Horse readied the ponies. The two brothers then returned to the Suhtai camp.

"You found your vision," Little Raven declared when Cloud Dancer joined him near the women's lodge. "Soon your child will be born."

"Yes, Father," Cloud Dancer responded. "He'll be a tall son, a grandson for you to be proud of."

"Did you see his name?" Little Raven asked.

"I saw many swallows," Cloud Dancer explained. "We'll call him Swallow Tail. Later he will earn his manhood name."

"As is fitting," the Raven said, nodding proudly. "Come. Let's have a smoke on our good fortune."

"Gladly, Father. Gladly."

It was the following morning when Raven's Wing's cries announced the birth. Her aunts sent word, and Little Raven organized a feast. Cloud Dancer gave away two ponies, then hurried to meet his son. The child was little more than a brown bundle of flesh and hair, but his mother's proud gaze pronounced him healthy.

"Here is your son," Otter Woman, one of the aunts, said as she held out the boy to his father.

Cloud Dancer accepted the little one and held him close. The infant sucked air and moved its tiny arms and legs. The Dancer warmed at its touch, and he smiled down at the child.

"He wants his mother," Cloud Dancer announced as he passed the little one on to Raven's Wing. "His name will be Swallow Tail, for that is what my dreams told me."

"He'll be a strong son for you," Raven's Wing said, rocking the baby as she motioned Cloud Dancer nearer.

"Yes," the Dancer agreed. "And we'll make brothers for him. These children will make the People strong."

"Enough!" Otter Woman barked. "Away," she added, ushering Cloud Dancer from the lodge. "Busy yourself with men's matters and leave us to look after little one."

Cloud Dancer laughed as he left. He could have sat beside his wife and child for days, basking in the glow of their eyes. But Otter Woman was right. Other duties waited.

Cloud Dancer busied himself with the hunt, but deer were scarce in the flatlands. Always he brought meat for the family, but more and more often it was a goose or prairie hen. Many lacked his eye with a bow, and so hunger began to stalk the camp. Many among the Suhtai spoke for returning to the good country near Muddy River.

"We always had fish and game there," Yellow Bird argued. "I've seen no shadows in my dreams. They, too, hold power."

"The Arrows warn of death there," Cloud Dancer said. "You have dreams. Do they show you a people climbing Hanging Road? Are they full of weeping mothers and dead children? Mine are, and I trust their warnings."

"His dreams led us to Horse," White Horse pointed out.

"Are we boys to listen to the words of strangers," Yellow Bird complained.

"This is my daughter's husband," Little Raven replied. "He's shown our people only honor and generosity. He feeds the hungry, and I trust his power. Even so, I hunger for Muddy River."

"Death waits for us there," Cloud Dancer warned.

"We'll ask Buffalo Hat," Red Elk, a head man of the Suhtai, announced. "The Hat will tell us what to do."

Cloud Dancer nodded. He respected the power of the sacred Hat, and he knew it would advise prudence.

The men then approached White Calf, the keeper of the Hat, with a pipe. Once the ceremonies were conducted, Red Elk inquired of the Hat what should be done. The answer revealed caution, as Cloud Dancer had hoped.

"We'll send five men to Muddy River," Red Elk explained to the others. "I will go. Yellow Bird, who leads the young men, should come along."

"Take Cloud Dancer," Little Raven advised.

"Then, I come, too," White Horse volunteered.

"I'll go with my new brother," Painted Robe, the young brother of Red Robe Woman, added.

"Five men!" Yellow Bird objected.

"Some boy should come to hold the horses," White Horse answered. "I'll see he finds no harm."

"Be wary, brothers," Cloud Dancer urged. "I've seen Death riding Muddy River. We may none of us be safe on this ride."

"Soon we'll know if your dreams—or your words—hold any truth," Yellow Bird muttered. "We'll make the prayers and leave tomorrow. Agreed?"

"Yes," Red Elk answered. "Tomorrow."

They did just that. It was hard for Cloud Dancer to say farewell to Raven's Wing and little Swallow Tail, but he feared allowing anyone else to approach Muddy River. Only a man with the memory of that shade could keep its peril from the People.

Muddy River lay two days' riding east, and at first no sign of danger crossed their trail. Twice they paused to shoot a buffalo to satisfy their hunger, but otherwise they hurried along. Finally they came upon the first Mandan village.

"Here we'll be welcome," Yellow Bird declared. Cloud Dancer urged caution, though.

"I don't hear anything," he said, pondering the strange silence. "Look closely. Is anybody about? Where are the fires?"

The riders slowed. Soon they understood the silence of the camp. A forest of burial scaffolds occupied the rise above the huts. A few bodies — the last to die — lay where they had fallen, in their lodges or beside the ashes of their fires.

"Come no closer," Red Elk ordered. "It's as Cloud Dancer foresaw. Death has ridden down the Mandans, even as it would have struck down our people. Muddy River is lost to us. We must seek our summer camps elsewhere!"

The five riders turned and galloped away. For a time Cloud Dancer felt the shade's ghostly fingers reaching out to tear them from their horses. And when, at last, they made a resting camp, he recognized the terror in his companions' eyes. He knew thereafter none among the Suhtai would question his dreams.

Chapter Twelve

That year of Swallow Tail's birth was best remembered as the time the spotted sickness killed the Mandans. Those who survived bore its marks forever, and that tribe was soon little more than a memory to the People.

Fortunately the People fared better. Bull Buffalo painted the plains black with his children, and the ten bands benefited from his gifts of food, clothing, and shelter.

"All we have, you have brought us," Cloud Dancer spoke before each hunt began. "Give us the true aim, that we may be strong."

When not hunting, Cloud Dancer devoted himself to his growing son, and to making the medicine cures required by the Suhtai. His knowledge grew under the tutelage of Little Raven, and many ceremonies denied Touches the Sky for lack of a woman's aid were possible through Raven's Wing's help.

In time, too, the distinctions between the Suhtai and the other bands diminished. Young men and women took mates from the other bands, and the languages merged. Customs, too, were shared, though those born to the Suhtai would always retain that identity more than children born to the other bands.

Three snows passed, and Swallow Tail grew. His legs

steadied beneath him, and he grew venturesome as small boys will. More and more Little Raven took charge of the boy, guiding his learning with moral stories told with a gentle touch.

"It's good our son needs his mother less," Raven's Wing told Cloud Dancer. "Soon you must journey to the hills and seek another vision. I'll be going to the women's lodge before it snows again."

"Ayyyy!" Cloud Dancer howled. Soon the news spread through the camp, and much singing ensued.

"This, too, will be a strong son," Otter Woman pronounced when she touched Raven's Wing's belly.

"Perhaps I don't need to seek a dream after all," Cloud Dancer said, laughing.

"Old women see things, too, Nephew," Otter Woman growled. "And often they're more use."

That summer Cloud Dancer rode faster and surer as he led his companions on horse raids against the Kiowas and later to the buffalo hunt. White Horse was always at his side, together with Painted Robe, now a young man of sixteen snows.

"It's a good day to be alive," the Horse said often. For Red Robe Woman's belly was also swollen.

"I hope you, too, will know the joy of watching a son grow," Cloud Dancer answered.

"The boys will be brothers even as their fathers are," White Horse vowed. "I've always known that."

"Or maybe they'll be lucky," Painted Robe said, grinning. "They could be girls and resemble their mothers. It's enough trouble to have two ugly men among the Suhtai!"

When Raven's Wing's time came, Cloud Dancer took Swallow Tail into the hills. The boy was young to ride, so the Dancer helped the child up behind him on the same mount. White Horse, too, came along, and they made the fire as before.

"We come to make prayers," Cloud Dancer explained to the boy. "And to seek a vision that may tell of your brother's future."

"Will it be a brother, then?" the boy asked.

"Otter Woman says it will," Cloud Dancer answered.

"She knows," Swallow Tail declared.

Cloud Dancer fasted as before, but he didn't cut his flesh that first day. There was no need. The dream came easily.

It was different from the first. No dark clouds marred the vision, either. Instead there was a council held on a white sea. Beside the fire a boy danced, chanting in the old words of the Suhtai.

"I walk the brave-heart road," the words meant. "I see the dangers ahead, but I never flinch from my duties."

In the distance wolves howled, and ravens flew overhead. But it was the dancer that filled Cloud Dancer's mind.

He awoke next morning with the first rays of dawn. Swallow Tail had left his own bed and burrowed under one arm. Across the fire White Horse sat, feeding twigs to the embers.

"The dream came," the Horse observed. "I kept the boy away while you read its message. Later, when you calmed, I saw no need to keep him away. He misses his mother."

Cloud Dancer wrapped the boy in a heavy buffalo hide and left him to rest a moment. The Dancer then prepared himself for the dawn prayers. Even as he greeted the sun, though, Swallow Tail hurried to his side. In his

141

small voice, he echoed the words, taking care to preserve his father's reverent tone.

"Grandfather taught me," Swallow Tail whispered.

"It's a good thing to know," Cloud Dancer declared. "Come, let's eat. Then we'll go visit your new brother."

It was, indeed, a son Raven's Wing brought him that day. That alone was worth a father's remembering. But making the morning prayers with his son was also an event worthy of recalling, and Cloud Dancer noted it accordingly.

The new child was called Little Dancer. From his first moments he seemed particularly taken with music. Otter Woman sang to him, and Cloud Dancer blew tunes on his flute. Even Swallow Tail joined in the amusement, though he soon tired of the infant's wailing.

In other tribes a weeping baby might have been taken to the edge of camp and cured of crying; but the People held children high in their thinking, and every effort was made to satisfy the child. Sometimes Swallow Tail would go to Little Raven's lodge and sleep beside the old man. Other times he would sit beside his small brother and sing until the crying stopped.

That same summer Cloud Dancer accompanied White Horse into the hills, for it was Red Robe Woman's time. Prayers and preparations were made, but the Horse was given no dream. Instead Cloud Dancer's sleep was visited, and the dream passed on to his companion next dawn.

"Brother, I saw us small again," Cloud Dancer explained. "Dreamer and Corn Boy, swimming the river and catching fish. Later these children mounted ponies and chased Bull Buffalo."

"Yes? But what of my child?" White Horse asked.

"It wasn't me, and it wasn't you I saw. The boys were alike, but different. One was Little Dancer. The second was your son."

"It'll be as I've always thought," White Horse declared. "Our boys growing tall together."

"Yes, Brother, I saw it so."

"But what will I call him?"

"It's for a father to name his son."

"Then, I'll give him the name I set aside long ago," White Horse decided. "He, too, will be Corn Boy."

"It was a lucky name," Cloud Dancer said, smiling as he recalled those old times. "We should now go meet this boy."

"Ayyyy!" White Horse screamed. "My son is born!"

It surprised neither of them to learn Red Robe Woman had brought a boy into the world that very dawn. They were still not within sight of the camp when they heard Painted Robe's howling mark the event.

"I have a nephew," the young man screamed as he greeted his brother-in-law. "It's a fine morning, isn't it!"

"The best I remember," an eager White Horse said as he jumped from his horse. "The very best!"

"Go with him," Cloud Dancer urged as he took charge of the horses. "I'll see to the animals. On a day like this you should both feast and dance. The People are stronger for this new son."

Three additional snows came before Cloud Dancer made his third and final journey into the hills. White Horse came along as before, but there were three small ones as well. Red Robe Woman had borne White Horse a second son under the big-wheel moon of late winter, but that child was too young to follow his father. As for Swallow Tail, he was of a size to tend the fire, and he took

143

charge of the smaller boys as well.

This time the dream brought joy and sadness, for it foretold both of birth and death. Even as the small one took his first steps, Raven, whose wings sheltered the infant, fell earthward in final flight.

"We'll call him Raven Feather, in honor of your father," Cloud Dancer told Raven's Wing when he returned to her side.

"It's a good name," she agreed, smiling. "I wished for a daughter, but the people have need of strong boys."

"If this one is like his grandfather, he will know greatness," Cloud Dancer observed.

"Can his father's son be less?" she asked. "Now go and let me bring him into the light. Send Otter Woman to me."

This third child was no easy birth, and Raven's Wing cried and bled as he emerged from her. Little Raven and Cloud Dancer danced and chanted every invocation to the spirits they knew, hoping to chase pain from the women's lodge. Raven Feather was born, and his mother survived, but Otter Woman's frown attested to the struggle.

"He's small and weak, Husband," Raven's Wing said wearily, "but he'll grow under our care and attention."

"He will," Cloud Dancer agreed, relieved the fallen raven was not, after all, his wife. "And you, too, will mend."

"The old ones say it's so," she agreed. "But they also say there will be no more children."

"Man Above has given us three sons," Cloud Dancer noted. "A daughter would have been welcome, but we've known good fortune. It's enough."

"Yes," she agreed. "And in time, you could take a second woman to our lodge."

"No, we two are paired, like eagles. Our match is for always, and we won't one long outlive the other."

"You've seen this in your dreams, too?"

"No, but I know it for a truth, Raven's Wing. Just as I know our sons will make us proud and the People strong."

"Yes, maybe it is enough," she said, sighing.

"To judge by the trouble two boys have brought, you may think it burdensome even," he said, laughing. "I must go now. There's a feast to hold. I'll give away two horses in thanks to Man Above — one for the new son you've brought me and a second for returning you to our hearts."

From that moment Raven's Wing revived. Soon she was again helping with the medicine cures and looking after her younger sons. Swallow Tail, meanwhile, passed less time with his mother. More often than not he accompanied his grandfather around the camp or played at boys' games by the nearby streams. He added his voice to his father's dawn prayers, and for the first time he splashed into the river beside Cloud Dancer and washed with the other men.

"What's this?" the older boys cried. "A mouse has come into the river with us!"

They pulled at him and tormented him terribly, but Swallow Tail endured what he couldn't prevent and returned to the river.

"Grandfather says it's the hard things that make a man strong, Father," the boy explained later. "And even though they splash water in my face and call me names, they don't object when I join their games."

"You hurry yourself, Naha'," Cloud Dancer said. "You're but a boy of six summers. There's time before you walk man's road."

145

"Yes, Ne' hyo, but already I ride as well as many of the older boys. My heart longs to join you and White Horse when you hunt Bull Buffalo."

"There are other things to learn first," Cloud Dancer declared. There were, too. But the Dancer couldn't help nodding pridefully that his son was eager to walk tall.

Thereafter Cloud Dancer shared more and more with his eldest son. The two would sit by the fire, crafting arrows or stringing a boy's bow. Swallow Tail would toil diligently and then hold up the arrow for his father's approval.

"The shaft is straight, as it should be," Cloud Dancer would observe. "And the tip won't waver as the arrow flies. Any warrior would proudly carry it."

"Even my father?" the boy would ask.

"Especially so," the Dancer would reply.

Such lessons should have fallen to an uncle or grandfather. Raven's Wing had no brothers in the camp though, and White Horse was never far from Cloud Dancer's company. Little Raven had once tended to the instruction, but clearly the medicine man's days were now numbered. As the plum moon marked the time for the autumn buffalo hunt, so it cast a longer shadow across his face. Medicine chants and curing herbs could not long combat the ravages of time.

"Ne' hyo," Swallow Tail declared one morning, "where is grandfather? Why hasn't he come to make the morning prayers?"

"He tires easily now," Cloud Dancer explained. "He needs more rest."

"He's sick," the boy noted. "He says it's the long-road sickness. Soon his heart will be too tired, and he will step upon Hanging Road."

"Do you understand this?"

"No, Ne' hyo. I only know he's too tired to share stories."

"You've seen how it is with old horses," Cloud Dancer said. "Sometimes they are too weary to continue. They collapse and breathe out their lives watching the young ones race by."

"Is that how it is with Little Raven?"

"Yes, Naha'. Your grandfather has endured many winters. He's known hardships, and the years rest heavy on his shoulders. Soon he will give up the burdens of life and leave us behind."

"He's strong yet! He's told me so."

"He knows time is short, but he fights the approaching shadows because he knows you need his company. It's a hard thing, giving up a loved one to climb Hanging Road. But Little Raven feels great pain, and we must not keep him from finding his rest."

"I'll talk to him, Ne' hyo."

"Peace is a wonderful gift to give," Cloud Dancer declared. "And you will always carry him in your heart, even as you remember his stories to share with your son's sons."

It wasn't long thereafter that Little Raven sat with his grandsons and spoke of the long road he would soon climb. The boys left, their faces long and grim. And darkness covered the eyes of Little Raven and bore him away.

Otter Woman took charge of the body, dressing it in the finest clothes. Then Cloud Dancer helped wrap Little Raven in a fine elk robe, placing his medicine rattles and weapons at his sides. After the bundle was bound with many ropes, old men were summoned to sing the ancient

147

songs. Finally the body was placed on a travois and taken to its resting place — a nearby hill where Cloud Dancer had erected a scaffold.

In this place Little Raven was put — high up so that his shade might start its climb upward. Three horses were shot beneath the scaffold so their spirits might carry their master on the long journey.

There was great wailing when the Suhtai collected beside the scaffold, for their departed elder was a respected man. For three days the band kept to its camp, singing the mourning chants. Cloud Dancer and Raven's Wing put aside their finery and wore only old skins. As a dutiful daughter, Raven's Wing cut her hair and gashed her legs. The Dancer unbraided his hair and let it fall onto his shoulders out of respect to his father-in-law.

When the short period of mourning was over, Little Raven's possessions were taken from his lodge and given away to the People. Many treasured belongings were handed out, and it took much explaining for the children to understand.

"You must avoid these things," Cloud Dancer told Swallow Tail. "We are giving them away so your grandfather's ghost will not linger. To bring a remembered blanket or some knife with you would hold his ghost nearby. You must give the ghost up so that Little Raven's spirit can complete its journey."

"He would want it so?" the boy asked.

"Yes, and so we scream out our pain and cut ourselves," Raven's Wing added. "Then, when we have given up the ghost, we can continue on our own path."

"It's hard to understand these things," Swallow Tail said, "but I will do it. I'll help my brothers do so, too."

"You've done well by that boy," Cloud Dancer whispered that night as he stared at the stars lining Hanging Road. "Find peace, Father."

The only other change Little Raven's death brought was that Otter Woman came to live with her niece. The old woman soon busied herself helping with the camp duties, and she often attended to the young girls who took to the women's lodge for the first time. Still there was time for her to sew new garments for her nephews and mind the little ones' moral instruction.

"Mother's aunt is a quarrelsome sort," Swallow Tail complained bitterly. "She's never pleased with my behavior, and she torments my brothers. She won't ride a horse and so slows the whole camp when we move."

"She's old and doesn't understand change," Cloud Dancer noted. "But she's very dear to your mother, and she helped you come into the world. Her gift is the memory of old times and an understanding of what was. We must return that gift by offering her patience."

"It's a hard thing you ask, Ne' hyo."

"I know," Cloud Dancer agreed, smiling.

Fortunately there were new lessons to draw Swallow Tail's attention, and duties, too. As he grew older, he took a turn at minding the horses of his father and uncle. Often he shot his blunt arrows at small birds or stalked game, sharpening the skills that would make him a hunter when older.

As a rider he had no equal his age, and he won many races. As to wrestling, he was still younger than most he challenged, and he received a fair battering once or twice. He swam well and ran fast, which was good since he often incurred the wrath of the older boys by returning jeers and taunts in kind.

Swallow Tail was in his tenth summer when Cloud

Dancer first took him along to hunt deer in the thickets that lined the northern hills. White Horse went, as always, together with Painted Robe, who was no longer a boy. The three men dismounted and left their horses to Swallow Tail's care.

"We won't be far," Cloud Dancer assured his son. "This place is full of sign, and we should find an animal to kill soon."

"I know you'll kill a big buck, Ne' hyo," Swallow Tail said, grinning at the notion. "Next time maybe I can come along on the stalk."

"Next time," Cloud Dancer agreed as he turned toward his companions.

The men were well into the thicket and approaching three deer when Cloud Dancer halted. His nostrils detected an odd odor. The deer sniffed it, too, and they turned away. The Dancer nevertheless notched an arrow and killed the nearest buck with a clean shot through the shoulder that pierced the heart. White Horse killed a second creature.

"Look after the deer," the Dancer said as he turned back toward the horses. Already he could hear one stomping and screaming in alarm. White Horse nodded and started for the deer while Cloud Dancer backtracked toward the ponies.

He was too far distant to know the source of the peril, but he felt it just the same. And he had visited those hills often enough to know the wild creatures that lived there. He imagined Swallow Tail set upon by a grizzly. Or perhaps Kiowas were scouting the country in search of ponies to steal! Cloud Dancer hurried. But when he arrived, he froze in disbelief. Swallow Tail sat in front of the horses, quietly singing. A stone's throw away prowled a gray wolf.

"Uncle Wolf," the boy said, "I can't give you my father's horses to eat, but even now he is killing a deer. We'll leave a good piece for you and your brothers when we go. You'd make a poor meal of me. I'm nothing but bone."

The wolf seemed confused by the boy's calm, and yet interested. It crept closer. Swallow Tail sang again, then related an old Suhtai tale likely learned from Little Raven.

"Go now, Uncle," the boy concluded. "Ne' hyo comes, and he may not recognize you."

The wolf turned and left.

Cloud Dancer nodded his approval, turned, and rejoined the others. He didn't speak of the wolf until long afterward.

Chapter Thirteen

Those next three summers found Cloud Dancer often leading the hunt. At his side Swallow Tail rode proudly. Soon Little Dancer, too, took the first steps of manhood, as did his cousin, Corn Boy.

"It's as I've always known it would be," White Horse declared. "They tend our horses and follow us to the buffalo hunt. Can life be better?"

But along with birth and growth, there came death. That was the natural way of the world, and when the old were called to walk Hanging Road, Cloud Dancer joined in the chanting and attended the giveaways, knowing every story came to an end and all lives concluded. That summer, his thirty-fourth, death struck at the young, though, and his heart found no understanding of that.

First, lightning hit a small girl gathering summer plums. Then two young brothers were swept away in a sudden flood and drowned.

"It's a bad time that's come to the People," White Calf, who kept the sacred Buffalo Hat, observed. "We'll move camp north."

The move didn't end the misfortune, though. Sickness found the new camp, and fevers tormented the children. Cloud Dancer and Raven's Wing went from lodge to lodge, performing the ancient cures and offering what comfort they knew. Still the fevers spread. And little ones began to die.

"Man Above, the heart is going out of the People," Cloud Dancer chanted on a distant hill. "Give me a vision of what must be done."

White Calf called the headmen together and recalled hard times from the past.

"Soon it will be time to erect the New Life Lodge," he said, studying his companions with grave eyes. "Many are sick. Three men must construct the lodge, as always. Others can vow to suffer in the lodge so the children will be cured. Good health will surely return."

Cloud Dancer was among those who nodded his agreement.

The criers then spread out among the lodges, telling of the decisions made by the council. Again the camp would move. Each family with sickness was told of the need for vows. When the New Life Lodge was erected, as was the custom in midsummer, those who had promised must honor their vow by suffering.

White Horse promised to make the lodge, for his small daughter, Red Deer, was sick. As was fitting, Cloud Dancer made the same vow, for the small one was tormented, and he couldn't ease the suffering.

"Ne' hyo, I will also help," Swallow Tail promised. "I'll go to the New Life Lodge and hang by the pole."

"There's much suffering, and it's better you endure it when you're older," Cloud Dancer objected. "Man Above will send a cure. Other men have vowed to dance, and they will be enough. Someone else can en-

153

dure the torture. It's not a thing a boy of thirteen summers should undergo."

"But I have dreams, Ne' hyo," the boy said. "I see wolves. They call to me to take the steps of a man and put childhood behind me. I've hunted deer and buffalo. I've plucked the first hairs from my chin."

"You must follow your heart," Cloud Dancer said, sighing. He had never felt so old as now. Suddenly he saw the young man standing before him no longer as the small one who had sat at his side, crafting arrows or sharing tales. Here instead was the image of the youth who had followed Touches the Sky into the Arrow Lodge.

Swallow Tail read the reluctance in his father's eyes and gripped his hand.

"It's right, Naha'," the Dancer whispered. "You will make the lodge, and I will dance. Father and son together. The cure will come speedily."

And it did.

Among the many rituals brought to the People by the Suhtai, none carried the weight of the New Life Lodge Ceremony. Other tribes called it different names. Lakotas celebrated it as the Sun Dance, although the People had many sun and moon ceremonies. Other bands simply called it the Medicine Lodge. Cloud Dancer performed many curing rituals in medicine lodges, so he used the old Suhtai name for this one.

White Calf saw to the arrangements. First the warrior societies gathered on the south side of the camp circle. Two young men were chosen to lead each band. Next came the warriors, followed by their chiefs. Afterward the boys of the camp rode along on horses. It was

154

an inspiring sight, especially when they sang their brave-heart songs. They made one turn inside the camp circle and a second outside. Then they entered again, and the group broke up, each man going to his own lodge.

Once the parade was over, the people began packing up the camp. For four days the Suhtai broke down their lodges and moved short distances. This was a tedious task, but before the advent of skin lodges, Cloud Dancer supposed it must have been far more difficult. In each new place White Calf would pray and smoke.

The day before the New Life Lodge was erected, the Elk Warriors rode out and killed a jackrabbit. Strips of rabbit fur were cut and tied to the buffalo robes worn by the lodge-makers.

Next several structures were erected. First came the gathering lodge and the Only Lodge. Then the New Life Lodge itself was raised, as were two coverings for the use of the warrior societies who had charge of the ritual.

Once the ceremonial lodges were built, White Calf summoned all those who had previously made the New Life Lodge to the gathering lodge. It was time to plan the ceremony. Cloud Dancer and White Calf, who would sponsor the ceremony, came, too. Running Dog, whose three children had recovered from the sickness, was the other sponsor. These three were there only to learn, and so they kept silent.

On the day before the hanging pole was cut, White Calf again assembled this group. Now they went to the Only Lodge, and each new maker carried a pipe.

Every man who had made a vow had need of an

older man to advise him in the ceremony. It was required such an instructor had himself made the New Life Lodge. A lodge-maker acquired power from this gift of prosperity he provided to the People, and he gave up some of this power when he shared the ceremony with another. Therefore those making the New Life Lodge for the first time sought out a man who had not already served as instructor. The lodge-maker offered his advisor the pipe and promised payment for his services and compensation for the power he could expect to give up.

Cloud Dancer sought out an Elk Warrior known as Stands Long in the Sun for his instructor. Along with the pipe, Cloud Dancer pledged three good horses, for it was known Stands Long had himself presented two horses when entering New Life Lodge, and a man would be insulted not to receive at least as much as he had once offered.

"I'll show you the path," Stands Long said as he accepted the pipe. "It's good a man of power, one who sees the path ahead, should seek new life."

White Horse and Running Dog also offered presents to their advisors.

Now the lodge-makers and their instructors smoked a short-stemmed pipe in a special ritual. Then the advisors instructed the lodge-makers. An instructor spoke a sentence, and the lodgemaker repeated it. There were prayers and offerings, for all the powers and influences of the world were invoked. Each thing — animals, birds, hills, rivers — was prayed to and given small gifts. The prayers were spoken four times by each advisor, and the lodge-maker repeated them each time.

156

When these prayers and offerings were over, they smoked again. This time a long-stemmed pipe of black stone was used, and different ritual words were spoken.

Cloud Dancer drank in the meaning of these rituals and etched them in his mind. He knew, as did White Horse and Running Dog, that the time would come for them to instruct others.

The next day was spent in meditation. Few words were spoken, but few were needed. In the solitude of the Only Lodge, the lodge-makers pondered their vows and prepared for the suffering to come. Then, as the sun started its descent into the western horizon, the advisors led their three charges outside. They walked eastward, following White Calf and the other medicine chiefs across the plain. When they stopped, the lodge-makers were formed in a row, facing south. White Calf and his companions made a second row, facing north. The advisors took up places behind this second row. Finally, a small fire was kindled at the south end of the line.

White Calf, who was called Earth Maker, drew a small circle in the ground, representing Earth. After White Calf had whittled three pipe sticks, Cloud Dancer was instructed to fill a pipe and bring it to the Earth Maker. The Dancer did so, taking care to rest the pipe on the ground with the stem turned toward White Calf.

Next White Horse brought a coal from the fire and placed it before White Calf. The Calf moved the pipe around the earth circle before lighting it. Then the lodge-makers each took a smoke and passed the pipe along.

After they finished with the pipe, the lodge-makers moved away from the others, toward the southeast. There, sitting on their buffalo robes, they performed a second pipe ritual. When it was finished, they returned to the camp. In their absence, men from the camp had moved the Only Lodge into the center of the camp circle.

The lodge-makers entered the Only Lodge and were presented several sacred bundles to bring to the New Life Lodge. These contained medicine herbs and bone charms passed on by old ones, and their power would enhance the ceremony. Next the lodge-makers were instructed to remove all their clothes except breechclouts. They left the Only Lodge then.

Red Elk stood beside the New Life Lodge, holding a bull buffalo's skull. After a short ceremony, the head was taken inside the New Life Lodge and placed in the back, facing east. The lodge-makers were then brought in and made to sit on the southeast side. To the west sat White Calf, flanked by the three advisors. Again Earth Maker made a circle in the ground.

Another pipe was lit, but this time only Cloud Dancer, White Horse, and Running Dog smoked. Cloud Dancer sensed a difference in the attitude of the others now. There was growing anticipation and much remembering. He felt, too, the old closeness he'd often shared with White Horse.

Next men stepped outside and summoned the warrior societies. Each society promised dancers, and they carried on wildly outside while the old ones summoned Cloud Dancer to approach the buffalo skull.

The Dancer knelt beside Night Hawk, an old man

who took the lodge-maker by the right hand and guided him in reverently drawing a yellow line from the top of the skull, between the horns, down to the end of the nose. Next Night Hawk made ritual motions over arms, leg, and head. Then White Calf lit a pipe and beckoned Cloud Dancer come over and smoke.

This time the pipe ceremony was an odd one, with many complicated motions. White Calf also blew smoke over arms, legs, and head, as if to wash away the old with sacred smoke. Finally White Calf emptied the ashes in the heart of the fire and cleaned the pipe. The dancers entered, and White Calf turned to advise them.

"You will suffer much," Earth Maker noted, "but from pain we learn respect and patience. These hard times bring power to your dreams and strengthen your heart. It's good you suffer."

Cloud Dancer watched Swallow Tail's face as the Hat-keeper offered encouragement. The Dancer remembered how, just days before, he had led the boy out among the horses and picked out a fine spotted mare.

"Dancers need helpers, Naha'," Cloud Dancer had explained. "You should offer yours this gift."

"But who will I go to, Father?" the young man had asked. "You and White Horse keep your own vows, and I have no other uncle among the Suhtai. Grandfather is dead."

"Go to Yellow Bird," Cloud Dancer had advised. "He knows good horses, and he, too, accepts challenges."

Yellow Bird, who led the young men, had let it be known he hoped to keep his power for use in war. To share knowledge of the New Life Lodge was to share

159

the power one obtained through his suffering there. Nevertheless Yellow Bird had warmly accepted Swallow Tail's proposal.

"It's well you came to me," the Bird had said. "I know how it is to be young. It's hard, this thing you want to do. But it will help you stand tall among your friends."

Now Yellow Bird busied himself painting Swallow Tail's face and readying him for the dancing. Meanwhile a drum was brought in, and the smoking continued. Long periods of silence often filled the New Life Lodge, during which the men prayed. Four drummers came in and sat beside the drum.

A great amount of drumming and singing followed. Four wolf songs were sung. Then the lodge-makers and the dancers stood and danced, blowing on eagle-bone whistles which hung by a cord around their necks. The dance was restrained, with little more than the bending of knees as the bodies moved up and down to the beat of the drum.

The dance concluded, and Cloud Dancer took a pipe to the drummers. The music stopped, and the dancers rested. After smoking, the drummers resumed their labors. They sang four songs before the dancers rose. And then the dancing went on until Cloud Dancer again took a pipe to the drummers.

Four times the dancing started and stopped in this way. From time to time food was brought in, provided by the lodge-makers for those who had not vowed to undergo a starving. Cloud Dancer himself ate nothing, for hunger always enriched his power.

When the fourth pipe was brought back from the drummers, the day's activities were finished. The dancers lay on beds of white sage and rested. Spectators returned to their lodges. And such rest as would come was welcomed.

In the final four days of dancing and ritual, the interior of the New Life Lodge was transformed. The tall cottonwood pole that dominated the center of the lodge was joined by others — box elders and chokecherries. Branches formed a small forest. A large buffalo wallow had been ceremoniously cut in the earth. Strips of hide and medicine bundles hung suspended by rawhide strips.

All this time the medicine chiefs had made prayers. The People had sung and danced while warriors performed mock combat. Now came the climax of the ceremony — the torture dance.

The call went out, and dancers stepped forward to be prepared. First the young men were painted. Then they lay on their beds of white sage while the skin of their breasts was pinched and pierced with sharp pins. They were then made to stand on white sage while the ropes were attached to the pins.

Members of the family gave presents in honor of the dancers, and cries of encouragement were shouted by advisors and friends. Then the drumming and singing resumed, and the dancers began their suffering.

Cloud Dancer was busy bringing the pipe to the drummers and attending to the rituals. Raven's Wing was there now, too, helping in a hundred ways. Even so, they found time to glance at Swallow Tail.

The boy danced with the others, blowing his eagle-bone whistle and straining to tear himself loose from the hold of the rawhide strip. As he pulled, the pins opened the tears in his chest, and bright red blood trickled down his belly. Agony etched itself across his face, and he shuddered with pain.

Man Above, give him strength, Cloud Dancer silently prayed.

But the ordeal was only beginning. Even the bravest of the dancers winced at the initial pain. Eight songs had been sung when the first dancer managed to pull himself free. The dislodged pins dangled from the rawhide, and the People shouted. The dancer stared at the jagged scars left on his chest and steadied himself until his family came to carry him off.

A second dancer tore his way free, and three others, exhausted, collapsed and were cut free by their advisors. Still Swallow Tail danced. His bone whistle lost its energy, but he kept it in his mouth. He went on pulling back, and the blood continued to run.

Cloud Dancer felt Raven's Wing grip his hand. Her worries merged with his own. Yellow Bird fingered a knife, for the boy's legs started to wobble.

No, Cloud Dancer prayed. *Give him the strength. Don't let him fail at this, his first manhood task.*

No one would have thought ill of Swallow Tail had the boy fainted. He was the youngest there, and far from the first to falter. But Cloud Dancer knew his son expected more of himself. Demanded more. Here was the boy who had spoken with Wolf.

Take heart, son, the Dancer silently told his son. *Break free.*

Yellow Bird had seen enough. He drew the knife and approached the strap. Seeing him, Swallow Tail spit out his whistle and howled. Then, in a final effort, he

162

threw himself backward, tearing the pins from his flesh.

Little Dancer and Corn Boy were there to catch him. The boys held him for but an instant. Then Yellow Bird lifted his young charge into the air and shouted. Thereafter others cheered the young dancer as the Bird hurried to paint the tears in the boy's chest with ointment.

You've done well, Cloud Dancer thought, stepping over and resting a hand on the young man's bloody chest.

"Ne' hyo, I heard your words," Swallow Tail said, nodding reverently.

"Rest," Yellow Bird scolded as the boy fought to regain his feet. "You'll speak of it later."

"Yes," Swallow Tail agreed.

Chapter Fourteen

Two days Swallow Tail rested and ate—ate anything and everything Raven's Wing could cook.

"It's good you hunt the buffalo soon, Husband," she told Cloud Dancer. "We'll need a hump roast to restore our son."

Indeed the boy seemed no more than skin stretched over bone! But it wasn't the meat on a man's ribs that brought esteem. And no other boy of thirteen summers found such favor among his peers—or among the men, either.

"Can I touch the scars, Brother?" Little Dancer asked. The younger boy displayed a sense of awe never before shown toward his elder brother, and Cloud Dancer fought an urge to laugh.

"There's little to see," Swallow Tail said, pointing to the nearly healed marks on his chest.

"They'll always be there," Little Dancer observed. "People will remember you suffered in the New Life Lodge. I'll do so, too, one day."

Cloud Dancer believed that, although he hoped a few more years might pass first. If only the young ones could be more patient!

Later, when autumn arrived, and it was time to ride

out in search of Bull Buffalo again, Cloud Dancer watched with concern as Swallow Tail saddled four ponies.

"I've hung from the pole, Ne' hyo," the young man said. "It's expected that I go."

"You hurry yourself," Cloud Dancer said, frowning. "Isn't it enough to hunt deer and shoot rabbits?"

"You weren't much older when you brought Horse to the People."

"My dreams sent me, Naha'. I did no choosing."

"I'm not choosing, Ne' hyo," Swallow Tail explained. "I'm your son. Much is expected."

"Yes," Cloud Dancer said, sighing. "Gray Wolf, my father, is a chief. My uncle is Touches the Sky, he who keeps the Arrows. I know what's expected. Your grandfathers were great men. One day you'll follow me on the medicine trail or lead the young men to war. But now there's time to be a boy."

"Not for a long time, Ne' hyo. I, too, have dreams. Once, when I followed you and White Horse after Deer, Uncle Wolf found me. We spoke, Wolf and me. Since that time he's come to me at night, showing me many things. Even if the others didn't expect me to walk man's road, Wolf would."

"It's your heart sends you on the hunt, then?"

"Yes, Ne' hyo. And Wolf."

"I understand. I remember when you first met Wolf, in those hills where we went to hunt the deer. I heard sounds, and I hurried to help you. It was only Wolf, though, and you were in no danger. He and you were of one heart even then. You're his son now. It's he who'll tell you which path to travel. We'll hunt. And when we return, you and I will go into the hills and have a dreaming. It's time you carried a man's name. Your mother and brothers will miss you, as I will. My lodge will feel empty."

"Am I doing wrong, then?"

"A man who has dreams must follow them, Naha'. My son couldn't do otherwise. Come, let's make ready our ponies. We have the buffalo prayers to make and the hunt to begin."

Cloud Dancer would have kept Swallow Tail at his side on that first buffalo hunt, but the young man would not hold back. As for the Dancer, he and White Calf were often busy with the medicine prayers. Swallow Tail rode out with Yellow Bird and the other young men, scouting the plain in search of Bull Buffalo.

Once the herd was located, though, that changed. More prayers were made, and the hunt was organized. The warrior societies took charge, and blooded warriors led the initial charges on the great bands of hairy beasts.

"Ne' hyo, the others go without me," Swallow Tail lamented as he took his place between Cloud Dancer and White Horse. The brothers had ridden together for so many years. Now for the first time they made room for a son.

"We wait for the herd to turn," Cloud Dancer said, motioning for the boy to ride forward a bit. "When they do, White Horse and I will split off a group from the main herd. Look for a small bull or a calf and ride down on it, using your lance to cut below the shoulder. You know how?"

"Yes, Ne' hyo," Swallow Tail said, nodding solemnly.

"We boys practice it often. But—"

"In your games, Bull Buffalo cannot turn and gore you," White Horse observed. "Don't worry. We are with you. Pick a small animal for your first kill. It won't be so difficult."

Cloud Dancer nodded his agreement. By then the lead hunters had started the chase. A band was swinging around, and with a loud whoop Cloud Dancer started his charge. White Horse, as always, was at his side. The two of them drove a wedge into the buffalo and split off a small group of twenty. Other hunters swept in to kill the confused animals.

"There's a calf!" White Horse shouted, waving his lance in the direction of a bull calf. Cloud Dancer indicated another farther back. Swallow Tail, though, charged the largest animal of the band.

"He's your son," White Horse declared as the young man darted in and out of the thundering creatures, then drove his lance deep into the side of the bull. He pierced the animal's thick hide three times before the lance took hold. Abandoning the lance, Swallow Tail notched an arrow and fired it under one shoulder and deep into the bull's vitals.

Now the buffalo slowed. His chin dropped, and his forelegs gave way, leaving him to vault awkwardly forward while the other buffalo rumbled past.

"Ayyyy!" Swallow Tail howled as he rode by and drove the lance deeper into the dying creature. With a final shudder, the bull died.

"Ayyyy!" Cloud Dancer cried.

"Ayyyy!" White Horse echoed.

"I've killed my first bull!" Swallow Tail exclaimed.

The excited thirteen-year-old pried his lance loose and waved it skyward. Then the boy made a brief prayer.

"You did well, Naha'," Cloud Dancer declared as he rode over. "It's a big bull, and you made the killing clean and fast."

"His meat will fill our bellies, Ne' hyo," Swallow Tail replied. "And his coat will keep me warm through the hard-face moons of winter."

As the other young men honored Swallow Tail's kill, the boy took on a glow.

"Soon Little Dancer and Corn Boy, too, will join us," White Horse said, gazing with approval at his nephew.

"Yes, they grow taller each summer," Cloud Dancer agreed.

"Was there ever a better day, Brother?"

"Perhaps the day we made our first kills. But this day, too, I'll long remember."

"The day your son killed his first bull," White Horse said proudly.

"The day I first discovered I was old," Cloud Dancer argued. "Now, we have kills of our own to make, Brother. Look at those bulls grazing there on that hill."

"Ayyyy!" White Horse screamed. "Soon they'll be winter meat!"

Following the hunt, there was much feasting. The warriors recounted their exploits and recalled other hunts of the past. The camp was busy as women dried meat for winter or cooked roasts to fill bellies. Hides were spread on stretching racks. Boys worked to replace arrows lost in the hunt.

Swallow Tail killed a second bull that autumn, and he offered half the meat to the family of Lame Eagle, a warrior injured in the hunt.

"He's a boy no longer, Husband," Raven's Wing declared afterward. "He deserves a proper name. I would have him take my father's."

"He'd welcome it, too," Cloud Dancer admitted. "But his path isn't ours. Already he rides with Yellow Bird. No, he'll want a warrior name. Wolf speaks in his dreams."

"Then, we'll seek out your father," she suggested. "He and Wolf are well-acquainted."

"It won't wait for winter. I've watched him. The dreams come often, and they trouble him. He doesn't belong with us anymore. It's time for him to join the other young men."

"So soon?"

"And time for me to take him into the hills and seek a dreaming. Wolf may visit him. A name will come to me."

"Yes, Husband," she agreed. "Only go soon. Winter comes early this year. I feel its bite already, and it will be worse in the hills."

"White Horse will come and watch over us," Cloud Dancer explained. "Little Dancer and Corn Boy can tend the fire."

"They're too young," she argued.

"Before long, and surely before we're ready, they, too, will hunt Bull Buffalo. And I'll seek a name for a second son."

"A woman should be proud for her sons to ride with the young men," Raven's Wing said, drawing closer.

"But all I feel is the emptiness that will soon be our lodge."

"Not for always," Cloud Dancer said, wrapping an arm around her. "There will be grandchildren. You and I will be busy telling stories and showing them the sacred path."

"Yes," she said, sighing. "Old woman's work."

They left soon after that. Cloud Dancer made the dawn prayers with Swallow Tail at his side. Then they joined White Horse and the two younger boys at the fringe of the Suhtai camp. Horses were ready, and once Cloud Dancer was satisfied all preparations were complete, he climbed atop his pony and waved for the others to do likewise. Soon they were riding into the southern hills.

Raven's Wing had been right about winter. There was a chill to the air that morning. Even so, Cloud Dancer felt a warming glow spread through him as he glanced at Swallow Tail, riding straight and tall at one side. Little Dancer and Corn Boy trailed the party, their high childish voices singing warrior songs and sharing remembered tales.

"Yes, it's a good day," White Horse said as if reading his brother's thoughts. "They'll make good men, these young ones."

Cloud Dancer nodded his agreement. Inside he wished that day could be delayed. It wasn't possible, though.

They made a camp of sorts on a hillside half a day's ride from the Suhtai village. White Horse made a shelter of sorts by weaving buffalo grass into a thatch and laying it across a framework of cottonwood branches. Corn Boy and Little Dancer collected wood for a fire. Cloud Dancer spread hides out for himself and Swallow Tail, then painted the young man's face and chest.

"We'll eat nothing," Cloud Dancer explained. "The starving will help bring the dream. If it is slow, I'll hurry it by cutting my flesh."

"You must cut mine also, Ne' hyo," Swallow Tail insisted. "Wolf will expect me to suffer."

"That's for your father to decide," Cloud Dancer argued. "If you don't have your dream in two nights, then I'll mark you. First show patience. Man Above has much to do."

Swallow Tail respectfully lowered his eyes, and Cloud Dancer completed the preparations. Little Dancer and Corn Boy kindled the fire, and White Horse set off to scout the plain below. Kiowas were known to raid that country, and they would be a long time celebrating the death of their old enemy.

First, Cloud Dancer made the pipe ceremony. He contented himself with smoking and praying as the sun crossed the heavens. Later, while the others ate dried buffalo meat and attended to their duties, Cloud Dancer cut the first strips of flesh from his chest. As blood trickled down his chest, he stood and sang old medicine chants, inviting a vision. Swallow Tail joined in these songs, and they slowly danced around the fire, its yellow light dancing eerily on their bare chests.

"Man Above, show me the way," Cloud Dancer pleaded.

171

"Wolf, my uncle, visit my dreams," Swallow Tail added.

Cloud Dancer never expected the dream to come quickly. He did hope it would arrive the second night. Already he grew weak from starving and exertion, and Swallow Tail approached exhaustion.

"Cut me, Ne' hyo," the young man suggested. "Bring on the dream."

Cloud Dancer refused at first. He lit the pipe and smoked. Finally he drew out his knife and touched it to his son's flesh.

"Never cut deep," Cloud Dancer explained as he pierced the flesh above both nipples. Then he made cuts along the boy's thighs. The blood came, running bright red down Swallow Tail's belly and legs. The boy never flinched, though. Instead he took up the medicine chant and danced around the fire.

Little Dancer and Corn Boy looked on in awe. White Horse's eyes betrayed some concern, and he offered food and water. Cloud Dancer drank, but he waved aside the food. Swallow Tail did likewise.

The dream came to Swallow Tail first. The boy lay on a thick buffalo hide and restlessly turned on one side and then the other. He rolled over against Cloud Dancer's side and shuddered. Once not so long ago Cloud Dancer would have drawn the boy close and offered comfort. But there was no stepping back from man's road, and torment was part of receiving the vision.

Cloud Dancer fought back his own weariness until Swallow Tail quieted. Then, after dabbing the young man's cuts with healing mixtures, Cloud Dancer allowed himself to slip into a deep sleep.

Soon he was flying across the hills and prairies, dancing on the clouds, hearing the songs of Mother Earth and Father Sky as he watched Bull Buffalo blacken the plain.

Then he saw Wolf.

"Bring me your son," Wolf spoke. "I'll make him strong."

"He'll need this strength," Bull Buffalo said, climbing a tall hill. "Danger comes."

Now Cloud Dancer saw a party of men coming up Muddy River on a great long canoe. These were the hairy faces of Sweet Medicine's prophecy, and they brought many wonderful presents. There were knives of metal so hard it never chipped. They wore shiny beads and carried sticks that spoke with thunder.

"These are the first, the few," Bull Buffalo said sadly. "Now the People are strong, and these pale ones are nothing. Their hearts are good, these ones, and they hold no anger. But others, bad ones, are certain to follow. They bring death to my brothers, and to yours."

"It will take a man as hard as this new metal, this iron, to keep the People safe," Wolf added. "Will even that be enough?"

The vision fixed next on a slight-figured young man riding across the plain. He carried the stringless bow of the Foxes and his face was painted for war.

He appeared older, but Cloud Dancer saw it was his son. And he knew what name the young man must carry. Wolf had said it. A man as hard as iron. Iron Wolf, the young man would be called.

173

Cloud Dancer remembered it all when he awoke. But he said nothing to the others. Instead he roused Swallow Tail, and they ate some meat.

"We must talk, Ne' hyo," the young man said. "Wolf spoke to me."

"Yes, I know," Cloud Dancer said. "I've had a dream, too. We'll walk a way and speak."

They left White Horse and the boys to break camp and ready the horses for the return to the Suhtai camp. Once out of sight, Cloud Dancer sat on a large boulder and waved his son close.

"I saw many things," Swallow Tail began. "I understand little of it. There were people with pale flesh and great beards like Bull Buffalo. These people don't hunt buffalo and deer. Instead they draw Mother Earth on yellow cloth and speak strange words."

"Yes," Cloud Dancer agreed. He then revealed the prophecies of Sweet Medicine and shared his own vision.

"I feel they're close, Ne' hyo. Them and their iron knives and shiny beads. We should turn away from them."

"We'll try," Cloud Dancer said sadly. "But they'll come anyway. The future's often hard. When I was young, we fished the river and grew food in the nearby fields. Even the old ones couldn't remember a time when the People had been anywhere else. Since my first breath, we have traveled far, crossing many rivers and climbing many hills. Now Horse has come to us, and we hunt Bull Buffalo for food and clothing. It's not for us to say this is better than what was before. Different, yes. But a man doesn't decide what turns his road will take. It's his road, and he walks it."

"But you see what will come, Ne' hyo."

"Sometimes, Naha'. Maybe you, too, will see."

"But I won't be a healer, like you and Little Raven. I read that in your eyes. You're disappointed."

"No, not that," Cloud Dancer objected. "Sad. I'll miss my son now that he will take to the young men's lodge. But these will be exciting days for you. You've proven yourself. It's right you should start walking man's road."

"And will I carry a brave name like my father?"

"Yes, Naha'. When we return, we'll invite the People to a feast. I'll give away three horses, and you'll have your name."

"I'll learn it only then?" the young man cried.

"Only then," Cloud Dancer echoed. "Have patience, Naha'."

"You say that often," the young man grumbled. "But what young man was ever patient?"

They returned to the Suhtai, and White Horse went out to the Poor People and summoned them as well. Old Gray Wolf brought his band, and Touches the Sky greeted his nephews warmly. Later, the Arrow-keeper made prayers and blessed the young man who would soon receive his warrior name.

Two days and nights the People feasted and danced. Presents were given by Gray Wolf and Touches the Sky, and the three horses were presented by Cloud Dancer to young men in need of mounts. Finally, after much talk and smoking, the Foxes gathered. Criers came and fetched Swallow Tail, who was conducted to the Fox council where his grandfather, father, and uncle waited.

"This is my son, who comes before you," Cloud Dancer explained. "He's been called Swallow Tail; but that's a boy's name, and he has come to be a man. He has no use for this name, and I give it away to anyone who wants it."

"Wolf has come into this young man's dreams," Gray Wolf added. "Wolf speaks of many things, and he urges us to be strong. We'll need leaders to keep our hearts brave. And strong men to steady us when the fighting starts."

"The hairy faces bring a new metal from the land past the far rivers," Cloud Dancer said. "They call this iron, and it never chips like stone. As it is steadfast, may my son be so. I give him a brave-heart name, Iron Wolf. Iron Wolf, come meet your brother Foxes."

"Ayyyy!" the men yelled.

Gray Wolf handed his grandson a stringless bow, and others brought the sacred cord. The young man was painted, and much celebrating followed.

"I'm a boy no longer, Ne' hyo," Iron Wolf said.

"No, yours is now man's road," Cloud Dancer agreed. "Be strong as your name, Naha'. There'll be need."

Chapter Fifteen

The Poor People weren't the only ones to visit the Suhtai that autumn. Not long after Iron Wolf was inducted into the Foxes, a large group of Arapahoes arrived from the west. These Arapaho people were strangers to the Suhtai, but Gray Wolf's band knew them well.

"They're much like us," Gray Wolf explained. "We've hunted buffalo together. They, too, fight the Kiowas. Many of our young men have taken Arapaho women, and some of our girls have welcomed Arapaho husbands. So we're strangers no more."

The Suhtai nevertheless remained distant. These Arapahoes had adopted many strange ways, and their tales of trading with the hairy faces alarmed Red Elk and White Calf.

"I know of the grandfathers' warnings," Yellow Bird said when the men met in council. "I, too, heard Sweet Medicine's prophecies when I was a boy. But Arapahoes grow no hairs on their chins. Their flesh is brown under the sun as our own is. They dance well, and they make the dawn prayers. If I trade them a pony, no one objects. It's only if I take these hairy-face things the pale people have brought. Then I make bad medicine for my people!"

Other young men agreed with Yellow Bird.

"These iron knives are strong," Running Dog said. "They tear buffalo hide quick and straight."

"My wife admired the shiny beads they offer," Cut Forehead, leader of the Crazy Dog Warriors, added. "Can there be harm in making a woman to look more beautiful?"

"These things will steal from us Is'siwun's protection," White Calf warned. "Didn't Erect Horns, who brought this sacred Hat to us, say we should keep to our old ways."

"We accepted Horse," Yellow Bird argued. "We've left the places known to our fathers to come to this new country. I'll bring a pipe to Is'siwun. She may advise us to accept these new things."

"There's terrible danger here," Cloud Dancer said, rising slowly. "Many are too young to remember the Chippewa raids that left many dead. Some of you may recall the wails of the women and the cries of the children. My uncle, Touches the Sky, saw these terrible things in his dreams and spoke warnings; but some young men foolishly ignored this, and we suffered. Sweet Medicine and Erect Horns, who brought much power to us, told of the hairy faces long before they came to this country. They had the far-seeing eyes. Can we turn away from their wisdom?"

"Life is change," Yellow Bird answered. "I respect these old warnings, but I also know we can't allow these good things to come into the hands of other people and not our own. Can we give the Kiowas iron weapons and fight them with flint knives?"

There was a murmur of agreement among the warriors, and Red Elk quieted them.

"Take Is'siwun your pipe, Yellow Bird," the headman suggested. "If he says we can accept these things, then we will do it. But be careful. I value Cloud Dancer's advice. His dreams carry great power, and he's never led us into harm. As he said, many are too young to remember when the Chippewas murdered the Poor People. Most Suhtai were far from that place. But I know the warning Cloud Dancer gave us—that we should stay away from Muddy River. How many saw the Mandan camp of the dead? Is that what you would bring to us, Yellow Bird? No, you can't imagine such misfortune. It's for the medicine men to see the path ahead. So we must listen to their words."

Yellow Bird accepted this mild reproof without reply. But he and his companions were clearly far from convinced.

The council concluded with the decision to consult Is'siwun, and after a pipe was smoked, the men went their separate ways. Cloud Dancer wasn't invited along when Yellow Bird took the pipe to White Calf and consulted the sacred Hat, so he never learned what was said there. White Calf wouldn't speak of it, but he moved his medicine lodge from the camp. Many of the older Suhtai moved as well. Yellow Bird and the young men remained to trade with the Arapahoes.

"It's a bad thing, this trading," Touches the Sky told Cloud Dancer.

"Yes, Uncle," the Dancer agreed. "It can only lead to misfortune."

"Sometimes I think I've lived too long," the old man lamented. "My power's not strong as it once was, and I see only hard things and difficult times for the people."

"Maybe I should carry a pipe and ask the Arrows for their wisdom," Cloud Dancer suggested.

"You've had your dream," Touches the Sky said. "I've had mine. The Arrows would urge us to leave this place, and you won't do that. You have a son who rides with the young men, and young ones who don't belong in an old man's camp. Maybe they'll have eyes to see the consequences of ignoring medicine dreams. That's a thing worth knowing."

"Yes, it is," Cloud Dancer agreed.

A sense of dread filled Cloud Dancer's heart those next two days. He could feel tragedy creeping like a shadow upon the two remaining camps, but he could do nothing to fend it off. He passed the days walking with Touches the Sky and Gray Wolf, speaking of old times or sharing his sons with them. Little Dancer and Raven Feather had lost their shyness, and together with Corn Boy, they enjoyed the attentions of these grandfathers.

Iron Wolf was off hunting most of that time. He wouldn't abandon his new place among the other young men, but neither could he ignore his father's warnings. In spite of his name, Iron Wolf disdained the new tools and weapons the Arapahoes brought.

Not so the other young men. Yellow Bird flaunted the fine new knife he carried and the iron pots he acquired for his wife. Cut Forehead and the Crazy Dogs boasted they were now the strongest of the warrior societies.

"We don't pass our days brooding over old women's tales," Cut Forehead said contemptuously. "Soon we'll have other new things that will make us even more feared in battle!"

Cut Forehead wouldn't see those things, though. The very next evening he had cross words with Curly Bow, another young Crazy Dog. Each of them pulled a shiny new iron knife, and soon they slashed at each other. Cut Forehead seemed only to be playing at battle, but the Bow was deadly serious. He blocked two half-hearted thrusts and drove the knife deep into Cut Forehead's belly. A stone knife would perhaps have done mortal damage, too. The iron blade sliced through muscle and pierced vital organs. Cut Forehead gasped, looked up in surprise, and died.

A great wail rose from the People. The predicted calamity had come, for no misfortune was as great as for one of the People to take the life of another. No band could long survive the blood feuds which must follow, and the People collected around Curly Bow, their angry words and fearful eyes falling like heavy blows on the stunned Crazy Dog.

"It's as the old ones warned," Curly Bow cried as he withdrew the knife and tossed it away. "These iron things have brought bad medicine to us. I've killed my brother, and now the People will suffer!"

Curly Bow screamed and chanted and raced around the camp, seeking out advice from relatives. But before they could speak, he would race off toward another. As he ran, he kicked off his moccasins and stripped his leggings. He cast aside his deerskin vest and tore off his shirt. Finally he cut the manhood string which held the

Suhtai skin flaps. Naked and wild with madness, he continued to run about, tearing out his hair and screaming.

"Madness has taken him," Yellow Bird declared, avoiding the hard gazes of the old men who had warned him of such misfortune. "We must tell the Arapahoes to go, and we must tend Cut Forehead. We'll move camp, too, for this is a bad place."

"Curly Bow must be sent away!" Red Elk announced.

"He's gone already," Cloud Dancer observed. "Man Above has struck him senseless."

"There's other work to do, too," Touches the Sky said as he gazed upon the lifeless body of Cut Forehead. "The power of Mahuts, the sacred Arrows, has been broken. It must be restored."

"Yes," the other old ones agreed. "You must climb the hills and make them over."

"I've grown old," Touches the Sky said, turning to Cloud Dancer. "I'll need help. Nephew?"

"Yes, I'll come," Cloud Dancer agreed, noticing the change that now filled his uncle's face. It wasn't just sadness, or even fear. No, a terrible weariness seemed to take possession of the tall man, bending him under its weight.

"Bring the young ones," Touches the Sky then whispered. "And White Horse. We go a great distance, and their help will be needed."

"Yes, Uncle," Cloud Dancer replied, even as he would have twenty summers before when he first followed his uncle onto the medicine trail.

"Harden yourself for the trials to come," Touches the Sky spoke to the others. "Hold the little ones close. All that Sweet Medicine foretold is coming to pass."

Even the bravest of the young men shuddered as they read the future painted on Touches the Sky's face. Their gazes dropped to the ground, and the mourning chants that followed were not solely for Cut Forehead. No, the People now mourned their own fate as well.

Cloud Dancer delayed their departure until Cut Forehead's burial rites were completed. He then went among the Suhtai people, making his farewells. Soon the bands would part company, for it was well to disperse the People in winter. Cloud Dancer sensed his path would take him away from his wife's band and back to Gray Wolf's people.

"I, too, feel it," Raven's Wing said sadly. "It's for the best. I have only Otter Woman left of all my relations here."

"There's our son," Cloud Dancer pointed out.

"He'll soon take a wife and make his own way," she said, gripping her husband's hands. "Touches the Sky would long ago have given over Mahuts into your care if we had traveled with the Poor People. He's old. You must accept this new burden."

"It will be hard."

"Has the medicine trail ever been an easy one, Husband? Not for my father nor for me. I understand its ways. Let's talk no more of it."

He held her tightly, hoping that somehow the affection that passed between them might make the going easier. But a man was only a weak creature — nothing among the great powers of the world. Cloud Dancer worried even an Arrow-keeper could do little to change what was now fast approaching. And who save perhaps White Calf held similar power?

And so Cloud Dancer broke down his lodge and packed up his belongings. Little Dancer and Corn Boy, aided by Raven Feather, collected the horses and drove them to the edge of the camp. White Horse, by then, had made his preparations for the journey as well. The Horse and Red Robe Woman waited with her family, and there was sadness for the loss of such a good hunter.

"Mahuts needs me," White Horse had explained when his relatives objected.

"Then, you must go," they had agreed.

Now all that remained to be done was to mount the horses and begin the long ride westward.

"Where do we go, Uncle?" Cloud Dancer asked as Touches the Sky led them past the first line of hills. "Won't these hills bring us close enough to Man Above?"

"They would bring you dreams, but that's not enough," the old man explained. "Tonight I'll show you Mahuts. You can see how the power is tainted. It's necessary to take the Arrows to Holy Mountain. There I'll make prayers."

"Holy Mountain?"

"It's a distant place, in the center of the world. All my life I've heard stories of how Sweet Medicine received the Arrows there. I must go there and seek a dream."

"It's far, then."

"Yes, far," Touches the Sky said, sighing. "I've dreamed before, in other places. But dark times are coming. The People will need the strongest power."

Cloud Dancer nodded, although he didn't understand. He knew soon Touches the Sky would begin sharing the mysteries of Mahuts and the power that came to an Arrow-keeper. These things Cloud Dancer would one day pass on to a son or nephew.

They rode on and on, stopping only when the sun began to die in the west. The lodges were erected, and food was cooked. After eating, Touches the Sky summoned Cloud Dancer inside the Arrow Lodge and lit a pipe.

"Here is Mahuts, the four sacred Arrows," Touches the Sky said when he finished smoking. The old man opened the fox-skin covering and exposed the Arrows. The ancient shafts were straight and strong, but something was wrong with the stone points.

"There's blood on the points, Uncle," Cloud Dancer gasped. "How is that possible?"

"Mahuts is the soul of the People," Touches the Sky explained. "When blood is shed, can it help but stain the arrows? This summer we must renew them. We'll gather all the People and cleanse them by making the medicine prayers. You'll replace the feathers and purify the points. Then the buffalo arrows will again bring Bull Buffalo to our hunters. The man arrows can regain their blinding powers, too."

"Will there be much to learn?"

"Much, but you've always been an apt pupil."

"You'll teach me the rituals as we journey to Holy Mountain, then."

"Yes," Touches the Sky said, gazing solemnly at the Arrows. "It's one reason I chose to go there."

"And the other?" Cloud Dancer asked.

"It's said Sweet Medicine's spirit walks that place. I will climb Hanging Road there."

"You're not sick, Uncle?" Cloud Dancer asked in alarm.

"Weary," Touches the Sky explained. "And sick in my heart perhaps. I've seen too many things. I've known few comforts. I've lived long, keeping my feet on the sacred path so that the People would grow strong. But now I look upon them and see the dark days Sweet Medicine prophesied. A younger, stronger man should take up this burden. It's too heavy for me to carry."

"I'll try to be worthy, Uncle."

"You have never disappointed me, Cloud Dancer. Now, we must begin your instruction. There's much to learn."

Cloud Dancer became a student once more. He listened attentively to his uncle, and his understanding of Mahuts and the sacred ceremonies grew daily. Later he practiced the rites under Touches the Sky's watchful eye. Little Dancer, Corn Boy, and Raven Feather were introduced to the sacred Arrows.

"Little Dancer has his grandfather's eyes," Touches the Sky noted the next day when he and Cloud Dancer made the dawn prayers together as they had so long ago.

"A hunter's eyes," Cloud Dancer agreed.

"Those of a warrior," Touches the Sky added. "He'll be a leader of the Foxes maybe."

"With Corn Boy at his side, even as White Horse rides with me," Cloud Dancer declared. "It's a good thing, having a brother-friend. Raven Feather is still small. He'll soon find a boy to hunt with."

186

"He has the quiet, thoughtful eyes," Touches the Sky noted. "From his mother. The Suhtai make good healers. Already he takes an interest in the curing."

"He's curious, Uncle, as all boys are."

"He won't be the one to keep the Arrows, though."

"Uncle?"

"One obligation of a keeper is to pass on his knowledge. I had no son, so I chose my nephew."

"You suggest Corn Boy?"

"No, that boy will never own the patience."

"I have another son, Uncle. Iron Wolf. He, too, is destined to walk the warrior road, though."

"He'll have sons."

"I'll be older than you when they're tall."

"I pray so. It will be hard for a young man to hold the People's respect."

"Uncle, how will I know when it's time to pass on my burden? How will I know the one to choose? Iron Wolf may have many sons."

"You will know from the aches that won't leave you," Touches the Sky answered. "He'll be known to you, too. There will be a mark, a scar maybe, or is it? A red mark on his neck."

"You've seen all this?" Cloud Dancer asked.

"Long ago, before you left your father's lodge. I've had no woman to comfort me and no sons to grow. My power has brought many dreams into my head."

Cloud Dancer marveled at such notions. To dream of boys not yet born who would take up the Arrow bundle? And yet he didn't doubt the truth of Touches the Sky's words.

The first snow was falling when they finally reached Holy Mountain. The boys shivered in their buffalo robes as a harsh wind tormented them. Red Robe Woman and her smaller children hurried to unpack horses while White Horse and Corn Boy began erecting their lodge. Cloud Dancer set his own lodge alongside that of his brother, at the base of the butte. The Arrow Lodge would continue up the slope to the heart of Holy Mountain.

For days Cloud Dancer had prayed for the journey to end. Each new ridge had promised to be Holy Mountain, but each time Touches the Sky scanned the place and scowled.

"We must continue," the old man had announced.

And so when they had reached Holy Mountain, Cloud Dancer had found himself surprised.

"It's not so high a place as I'd supposed," he remarked. "You're certain?"

"Look at it and ask yourself," Touches the Sky advised. "What does your heart tell you?"

Cloud Dancer concentrated on the rough outline of the mountain. Slowly a wondrous peace began to fill him. He smiled.

"Yes, you feel it," Touches the Sky said, nodding. "We must climb the slope and seek our vision. We'll practice the Arrow renewal, too. Then, when all is done, and you are satisfied that you know the ceremonies and understand the rituals, you will erect a scaffold for me."

"Before you . . . need it?"

"When you have it finished, I will have need," the old man said. "I grow numb already. We should hurry."

Cloud Dancer did just that. He rode with the boys and his uncle up Holy Mountain while White Horse kept watch below with the women. Touches the Sky instructed Cloud Dancer in the remaking of the Arrows, and they reviewed each ritual in turn.

"Now there can be harmony in the world again," Touches the Sky said when the Arrows were returned to their foxhide bundle. "Build the scaffold, nephews. Soon I begin the long walk."

Little Dancer and Corn Boy built the platform. Cloud Dancer passed that time in the Arrow Lodge, sharing his uncle's final day.

"Carry me outside, that my ghost won't know this lodge," Touches the Sky said when death's shadow fell across his face. "All that's inside, you will need, Nephew. My other things I've given away already. Make the mourning prayers, and don't travel three days. Then go back to the People. Gather them this summer and renew Mahuts."

Cloud Dancer helped Touches the Sky outside. The old man sat beneath a tall pine and drank in the crisp cool air. Snow fell on his shoulders, and he laughed as he recalled the snows of his boyhood. Soon, though, the laughter died as Touches the Sky's head fell against the pine.

"Man Above," Cloud Dancer prayed, "hurry the shade of this good and reverent man to your side. Give me strength to walk in his footsteps the path he has guided me to."

He then took up the great tall body of Touches the Sky, Arrow-keeper and medicine chief of the People. With Corn Boy's help, Cloud Dancer wrapped the old man in a buffalo hide and carried him to the waiting scaffold.

"Ayyyy!" Cloud Dancer and the boys howled as they unbraided their hair and began the mourning chants. Later they rested a stringless bow beside the body. White Horse slew three horses and tied their tails to the scaffold.

"Hurry him up Hanging Road," White Horse whispered.

There were no others to share the mourning feast, but it was held all the same. They observed all three days of mourning, too. Then they packed up the Arrow Lodge and their possessions.

"Where will we go, Ne' hyo?" Little Dancer asked. "Mahuts belongs with the Tsis tsis tas."

"We'll erect our lodges in the camp circle beside Gray Wolf," Cloud Dancer explained. "It's a good place."

"Yes," White Horse agreed.

They then turned to glance back one last time at Holy Mountain before starting the preparations for the return eastward. That summer Cloud Dancer would renew the Arrows, and the People would continue.

Chapter Sixteen

Five times the snows cloaked Mother Earth and melted under the summer suns, and all that time Cloud Dancer kept the Arrows. Mahuts, in turn, brought prosperity and peace to the People. The bands grew as new children were born, and the warrior societies became strong as young men took their places beside brothers and fathers.

"Has there ever been such a good time?" White Horse asked the day Corn Boy struck down his first buffalo calf.

"Yes, it's good to have strong sons," Cloud Dancer agreed.

But there was sadness, too. First Little Crane climbed Hanging Road. Next summer, only days after Gray Wolf gave his war name to the boy who had been called Little Dancer, the chief of the Poor People asked to be carried to Holy Mountain and placed beside his brother.

"So often we rode together in life," the old man told Cloud Dancer. "It's right our bones should lie in the same place."

Now, with the dispersed bands gathered for the New Life Lodge ceremonies, Cloud Dancer gazed with pride at his three sons. Iron Wolf was now a famous horse-stealer and an acclaimed hunter. Soon the young man would marry, and the cycle of life would continue.

Young Gray Wolf, straight and certain as a young man of fifteen snows should be, rode beside his cousin. Hairy Mane had given away his boyhood name, Corn Boy, to the small child Painted Robe's wife had brought into the world. Now the Wolf and the Mane joined the Elk Warriors in every hunt and raid.

Of the three boys, only Raven Feather remained in his father's lodge. Cloud Dancer remembered old Touches the Sky's prediction and taught this youngest child the use of medicine roots.

"You're the grandson of Little Raven, a great medicine-maker," Raven's Wing often told the boy.

But although Raven Feather demonstrated an interest in the curing rites, his eyes soon drifted to the excitement of the hunt and the stories his older brothers shared of young man adventures.

"He'll be a healer," Raven's Wing assured her husband. "He has the heart to make others well."

"But he'll never be one to live for the People," Cloud Dancer said, sighing. "I'd hoped for a son to take up my burden."

"Your uncle told you it would be another," she argued. "You have been an Arrow-keeper for just a short time. There are years remaining."

"Yes," Cloud Dancer admitted. "But Mahuts should pass into the hands of a man who has acquired wisdom from much living. I sometimes feel I'm too young myself. To wait for a grandson not yet born—ah, it will take a long time."

"Maybe not so long," she said as she pointed to Iron

Wolf. The young man carried a courting flute. "He's often seen on the water path, tormenting the water-carriers. He shares a buffalo robe with many maidens. No, it won't be so long, Husband. It will be nice to have him near again."

"Near?" Cloud Dancer cried. "He rides with Yellow Bird and the Suhtai."

"But his eyes rest on the Bird's niece, Yellow Robe, whose family is of the Poor People."

Cloud Dancer matched her grin. It took a mother to notice such things. In time there would be grandsons to teach the sacred path, even as Touches the Sky foretold.

All that would come later, though. Once the New Life Lodge was constructed, and the dancing carried out, the People once again split into their many bands. Is'siwun promised success to the hunters, and many bands set out to bring meat to their camps.

Cloud Dancer and White Horse organized the Foxes that summer. The Dancer felt strange, looking around and seeing so few of the old men remaining. It was a hard thing, realizing he himself might soon be a grandfather. Already Raven's Wing's hair showed streaks of white. She, who had not yet passed her fortieth summer!

While White Horse discussed tactics with the other Fox chiefs, Cloud Dancer readied the two sacred buffalo arrows which would lead to a successful hunt. As he unwrapped the sacred bundle, though, his head began to ache. The Arrows felt warm to his touch, and he sensed great harm.

"Go and bring your uncle," Cloud Dancer told Raven Feather.

The boy quickly rose and hurried off to do as instructed. "What's wrong?" Raven's Wing asked.

"I'm not certain," Cloud Dancer admitted. "But my head hurts. The Arrows aren't right."

When White Horse arrived, Raven Feather showed him inside and then left. Raven's Wing offered the two men some tea and moved off so that they might talk.

"It's only prudent to delay the hunt," White Horse said after Cloud Dancer shared his concern. "We'll go to the hills, and you can seek a dream."

"The young men will be impatient," Cloud Dancer said. "Some may go out on their own."

"They can make scouts instead," White Horse suggested. "If trouble is coming, it's sure to come from others. Maybe the Arapaho traders have returned. Perhaps the hairy faces have come up Muddy River. Or the Kiowas may be after our horses."

"It's a good idea," Cloud Dancer agreed. "Go and tell them. I'll make myself ready for the journey."

The young men grumbled, as expected, and some defiantly challenged the chiefs. But when Cloud Dancer joined the council and explained the warning came from Mahuts, all arguing ceased. No one had forgotten Curly Bow. No one wished to share his fate.

As they had done so often before, the brothers rode into the low hills to the west. Raven Feather came along to tend the fire, but otherwise they were alone. Cloud Dancer made prayers and smoked the pipe. Even before cutting his flesh, the dream came. It struck sudden and hard, like a lance thrust, and the Dancer cried out in horror.

"Brother, what have you seen?" White Horse asked as

194

he brought water to bathe Cloud Dancer's feverish forehead.

"The camp," Cloud Dancer explained. "Kiowas."

"See to your father," White Horse told Raven Feather. "I'll make the horses ready."

"Ne' hyo needs rest," the boy argued.

"There's no time," White Horse replied. "The camp's in danger. We must warn them."

"He must rest," Raven Feather said as he applied the cool cloth. "Go ahead. I know what to do."

"You can't stay here alone," White Horse said, frowning. "A watcher's necessary."

"I'm not helpless," Raven Feather insisted. "I'll ride to hunt buffalo next summer and win a name. Even now I can pull Ne' hyo's bow. Test me, Uncle."

"Go," Cloud Dancer moaned. He tried to stand, but he was weak from fasting, and the dream unsettled him. "Warn the helpless ones, Brother. Naha' will help me."

White Horse nodded, then rolled up his hides and set off to find his horse. Soon the Horse was riding down the hillside, hurrying toward the distant camp.

If the dream had been less unsettling, Cloud Dancer might have learned more. As daylight lit the eastern horizon, he could only recall skin lodges falling, women and children screaming, and young men rushing to battle the enemy. He searched his memory for the sound of singing arrows, for the sight of lance-carrying riders. He didn't find them. No, instead there was fire and thunder. He soon learned why.

That morning, after making the dawn prayers, Cloud Dancer chewed dried buffalo meat and waited for Raven Feather to collect their horses. Then, after packing their skins on the animals, the Dancer climbed atop his pony and led the way home.

The dream had been real in a way he didn't fully understand, and he feared the raid might have already occurred. Soon, though, he smelled the campfires, and later he heard the laughter of children splashing in Fat River. Criers announced their return. Raven's Wing emerged from the Arrow Lodge, concern etched onto her face.

"Where's White Horse?" Cloud Dancer asked as he dismounted.

"Gone with a band of young men," Hairy Mane answered. "There were sounds from upriver. Much screaming, and noise like thunder."

"Is there another camp close by?" Cloud Dancer asked.

"Suhtai," Painted Robe explained. "A small band, led by Yellow Bird. Hunters mostly."

"They were here to visit the girls this morning," young Gray Wolf explained. "Iron Wolf, my brother, was with them."

"There's been trouble there," Cloud Dancer said, walking toward his lodge. "Wife, we'll be needed there. Many will want curing."

"I'm to go also, then?" Raven Feather asked.

"Yes, you can help," the Dancer explained. "Painted Robe, watch the camp carefully. There are Kiowas close by, and we are rich in horses. They may visit us next."

"Ne' hyo, we'll protect the helpless ones," Gray Wolf vowed. "And guard the horses, too."

It was not without a trace of pride that Cloud Dancer gripped his son's slender shoulders. Names sometimes brought power with them. Could anyone doubt there was much of the old Gray Wolf in the younger one?

They rode slowly, cautiously, along Fat River. The smell of smoke again attracted Cloud Dancer's attention, but this odor had none of the pleasing traits of burning wood. Scorched hides outraged the nostrils and alarmed the soul. But soon his eyes brought Cloud Dancer greater pain.

It was, as Painted Robe had said, a small camp. The circle, or what remained, had only held seven lodges. There were also smaller shelters inhabited by young, unmarried men. Now only two tipis remained erect. The others smoldered atop charred lodge poles.

Nearby brownish clumps lay strewn like so many discarded sacks. Coming closer, Cloud Dancer saw these were bodies. Dried blood stained bare backs and shoulders. Foreheads were split open where scalplocks had been cut away. A boy of ten summers the Dancer recognized as Yellow Bird's son, Rabbit Tail, sat beside a slain woman, holding his left arm and fighting back tears.

"What manner of wound is this?" Cloud Dancer asked as he examined the boy's forearm. A terrible swelling above the wrist was stained black with flecks of burned powder.

"It was the Kiowas," Rabbit Tail said, wincing as Cloud Dancer touched the arm. "Ten maybe. With them rode a hairy face and another of the pale people. They pointed sticks at us that exploded like thunder. Beaver Tooth, my brother, was killed. Also Sky Bow

197

and Prowling Bear. Next they set fire to the lodges. Many defenseless ones were killed. Others were taken captive. I tried to stop them, but the hairy face touched his fire stick to my arm, and I was thrown back. My mother ran over and was killed."

"Where's your father?" Cloud Dancer asked as he eased the boy onto the ground.

"He and the others fought hard, but the fire sticks struck down many. Then the Kiowas left. Ne' hyo went after them."

"Iron Wolf? White Horse?"

"Yes, Iron Wolf went with Ne' hyo. White Horse came later, to warn us. But it was too late. He went to visit the other camp and tell them what's happened. There are more Suhtai near."

"They can help," Cloud Dancer said. He then cleaned the wound and began searching for what had done the damage. Deep in the boy's flesh a soft gray lump rested beside the bone. With Raven's Wing's help, the Dancer extracted the foreign matter and began making the healing cures.

"What magic did they use against us?" other Suhtai asked as they examined the gray lump. "Has Thunderbird joined our enemies?"

"This comes from the hairy faces," Cloud Dancer grumbled.

"Ne' hyo will punish them, then," Rabbit Tail cried. "For killing my mother and brother. For all these others."

"Perhaps," Cloud Dancer said, doubting a few sickhearted riders could catch a determined band of raiders. "As for us, there's much work to be done. We must build burial scaffolds and tend the dead. The mourning prayers must be spoken. Then we'll summon others. This deed must not go unpunished!"

White Horse said much the same thing when he returned with twenty Suhtai Fox Warriors. The Crazy Dogs and Elks followed. All were hungry for vengeance.

"These Kiowas will long remember the day we visit their camps!" Low Dog, who now led the Crazy Dogs, boasted.

But once they examined the shattered bodies of the wounded survivors, they shrank back. There was always some fear of the unknown, and these fire-stick weapons were terrible.

Their spirits revived when Iron Wolf arrived with news of the Kiowa camp.

"Yellow Bird and the others wait there now," Iron Wolf explained. "It's only for us to join him. Twenty of our people are captives. We'll rescue them and punish the Kiowas."

"Ayyyy!" the warriors howled.

"Ne' hyo, will you make medicine to confound our enemies?" Iron Wolf asked.

"Mahuts is in the other camp," Cloud Dancer explained. "The blinding magic is best used against an enemy fought on the plain. For raiding a camp, you should make yourselves invisible. It's an old Tsis tsis tas trick. We'll join Yellow Bird. I'll show you how once we're together. Then we'll fall on the Kiowas."

It sounded simple, but it wasn't. First of all, the Kiowa camp was well to the south of Fat River. It was also well guarded. The Kiowas had lost many horses to raiding parties, so even the horse herd was watched by a band of young men. The main encampment contained three great circles, for it seemed here was a major gathering of the tribe.

"You've brought only a few men," Yellow Bird complained when he saw the thirty riders who followed Iron Wolf to the camp. "How can we regain our honor?"

"Ne' hyo will make us invisible," Iron Wolf answered.

Yellow Bird dropped his head. His eyes had seen too much Kiowa power to believe in miracles. The others respected the Arrow-keeper's medicine, though, and they gathered close. Cloud Dancer made two silent prayers. Then he produced a pouch of crushed buffalo horn.

One by one the warriors appeared. Cloud Dancer bared their chests and painted them with his magic. When he finished, the men split into four bands. They would strike by nightfall, from each of the four cardinal directions. Their invisible cries would strike the enemy numb with fear, and victory could only follow.

Yellow Bird himself led the northern group. Low Dog and the other Crazy Dogs would strike from the south. White Horse and Cloud Dancer, together with Iron Wolf and the other Foxes, would strike from the east. The Elks would come from the west.

"I must warn you of two things," Cloud Dancer said as the bands prepared to take their positions. "Strike only men. Leave the helpless ones—the women, children, old people. And take nothing from the camp except our people who were taken captive. Do otherwise, and the invisible paint will lose its magic."

The warriors muttered impatiently, but all nodded their agreement. Then the leaders led their men off, and the surround was made.

Cloud Dancer stood between his brother and Iron Wolf. He silently prayed Man Above would bring the People good fortune that night. His companions readied themselves for the attack. Suddenly Yellow Bird's scream shattered the silent evening, and the first warriors hurled themselves upon the Kiowas. Confusion swept the camp as other voices shouted. The Kiowa guards ran one direction and then another. Arrows danced through the air, and one guard after another fell.

The Crazy Dogs reached the captives first. For a time there was furious fighting. Low Dog was wounded, and Coyote Eye was killed. The Kiowa line was broken, though, and with the help of the Elks, the captives were led safely away.

The Foxes had encountered some trouble at first, but they were able to blunt the enemy charge and drive them away. The horse guards managed a brief attack, but in the darkness, they lost their heads and ran away.

Yellow Bird should have been satisfied with the rescue. His young men struck the heart of the Kiowa camp, counting many coups and killing one of the hairy faces. Yellow Bird was mad with grief over his slain wife and son, though, and he lit a torch. Waving it wildly, he began burning lodges. A small boy ran past, and without thinking, Yellow Bird struck him down.

"Our power is broken," Iron Wolf cried, witnessing the killing.

Indeed it was. The flaming lodges illuminated the riders, and Kiowas rushed to beat back their attackers. Now, too, they saw how few the enemy were.

Yellow Bird might have retreated with the others of his band, but he refused. Instead he staked himself in the ground and fought savagely as Kiowas encircled him. He killed one, perhaps two. Then they fell on him and cut him to pieces.

Iron Wolf twice tried to rescue the Bird, but there were too many Kiowas drawn to the burning lodges. Cloud Dancer and White Horse strove to protect the young man's back, but soon they were heavily attacked. The Dancer lost sight of his son, and his heart was heavy with concern. Then he glimpsed Iron Wolf counting coup on a huge, hairy-faced giant. The pale figure stood a head taller. His bare chest and back were thick with curly hairs, and his dark eyes promised every sort of menace. Still the stringless bow flailed away, knocking the giant back.

"Jacques!" a younger man cried, waving a pair of strange sticks in the air. Here, then, were the magic weapons. The young man lacked his companion's hairy chin and chest, but he was a fine runner and quick at dodging arrows. Twice White Horse shot at him, but the young man dove under the first and hopped over the second.

Iron Wolf, seeing himself outnumbered, managed to turn the giant at the instant the smooth-cheeked young man fired his first stick. The air exploded, and Cloud Dancer's ears ached. The impact of the blast broke the hairy giant's back and dropped him to the ground.

"Naha'!" Cloud Dancer yelled. "We must go!"

Iron Wolf hesitated but an instant. Then, before the pale-skinned young man could make ready his other fire stick, the Wolf vanished into the shawl of darkness. His father and uncle followed.

Chapter Seventeen

Among the People, that summer would always be counted as the time the fire sticks fought Yellow Bird. Iron Wolf had his own reasons for noting the year. He counted his first coup on the enemy in the attack on the Kiowa camp. And he first asked Yellow Robe to share his buffalo robe.

As summer progressed, the two young people took on a glow. Rarely was one without the other in the evenings. Even while off hunting, Iron Wolf carried his flute and sang to the wind of the woman he wished for a wife.

The first breath of autumn was on the land when Iron Wolf spoke to the Foxes of making a horse raid against the Kiowas.

"Their ponies will be fat," the Wolf declared. "Their camps won't be far. We can do it easily."

"Yes," others agreed.

"We should punish the Kiowas," Painted Robe added. "They haven't suffered for the death they brought the People."

Others counseled caution.

"Brave words are easily spoken," White Horse said. "But raiding the Kiowas won't be the same now that they carry fire sticks. I've seen the holes their magic put in men. They strike from far off, killing a man as easily as I might snap a brittle willow twig."

"Take Mahuts a pipe," young Gray Wolf suggested. "Ask the Arrows, Brother."

"Yes, seek their advice," White Horse agreed.

"Winter comes," Iron Wolf objected. "We must start soon or the snows will find us."

"It's foolish to hurry a thing," White Horse argued. "A successful raid will bring you many horses. You will stand tall among the People. But you must lead wisely. Know what lies ahead. Take the pipe to your father and ask Mahuts to advise you. The Arrows are never wrong."

There was a murmur of agreement, and Iron Wolf accepted the council's opinion. He would take a pipe to Mahuts.

Usually an older man led raiding parties, and Iron Wolf hesitated to approach Cloud Dancer alone. How, after all, should questions be put? Often Iron Wolf had been present when warriors sought out Mahuts's aid, but a boy pays too little attention to ritual and ceremony. He didn't remember enough.

Iron Wolf approached White Horse, his uncle.

"I promised to bring Ne' hyo a pipe," the young man said. "But how's it done? How do I act. Will I ask Mahuts, or will my father do it?"

"You've done well to ask," White Horse replied. "Many young men make mistakes because they ignore their elders' counsel. To offend the Arrows would bring misfortune. We'll talk, and I'll explain what must be done."

They then did just that. The following day, just after

Cloud Dancer returned from making the dawn prayers, White Horse conducted Iron Wolf to the door of the Arrow Lodge. In the young man's hands rested a fine pipe adorned with eagle feathers.

"Ne' hyo, I would smoke," Iron Wolf said solemnly. "Then I would ask for Mahuts to guide me."

"Yes?" Cloud Dancer asked.

"We bring you these fine buffalo hides as a present," White Horse said, setting two hides inside the lodge. "The spotted pony you much admire is now yours, too."

"It must be an important matter you would share with the Arrows," Cloud Dancer said, welcoming them inside. The three men warmed their hands over a small fire while Raven's Wing offered tea. Raven Feather brought a tobacco pouch, then left to join the other boys.

For a time they drank silently. Then Cloud Dancer filled the pipe and performed the brief ritual that invoked the great mysteries. Finally, after the smoke was finished, Cloud Dancer drew his son closer to the Arrows.

"Ask Mahuts," the Arrow-keeper urged. "Speak of your concerns and hopes. The Arrows will consider these things."

Iron Wolf then spoke of the proposed horse raid. He told of the many ponies he would bring to the People. He explained his tactics. He would take only seven men, all of them young and strong. Three came from poor families and would share their good fortune with cousins and brothers.

"Your family is rich with ponies," Cloud Dancer noted. "Why would you lead this raid?"

206

"I wish to take a wife," Iron Wolf answered, shyly dropping his eyes. "Ne' hyo, I intended to speak to you, and to her father, but a man must own more than a name of his own. He should stand tall in the eyes of his friends. I have horses, but that's because my father is Cloud Dancer, a famous raider. You were younger, Ne' hyo, when you brought Horse to the People. It's for me to prove myself now and win a wife."

"These others who go with you," Cloud Dancer spoke quietly. "Your brother would be one of them. Your cousin?"

"Hairy Mane and Gray Wolf are boys no longer," White Horse said. "It's hard for us, their fathers, to see it, though. They hunger for man's road."

"The Arrows tell me this," Cloud Dancer said, reading signs from the way they turned. "There will be danger, perhaps death. You'll make medicine prayers before leaving our camp. You must avoid the Kiowa village. It's there death waits. Take nothing besides horses. You'll be tempted, as will the others. Are you strong enough to keep your band safe?"

"Yes," Iron Wolf vowed. "Strong as the name you gave me."

"Once I would have ridden with you, Naha'," Cloud Dancer said. "My medicine would have protected you. If not that, my bow arm. Rivers run, though, and my raiding days are gone."

"You're needed more here, as keeper of Mahuts," Iron Wolf said. "Boys can steal Kiowa horses. Few have the far-seeing eyes."

"Go, Naha'. Lead well. And remember what Mahuts counsels."

207

"I will," the young man promised.

The next day Iron Wolf made the promised prayers. Cloud Dancer provided medicine paint and charms for the young raiders. Then, following a feast offered by the Foxes, the young men departed.

Fifteen times Sun was born and died before the horse stealers returned. Many times Cloud Dancer felt his heart weaken with concern. Could he have misread the Arrows? Was there some magic he might have given his sons to shield them from the Kiowas?

"Believe in them, Husband," Raven's Wing scolded. "You taught them well. They're your sons. How can you doubt they will have success at a thing you yourself did so well?"

He knew, though, that she had troubled dreams. Only Raven Feather was unconcerned.

"They're my brothers," the boy boasted. "They'll bring many horses. Maybe next year I'll go with them."

That was an unsettling notion!

It was during this time of great anxiety that Touches the Sky first visited Cloud Dancer's dreams. The long-dead Arrow-keeper once again stood tall and proud. He sang a medicine chant and gazed deeply into the Dancer's eyes.

"Didn't I tell you this son would live long?" Touches the Sky asked. "His sons and their sons will remember this raid."

Indeed it seemed likely, for the riders drove a hundred ponies past the camp when they returned. Screaming and performing wild antics, the raiders drew every man, woman, and child to the river.

"Ne' hyo!" Iron Wolf shouted as he jumped from his

horse. "Your medicine paint confounded the Kiowas. Their fire sticks were useless. Look at our new wealth!"

"We must feast to celebrate this happy return," Cloud Dancer declared. "No one was harmed?"

"No one but a single Kiowa," Gray Wolf said. "He tried to grab my bow, and I struck him on his ear."

"We took nothing but horses," Iron Wolf added. "And they were too confused and surprised to follow."

Cloud Dancer smiled with relief, but he nevertheless argued the warrior societies should send scouts to watch the country north of Fat River. He himself was soon too busy to tend to such matters. Iron Wolf brought Yellow Robe's family three good horses, and Spotted Eagle, her father, agreed to the betrothal. Afterward Cloud Dancer honored his son with a great feast and giveaway.

"My hope is your road together may lead you to the happiness I've known with Raven's Wing," Cloud Dancer told the young people. "Walk the world in harmony, and all you seek will come to you."

The whole band joined in the dancing that followed. The singing and drumming lasted well into the night. Exhausted dancers lay in small groups, unable even to return to their lodges. Young Fox Warriors saw they were covered with blankets or conducted to their lodges. Meanwhile Raven's Wing offered her daughter-in-law such pots and hides as could be spared. Yellow Robe Woman, as she would now be known, had few female relatives to provide them. The camp women had crafted a fine lodge for the newly marrieds, though, and Cloud Dancer had painted one side with wolf figures.

"We'll be very happy here," Yellow Robe Woman told Raven's Wing. The words were meant for Cloud Dancer, too, but out of respect she would now avoid addressing her father-in-law directly.

"He's a good hunter and will provide for you well," Raven's Wing replied. "After a time, we'll visit. It's good to have a daughter at last."

Yellow Robe Woman smiled shyly, then entered the lodge. Iron Wolf followed. Once inside, he closed the flap, and the relatives exchanged grins as they went their separate ways.

That year the hard-face moons brought deep snows, and game became scarce. Even in their small bands, the People were hungry. Children grew thin, and some of the old ones took the long walk from camp into the snow drifts. There they would slowly grow numb and start the long sleep that led to Hanging Road. In this way they would ease the band's burdens.

"Ne' hyo, the little ones are starving," Iron Wolf declared when the sun brought a bright glimmer to the land after days of snow thick as geese feathers.

"It's a hard time," Cloud Dancer agreed. "Bull Buffalo is far down the valley, and Uncle Deer has left the thickets."

"There's little meat left. We must hunt, even if we have to ride to Fat River."

"First cut wood so there will be warm fires in our absence," the Dancer suggested. "See the children all have warm hides to keep off ice's touch. Then gather those men who aren't needed with their families. I'll seek a

210

dream. Man Above will send us animals to hunt."

"That would be a good thing, Ne' hyo," Iron Wolf agreed.

As the young man went to gather the Fox Warriors and enlist their help, Cloud Dancer told Raven Feather to build up the fire.

"Ne' hyo," the boy said solemnly, "you won't go to the hills?"

"It's too hard a journey," the Arrow-keeper answered. "Many times I've prayed to Man Above. He knows the Arrow Lodge. He'll find my dreams here if he wishes. I'll cut myself and take no food. Such sacrifices are always honored."

"Husband, you're already weak with hunger," Raven's Wing scolded. "It's good to be a man of the People and share food with the helpless ones. But you're an important man."

"No, not that," Cloud Dancer said, laughing. "Just old."

Raven Feather and his mother nevertheless tried to offer such food as remained, but the Dancer disdained it. He drank only melted snow as he chanted and danced. As the west swallowed Sun, he cut strips of flesh from his arms and let the blood run.

"Heammawihio, send me a dream," he pleaded. "Show me the way to ease my people's suffering."

He chanted and danced and sank, exhausted, onto buffalo hides spread out in a bed. Quickly Raven Feather covered his father.

"Nah' koa," the boy said, gazing anxiously at Raven's Wing. "We must make him eat. I'll go and bring White Horse. He can maybe force Ne' hyo to break his fast."

"Only Man Above can do that," she answered, stopping the boy as he crawled toward the door. "Naha', I've known this man a long time. I trust him to know these things. Man Above holds his spirit gently in the clouds even now. An Arrow-keeper's life is not easy, but it's rarely short. We've known worse days, and these are not the last hungry ones. But the People will endure. That's the one truth I know."

Cloud Dancer was less certain. Three days he fasted, chanted, and danced. But the spirits were elusive. The dream failed to come. He walked the camp in despair, gazing at the empty eyes of the boys, hearing the cries of the youngest ones, knowing he was unable to bring the suffering to an end.

"Heammawihio, hear us!" he pleaded again at sunset. "The People are dying. I've kept to the sacred path, and we have avoided the iron pots and fire sticks of the pale people. We grow weak, and our enemies become strong. Send me a dream! Let me lead the young men on a hunt. Don't make our task an easy one, Man Above. Bring us hard fights to make our hearts strong. But this hunger robs us of the children, of the future. Hold them close to your heart and bring me a dream."

Whether it was Cloud Dancer's words or his suffering that brought on the vision, he could never be sure. He didn't care. He thrashed wildly in his bed that night as ravens picked at his bones. He saw a forest of burial scaffolds. Many bundles were small, for they sheltered young boys and girls wrapped in deer hides.

Bull Buffalo appeared snow white on a cloud and bellowed out, "This will not be! Come, my brothers. Give yourselves to these children and make them strong."

Bull Buffalo then charged from the northern hills toward Fat River and fell into the camp of the People. The scaffolds melted into a mist, and the young ones returned to life.

When he awoke, Cloud Dancer found White Horse and his three sons sitting beside him.

"Eat, Ne' hyo," Iron Wolf urged. "You've grown weak."

"I will eat," Cloud Dancer agreed. "My suffering is finished."

"The dream came," Raven Feather explained. "Now we'll hunt."

"The men are ready," Iron Wolf explained. "The horses are gathered."

"They must be left behind," Cloud Dancer declared. "This time we'll hunt in the ancient way. We'll gather near the high bluff above Fat River. Soon Bull Buffalo will charge from the northern hills, and we'll drive him over the cliff."

"Ne' hyo, we've scouted that country," Gray Wolf complained. "We found no game."

"Bull Buffalo will come," the Dancer insisted. "I've prayed, and Man Above has asked Bull Buffalo to save the People. It will be as I say. Go and tell the others."

The young men left to spread the word. Many doubted its truth and went off to hunt on their own. One or two returned with some small animal dug out of its hole. But the children went on suffering.

Cloud Dancer, though, made medicine prayers. Then he called Iron Wolf to him. The Wolf appeared as instructed, carrying his Fox bow. The Dancer opened Mahuts's sacred skin and drew out the two buffalo Arrows. They had been used only rarely, and now as Cloud Dancer tied them to Iron Wolf's stringless bow, they were both struck by the moment.

"Guard them well, Naha'," Cloud Dancer warned. "Hold them high so Bull Buffalo can see. Hold them high, stand firm, and Bull Buffalo will give himself over to our need."

The sight of the buffalo Arrows silenced the hunters. They saw, too, that their Arrow-keeper's hair now showed streaks of white. The starving had aged Cloud Dancer, and even the unbelievers respected devotion to their welfare.

"Ayyyy!" they yelled. "Bull Buffalo will come!"

Cloud Dancer felt the power of their new confidence, but he also read the despair painted on the women's faces. Few of the little ones now left their lodges.

"Come, Brother," the Dancer said to White Horse. "Let's show these young ones how we hunted before Horse came to the People."

The men listened attentively. Then they split into smaller bands, each led by a warrior chief. The Elks and Crazy Dogs, Bow Strings, Red Shields, and Foxes — all were represented. Each group built a fire and waited for Bull Buffalo. Then, when the promised herd arrived amid a white cloud of pounded snow, the warriors circled in behind and drove the animals toward the bluff. It wasn't a huge herd. No, there were perhaps fifty buffalo altogether. That number of men, maybe a few less, chased them. It was a strange sight, eerie figures of man and beast, all near-shrouded by the snow clouds thrown up by the stampede. No one shot an arrow or hurled a lance. No, the bluff would do the

214

killing. Bull Buffalo was giving up his life. It wouldn't be taken by the People.

Among the Fox Warriors, Cloud Dancer stood behind Iron Wolf as the young man waved his bow. The sacred buffalo Arrows hurried the animals on toward Fat River where they plunged headlong over the bluff and fell to their deaths below, on the banks of the river.

Bull Buffalo had come upon them suddenly. Just as quickly, the herd was gone. Now started the hard work — skinning and butchering while the sun remained in the sky. Soon blood and flesh would freeze in a way no stone knife could cut. Great urgency attended the skinning. Women arrived shortly to carry the meat back to camp. Before long, hump roasts and ribs were sizzling over fires.

"Ne' hyo, you've brought life back to the People," Raven Feather said, resting an arm on his father's shoulder. "You've taught me much of the curing ways. Will you show me how to bring on the dreaming?"

"Soon," Cloud Dancer promised.

"When?" the boy implored. "Already I've plucked two hairs from my chin. I'll win my name when next we hunt Bull Buffalo. Already Gray Wolf speaks to me of raiding ponies. I'll set off on man's road before long."

"There's time yet," Cloud Dancer argued. But he read in his youngest son's eyes the terrible truth. Even as he himself once left old Gray Wolf's side, Raven Feather, too, would soon seek his own path.

"Husband, you should take some of this," Raven's Wing said later, when they sat beside the fire and stared past the amber flames to where meat bubbled over a bed of coals.

215

"Yes," he agreed, cutting a slice and setting it aside for the great mysteries. He accepted a second slice and chewed on the warming meat.

"It's a hard turn our road's taking," Raven's Wing observed. "Our sons are leaving one by one."

"We should have made others," Cloud Dancer grumbled. "A lodge is empty without children."

"Man Above decided otherwise. It's natural for them to go, and we'll have grandchildren."

"My hair's growing white," Cloud Dancer lamented. "I feel winter deep in my bones. Even the fire fails to warm me. Old age is a curse."

"No, life is never that," she argued. "My father mourned his passing, for he knew he would never see our children grown. We may perhaps see our grandchildren tall and strong, as our sons have become."

"Yes, that would be a good thing," Cloud Dancer agreed. But even that warming thought didn't chase the cold from his bones.

Chapter Eighteen

Those were the wandering years for the People.
They drifted across the plains between Fat River and
Holy Mountain, following Bull Buffalo. From the
tribes to the south and west they raided horses. These,
in turn, were traded to the neighboring Arapahoes
and the peoples who camped up north on Muddy
River.

In this way Cloud Dancer came to meet the Dakota
and Lakota bands. These new people had also inhabited the pipestone country of the east. They, too, re-
vered the holy places, and often small bands shared
the hunt. The People first introduced their new
friends to Horse, and much good trading followed. .
Young men of these different tribes often hunted and
raided together, and many took sisters or cousins of
their new allies as wives. In this way, a strong bond
was forged.

"It's good we make strong friends," Cloud Dancer
remarked to White Horse. "The road ahead is hard,
and we'll need help fighting the new enemies that are
coming."

"The pale people?" White Horse asked.

"Yes, Brother. The danger comes closer each dawn."

White Horse nodded gravely.

In truth, the threat was there already. The Hill People and the Suhtai were well acquainted with the pale traders who paddled canoes up Muddy River to swap beads and iron axes for beaver skins. Other bands had gone so far as to acquire fire sticks.

"We, too, need these weapons to battle our enemies," Winter Lance, an Elk Warrior chief, argued often. "The grandfathers accepted the bow when it was given to them."

"Man Above sent the bow," Cloud Dancer pointed out. "These pale people can't be trusted. Don't you know they have come like locusts to drive our relatives from the eastern country? They offer you fire sticks so you will let them stay. Soon another and another come. They won't give presents tomorrow. No, they will say this is their country, and we must go."

"Then, we'll fight them!" Winter Lance vowed.

"Ah, but will you win?" Cloud Dancer asked. "Have you forgotten the spotted sickness that killed the Mandans? Nothing good comes from trading with these pale people. I say touch nothing that is theirs and keep them out of our country."

But the young women, glancing at the shiny trinkets and fine beads brought by these traders, urged trade. Those who saw the power of the fire stick longed to own one.

"These old men see only the times before," Corn Planter, another Elk chief, grumbled. "They think that if we make the dawn prayers and dance in the New Life Lodge, good fortune will rain down on us.

We must win prosperity for ourselves. If we hunt and make war as we always have done, the Crows and others who own fire sticks will kill us!"

Those who felt strongest the pull of the new ways broke away and joined other bands. Others, though, feared leaving the protection of Mahuts. And even the most stubborn respected Cloud Dancer's visions.

As for the Dancer, he passed his fortieth winter in peace. Raven Feather, who at thirteen was eager to follow his brothers on man's road, remained to help his mother and father with the curing ceremonies. White Horse, Gray Wolf, and Hairy Mane stayed close when not hunting. Iron Wolf busied himself with the other young Foxes—and with Yellow Robe Woman, whose belly was swollen with the child she carried.

"It's sure to be a son," Raven's Wing announced. "Only a boy kicks so often. I know that well, for I brought three of them into the world myself!"

As the snows thawed that spring, Cloud Dancer was forced to cast from his mind the anticipated arrival of this first grandchild. A more important matter stole his attention. Gray Wolf and Hairy Mane, together with Painted Robe, had come upon a pale-skinned man while hunting deer.

"Ne' hyo, what should we do with him?" Gray Wolf asked after explaining the discovery.

"Where is he?" Cloud Dancer asked. "Is he alone?"

"Yes, and Painted Robe has taken his fire stick," Hairy Mane answered. "He speaks strange words and makes medicine motions with his hand. We haven't

219

harmed him."

"You've told White Horse?" the Dancer asked.

"He's away, as are the warrior chiefs," Gray Wolf added. "We thought perhaps you could ask Mahuts what we should do."

"I will," Cloud Dancer agreed. "Bring him to our camp. We'll make a smoke and consult the Arrows."

It was a sight long remembered, the entry of the pale-skinned man. Painted Robe had looped a rawhide rope around his neck. The Robe held the other end as he led the unfortunate captive along. Gray Wolf and Hairy Mane rode on either side. The pale man stumbled along, moaning and pleading in his foreign words.

Once at the camp, a crowd gathered to stare at this strange one. Painted Robe had taken his clothes, leaving him only a small shiny chain with a cross hanging around his neck.

"That's strong medicine," Painted Robe explained. "The Arapahoes say the man on the cross is a powerful spirit chief."

There was a murmur of amazement as the pale man followed their eyes to the charm. He touched it, made a motion across his chest, and dropped to his knees, sobbing miserably.

"Bring him," Cloud Dancer said, and the hunters escorted their prize to the Arrow Lodge. Once inside, the man collapsed at Cloud Dancer's feet and muttered a plea.

"Bring food," the Dancer told Raven's Wing.

Once the woman left, the pale man seemed to gain

some control.

"Give him a buffalo robe," Cloud Dancer suggested. "Let him cover himself."

Raven Feather handed the pale one a robe, and the stranger kissed the boy's hand and wrapped himself in the warm hide. Cloud Dancer stepped closer and examined the captive closely. At first he thought the light-colored skin some sort of trick, but when he rubbed the flesh, it merely reddened a bit. This wasn't paint.

The stranger's hair was yellow, like a cornstalk. His chin was smooth, but there were small hairs growing at the corners of his upper lip. Cloud Dancer stood the captive up. The buffalo robe fell away, betraying a thin frame scarcely covered by pinkish flesh.

"He's a boy," Cloud Dancer observed.

"Old enough to hunt alone," Painted Robe said, holding up the fire stick.

Cloud Dancer motioned for the boy to sit again, and he quickly wrapped himself in the buffalo robe and made the sign of the cross again.

"Vous ettes chien?" the young captive whispered. He made a dog sign. *"Sahiyela?"*

That was the Lakota word for the People. Cloud Dancer nodded.

"Ami," the boy added. *"Kola."*

Friend? When had the pale people ever been friends? They hunted with enemy bands and brought sickness to Muddy River.

"Ne' hyo, Night Hawk's wife, Gull Woman, is Lakota," Raven Feather said. "Maybe she can talk to this strange one."

"Bring her, Naha'," Cloud Dancer urged. "I would know why he comes into our country."

Raven Feather crawled around the rim of the lodge and made his departure. Later, after Raven's Wing had provided the young captive with dried buffalo meat and some fry bread, the Feather returned with Gull Woman.

Gull Woman first recognized the small cross. She had only recently come among the People, for Night Hawk, a Fox Warrior chief, had traded two good ponies to her Lakota father after the summer buffalo hunt concluded. She spoke her old tongue far better than that of her husband, and Cloud Dancer had difficulty making his own needs known.

She didn't have much luck with the pale-skin boy, either. But an Arapaho boy, who had come to share the winter lodge of his sister, Winter Lance's wife, arrived and took over the duties of translator. Soon strange talk filled the lodge, and the pale boy seemed to revive. He ate a little more, took some water to drink, and opened his heart to the young Arapaho, Beaver Tail.

"He came up Muddy River from a big village of the pale ones," Beaver Tail explained. "He paddled a big canoe with his father, one uncle, and one brother. They made a good summer camp, but they stayed too long on Muddy River. The snows came, and a storm sank their canoe. All but he drowned. Since that time he has wandered, shooting game and searching for help."

"He should have stayed on Muddy River," Painted Robe grumbled. "No pale skins come north of Fat River, into this holy country."

Beaver Tail turned and rebuked the captive, but the pale boy gripped his charm and barked an answer.

"His god sent him to us," Beaver Tail explained. "And you have saved him."

"No, we haven't," Cloud Dancer said, gripping the stranger's shoulders and making signs to show he was not welcome among the People.

"I can take him to my father," Beaver Tail offered. "These pale people sometimes buy captives. He says he has a grandfather in this big village who owns many fine things. This grandfather will pay much."

"These ways are strange to me," Cloud Dancer grumbled. "I'll ask Mahuts what should be done with him. We'll make a council, smoke on it, and make a decision."

"This will take time, Ne' hyo," Gray Wolf pointed out. "What do we do with him?"

"Find him some clothes," Cloud Dancer replied. "Tell him he's now under my protection. He won't be harmed. We'll make a bed here. Raven Feather can look after him."

"I'll bring his clothes," Painted Robe said, preparing to rise.

"No, find him something of the People," Cloud Dancer instructed. "Take his other things away. Nothing of the pale people must pollute our camp."

Painted Robe stared at the fire stick and frowned. He voiced no objection, though. White Horse had taught his brother-in-law to respect Cloud Dancer's advice.

Cloud Dancer entrusted the pale boy to Raven Feather and set about performing the Arrow rituals. This was a matter for Mahuts to consider. Even as he smoked and prayed, though, Cloud Dancer felt a disturbing presence in the camp. He had long dreaded this intrusion. Now that it was here, he feared the aftermath.

The Arrows predicted no bloody outcome. The points remained untainted. Nevertheless, they seemed unsettled.

Cloud Dancer sought an answer in his dreams, but none came. And now that the stranger was dressed in hides, he appeared less alien. He learned quickly, too, and soon he demonstrated respect toward Cloud Dancer and even spoke some of the People's words.

"I'm thankful," he managed. "For food. Protection."

These things Cloud Dancer accepted with a nod. He watched the amusing way that Raven Feather adopted the pale newcomer. It was the way a small boy took in a stray dog, seeing to its comforts and sharing his food.

"It's good he's here, Ne' hyo," Raven Feather declared. "We can learn about his people."

"No, we must avoid that," Cloud Dancer objected. "They are strangers to the sacred way. They kill without making the medicine prayers, and they bring sickness and death wherever they walk."

"Not Philippe," Raven Feather argued.

"Not yet," his father grumbled. "He's been here only

a short time."

But clearly long enough to endear himself to some. Raven Feather called him Brother, and Raven's Wing stuffed him with food.

"He was starving when he came to us," she said, frowning. "He has fifteen summers, but he's no bigger than Raven Feather. Beaver Tail says the pale people are mostly large, too. Man Above did well, leading him to our camp."

Cloud Dancer wondered. And when at last all the chiefs had returned, and a council was held, he spoke his own grave concerns.

"I've said it often," Cloud Dancer said, gazing past the roaring fire into the faces of his companions. "The People won't long survive contact with these strange ones. Sweet Medicine warned us of their coming. We should turn away from their odd medicine, avoid them, burn their possessions, and chase them from our country."

"Kill them even?" Winter Lance, the leader of the Elk Warriors, asked.

"Even that if they don't go," Cloud Dancer agreed.

"Shall we kill this small white face you've taken into your lodge?" Dancing Bear, a young Fox chief, asked.

"He's under my protection," Cloud Dancer said, shaking his head. "We must bring him no harm. That would be the same as slaying one of the People."

"You'll keep him, then; adopt him as a son?" White Horse cried in disbelief.

"No, he can go to the Arapahoes with Beaver Tail. The Arapahoes can return him to his family," the

Dancer explained. "He's brought us no harm, and we've been taught to help those who need aid. But to keep him would be to taint all we are. No, he must go."

"If you've decided, why summon a council?" Dancing Bear asked. "Are we to have a voice in these decisions?"

"We're chiefs," Night Hawk insisted. "My wife, Gull Woman, says this boy is valuable. His grandfather is a wealthy trader. He may pay us many good iron pots, ten fire sticks —"

"Yes, fire sticks!" Winter Lance exclaimed.

"Will you all ignore my warnings?" Cloud Dancer cried. "We must turn away from these foreign things. They will bring us misfortune."

"Yes, they will," Winter Lance agreed. "In the hands of our enemies. We must have them to defend ourselves. A man who holds a bow may kill a deer, but he has little chance of killing a Crow armed with a fire stick. Long before the strongest bow arm may loose an arrow, the fire stick strikes him down! We must make use of these weapons ourselves or else die as a people!"

"To adopt these new ways is to begin the long walk up Hanging Road," Cloud Dancer argued. "To die a slow death."

"Ne' hyo," Iron Wolf said, rising from his place among the Fox Warriors, "others among the People already take up the fire stick. We alone keep the old ways. Our numbers are few. Soon many of my brother Foxes may leave to join other bands. Will you not see we must accept these new tools and use them?"

"I see only death," Cloud Dancer explained. "Naha', I've read terrible things before. I sat beside my uncle, Touches the Sky, when he warned of the Chippewa attack. Many of us were killed because the chiefs had no ears for his words. I spoke to the Suhtai of danger on Muddy River, and we moved our camp. The Mandans, who took up our village, died. Soon I'll be old. I've hunted Bull Buffalo, known a good woman, raised my sons. If I close my eyes this night and never again open them, it won't matter. But hear me, you young men. You've tasted little of life. Will you hurry your death?"

"Nothing lives long," Winter Lance said, reciting the old warrior song. "Only the earth and the mountains. I'm a warrior and accept my death. I only ask my enemies to stand against me, and I will kill them. But fighting these fire-stick carriers is hopeless. They strike at us like lightning. There's no defense."

"Mahuts will blind them," Cloud Dancer vowed.

"The Arrows don't always lead us into battle, Ne' hyo," Iron Wolf said solemnly. "Seek a way for us to take these new weapons. There are many of us who would hang in the New Life Lodge and suffer to bring favor to our people. Can not this suffering allow us to adopt the fire stick?"

"It can," Cloud Dancer replied. "Perhaps nothing can keep fire stick from us. I only remember Sweet Medicine's warning, and I see the warriors dying in my dreams. Many men. Women and children, too.

The heart of the People stolen from us."

"Mahuts?" men murmured.

"These things lie ahead if you take the forbidden path," Cloud Dancer warned. "I'm only one voice. I can't stop you."

"No iron pot or fire stick will ever enter Arrow Lodge," Winter Lodge promised. "But this pale one will bring us fire sticks. We, Elk Warriors, and others besides, will use these new weapons to guard the helpless ones. To fill the children's bellies in winter with good meat."

"Ayyyy!" the Elks howled.

"We'll still make the medicine prayers, Ne' hyo," Iron Wolf pledged. "And we'll dance in New Life Lodge. It will be enough."

"Will it?" Cloud Dancer asked. "I pray so."

Beaver Tail led Corn Hair, as the People had come to call Philippe Freneau, to the Arapaho camp once the snows melted. It was later, while in the midst of the first buffalo hunt, that the pale boy returned, accompanied by an older brother and several hairy-faced giants.

"My grandfather is very grateful for your kindness, Ne' hyo," the young man told Cloud Dancer.

The Dancer nodded, though the thought of himself as father of one of these strange ones tore at him like an eagle's claw.

The pale people then made a great giveaway, offering many fire sticks, which they called muskets, and spreading great mountains of beads, iron kettles, and other treasures out before them. The trading was brisk, and the pale people departed with many good horses laden with fine buffalo robes and all manner of pelts.

"This musket is for my brother," Corn Hair said as he made his farewells. He set the weapon at Raven Feather's feet, then turned with a second musket toward Cloud Dancer.

"No!" Raven Feather said, blocking the young visitor's path. "He must not touch anything made by pale people."

"Why?" Corn Hair asked, confused.

"His dreams warn him," Raven Feather explained. "Terrible disaster will follow."

"If he touches a musket?" Corn Hair asked.

"If you come," Raven Feather answered sadly. "He fears even now this trading brings peril."

"This is so?" the pale boy asked, turning to Cloud Dancer. The Arrow-keeper nodded, and the yellow-haired young man frowned gravely. "I was happy here before," he said. "I thought perhaps to stay next summer. But I'm not welcome."

"It's not your doing," Raven Feather said. "Ne' hyo isn't angry with you."

"I've lived in your lodge. I know of his fears. He prays as I have prayed, but not for himself. He worries for you, my brother, and for the other people. We don't make the same prayers, but we feel the same faith. If I'd known, I wouldn't have come back."

"If you hadn't come, someone else would have," Raven Feather argued. "Ne' hyo knows it, too. Sweet Medicine spoke of it long ago. We know change is

229

coming. And death."

"Yes, I've heard of the sickness on the Missouri — Muddy River, you call it."

"I'll take this . . . musket . . . and remember my brother when I fire it," Raven Feather promised. "Later, after I walk man's road. Now I will give it over to Gray Wolf to keep. I'm my father's son."

"I won't come again," Corn Hair said sadly.

"Find happiness, Brother," Raven Feather said, stepping over and gripping the young pale skin's arms.

"Find happiness," Philippe Freneau whispered. "Walk man's road in safety."

"Only Man Above can know what will be," Raven Feather answered. "I won't forget your time here with us. Maybe a better day will come when we can share a camp on Muddy River and hunt Bull Buffalo."

"Your father would see it if it was to come, Raven Feather. And your eyes would believe in it."

"Then, we must wait a little longer," Raven Feather said, nodding gravely. "All men climb Hanging Road. I'll see you again on the other side, Philippe."

"In time, Brother. No need to hurry it."

Chapter Nineteen

While most noted that summer as the time Corn Hair came to trade, Cloud Dancer counted it as the season Yellow Robe Woman brought his first grandchild into the world. As Raven's Wing had predicted, it was a boy. Cloud Dancer, as he had when Raven's Wing took to woman's lodge, sought a dream. He envisioned many things for the child, and more for the man he would grow to be.

Here was the boy Touches the Sky had said would come. Here was the one to take up his grandfather's burden.

But when Cloud Dancer first looked upon the little one, he found it hard to believe in such promise. He was little more than a brown bundle with a fine splash of black hair on top.

"I'll call him Wolf Boy," Iron Wolf said. "My first son."

"It's a good name," Cloud Dancer observed. "Wolf still brings strong medicine to my son."

"It's a good day to be alive, Ne' hyo."

"They are all good days when a man has sons to share his lodge," the Dancer noted. "And grandsons to sit beside the fire and hear the old tales."

From his first days, Wolf Boy was seen frequently in the Arrow Lodge. Iron Wolf had become a respected warrior, and he often led the Foxes on horse raids against the neighboring Crows. Later, as the two tribes skirmished more and more, Iron Wolf was given one of the painted lances to carry into battle.

"Ne' hyo, I may not live long," Iron Wolf told Cloud Dancer. "I know you and my brothers will see Wolf Boy started up man's road if I am gone."

"Yes," the Dancer pledged. "But don't rush toward early death, Naha'. The People have need of strong fighters."

Wolf Boy and the younger brother, Two Feathers, who arrived two summers hence, were welcomed by their grandfather. Raven Feather had now joined the young men, taking man's road as Little Sky. The winter air rang hollow without the sound of running feet and childish laughter. As for the young brothers, they shared a spiritual bond from Two Feather's first moments.

"They put me in mind of other boys," White Horse often remarked. The Horse, too, had slowed with age. Hairy Mane had taken an Oglala Lakota woman for his wife, and the young man was missed. Red Deer Woman kept her father's lodge now, for her mother had climbed Hanging Road. Two younger sons rode with Winter Lance and the Elk Warriors, and their father rarely saw either.

"The winters grow colder, old friend," Cloud Dancer observed. "And the days are shorter."

Still there was much to do. In addition to following Bull Buffalo's restless wanderings, the People had become great traders with the peaceful bands that camped along Muddy River. These tribes—especially the Rees, Hidatsa, and what remained of the Mandans—hungered for horses. They had always eagerly traded corn, beans, melons, and tobacco to the People. Now they swapped iron tools, powder, and muskets, too.

The bands that visited Muddy River often found pale-skin trappers there, too. Some of these strangers took wives and lived among the Rees and Dakotas. Sometimes a Windpipe girl would wed one, too.

Even men like Winter Lance, who welcomed the pale-skin traders for the muskets and powder they provided, spoke loudly against such matches.

"These men are strangers," Winter Lance complained. "They will bring into the world children who aren't welcome among any people. The pale skins will shun them, and they won't belong to the People, either. As outcasts they can know only misfortune and unhappiness."

Matters weren't made better by stories that these pale people often abandoned their new wives and returned down Muddy River to winter in the big villages the pale people built in the south.

"If you see this trader called Broken Foot, send word to the Oglalas," Hairy Mane said as he led a band of Lakotas in search of the man. "He has dishonored my wife's family and stolen horses from the

Rees. When we find him, we will whip him badly!"

The Rees, who weren't related to the trader, found him instead. The horse thief was later discovered cut into pieces and pierced by Ree arrows.

"Even the wolves won't touch him," Winter Lance said scornfully.

When Cloud Dancer learned of it, he frowned.

"What other misfortunes will these pale people bring to us?" he asked. "And to themselves."

Wolf Boy's third summer, and his grandfather's forty-fourth, brought other worries. Many of the People went westward from Holy Mountain to hunt Bull Buffalo with their Oglala allies. Large bands of Dakotas and Lakotas were forcing the People to seek new camps in that rich country, and Cloud Dancer encouraged the migration. Pale traders casually crossed the lands to the east, but they were rarely spotted farther west. Still the Arrow-keeper sought to remove his family from the fate promised by Sweet Medicine.

Now the People found their path never far from the sight of Crow scouts, and the fighting grew fierce. Finally one of the Crow chiefs brought a pipe and made signs for a parlay.

"This is our country!" the Crow chief demanded. "We'll fight to hold it."

"Man Above has given it over to us," Winter Lance answered. "If you stay, we'll kill you. Already we take your horses and your women. Fight us? You're no more trouble than a sleeping snake. We

234

step past you or crush you, whatever is easiest."

The Crows, angered, rode away vowing to make war. Every party of hunters to leave camp kept watch for them, for the Crows were great tricksters. Coyote must have taught them the art of war, for nothing was ever as it seemed. A small party might suddenly become a hundred armed men! Once the Elks were badly mauled in a skirmish, and the Oglalas lost three young men in a hard fight late that same summer.

"You should bring Mahuts to help us," Winter Lance told Cloud Dancer. "We should use the blinding magic to ride down all the Crows. We should kill the men and take the women and little ones into our lodges to take the place of the many dead. Come, help us."

But Cloud Dancer's dreams warned of failure, and Mahuts remained in the Arrow Lodge.

That summer Iron Wolf counted his third coup on the enemy. As a lance carrier, he was much admired by the young men, and their brave words stirred him to charge the enemy. Sometimes the young men would follow. Other times they would wait and watch. Twice Iron Wolf was wounded by lead balls — once in the foot and once in the hip. Neither injury was serious, but Cloud Dancer thought them a warning.

"Crows are cowards," Iron Wolf muttered. "They fire their muskets and run away. The grandfathers tell of brave hearts who would stand and fight a man. Where are the brave-heart Crows?"

He soon discovered one. A party of Crows prowled the holy country near the high, flat-topped mountain the Lakotas called Bear Lodge. Mostly these Crows were young, but their leader was a scarred fighter known as Snake-eater for his fierce look.

Iron Wolf rode out with six young Fox Warriors to hunt Bull Buffalo, and he found the larger Crow party in his path.

"Chiens, come fight us!" Snake-eater taunted, using the Lakota language many of the People now understood. The Crow chief's mother was Oglala, a stolen woman it was said. Snake-eater rode out ahead of the others and dismounted. Once on the ground, he turned and bared himself at the enemy, shouting insults all the while.

"I'll fight you!" Iron Wolf shouted. He rode to within a short distance of the Crow chief, then climbed down from his pony. The two enemies now faced each other with lances, and the fight began.

Snake-eater was older and heavier, and his blows held more force. Iron Wolf was quick afoot, though, and he skillfully avoided the Crow lance. Then, as Snake-eater tired, the Wolf made his own move. He ducked his head under a blow, then knocked the Crow chief's lance from his hand. Snake-eater froze, and Iron Wolf butted the Crow to earth and dropped both knees on his chest.

"Ayyyy!" Iron Wolf shouted. "I'm first," he added,

touching the point of the lance to the Crow chief's shoulder.

Snake-eater stared hatefully at his attacker, but there was nothing to be done. Iron Wolf had won.

Slowly the Wolf retired, taking time to collect the Crow chief's lance and horse.

"Ayyyy!" the other Foxes yelled. "This is a good day for the People."

"Yes," Iron Wolf agreed.

When the Fox Warriors returned, bringing with them much meat and the tale of the Crow battle, a feast was held, and much dancing celebrated the coup.

"Now I wear three feathers," Iron Wolf told his young sons.

"I'm proud of these remembered deeds, Naha'," Cloud Dancer said, drawing his son close. "But this won't be the end of this Crow."

"No," Iron Wolf agreed. "We'll fight again."

The second green-grass moon hadn't gone when the Crows raided the Poor People's camp. Winter Lance and the Elk Warriors were watching, but Coyote was again with the Crows. They avoided the guards and fell upon the village unseen. The raiders were young, and they screamed when they charged. Otherwise the sleeping camp might have been at their mercy.

It was White Horse who organized the Foxes and drove back the Crows. The old man, a grandfather now, struck down two of the raiders himself and crippled a third with a well-aimed arrow.

Cloud Dancer hung back at first, looking after the helpless ones. But once others arrived, and the women and children gathered their wits, the Arrow-keeper, too, joined the fight. He hadn't carried a lance against an enemy in many summers, but his blood was hot with anger. He read the fear in his grandsons' eyes, and he was determined to punish those who put it there.

A Crow chief saw the old man leave the Arrow Lodge and guessed he might be a man of importance. Quickly he aimed a musket, but Cloud Dancer turned the ball aside with the magic of his medicine. He then charged, slapped the musket from the Crow's hands, and killed him with a single lance thrust.

Even as the Crow chief died, a vengeful Winter Lance and the Elks fell upon the Crows' flanks. Nearly surrounded, the raiders scattered. Those who could escaped. Others stood and died. No mercy was extended the raiders, for they had cut down women and children at the far edge of the camp. Among these were Winter Lance's wife, young sister, and three children.

Not since the Chippewas had fallen on the People in Cloud Dancer's youth had an enemy struck down the helpless. Some had been captured, but never was there anything to match the butchery of Winter Lance's family. The youngest boy was brutally cut open, and the oldest boy's hands were gone.

"My heart is heavy with mourning," Winter Lance said. "I must tend the bodies and make prayers. Will some man pledge to punish these Crows?"

Corn Planter, another Elk chief, vowed to pursue the raiders, and many of the Foxes joined in the hunt. Women searched the prairie once daylight arrived, and they restored the bodies as best they could. Others dragged the slain Crows from the camp and mutilated them in retaliation.

What murder was done in the Crow camp, Cloud Dancer never learned. Corn Planter and Night Hawk, who had led the revenge raid, brought with them fifty ponies, great stores of meat and hides, ten muskets, and much powder. The smoke of a burning village marked the western horizon. They also brought along fifteen young boys and three girls whose solemn, empty gazes testified to the brutal death of their people.

"I bring you a gift, Winter Lance," Corn Planter said as he handed a deerskin bag to the grieving Fox chief. "Snake-eater's heart. We cut it from his body. Take three of these Crow boys to fill your empty lodge. They now will be your sons."

"No," Winter Lance objected. "My heart is empty. Nothing can ever fill it again."

"These will help," Corn Planter argued.

Others who had suffered loss also took in captive children. The four oldest boys remained, though, and angry women suggested cutting them as the Lance's boys had been treated.

239

"No," Cloud Dancer barked. "They've been taken into our camp. Now they are of the People."

But men had also been killed, and there were too many little ones already given over to grandfathers and uncles.

"We go to trade horses to our brothers, the Rees," Iron Wolf pointed out. "We can tend to these four until then. The Rees and the Mandans have lost many children to the spotted sickness. They'll gladly accept these Crows."

"Yes," Corn Planter agreed. "They'll bring a good price."

So it was decided to take the boys north.

Cloud Dancer frowned at this notion. His band had never traded children, captives or not. But among the Muddy River tribes, it was a common practice. Pale traders offered high prices for women and boys old enough to work. These four were aged ten summers perhaps. No one could be certain, for they didn't speak.

"Their dreams are troubled, Ne' hyo," Iron Wolf observed. "They saw too much. I'm sick of fighting myself, and those slain were not my family."

On the northward journey to the Rees' Fat River village, Cloud Dancer smoked and prayed for the welfare of the captives. Gradually their minds returned, and they joined the other camp boys, especially the adopted Crows, in swims at the river and such games as were permitted.

For a brief time the four knew some rest. That

ended when the band arrived at the Ree camp. The People wasted no time taking them around the village, boasting of the Crow fight, and seeking a good price.

"We could keep them, Husband," Raven's Wing argued. "You've seen how they look to you. They'd make good sons."

"Once I would have welcomed them," he confessed. "Soon we'll have grandsons to raise, though. Let them fill the sorrowful hearts of these Rees."

"What have you dreamed?" she cried. "Our son? What will happen?"

Cloud Dancer gripped her hands tightly, but he wouldn't explain. Nor in spite of her pleas would he warn Iron Wolf.

The People were not the only visitors in the Ree camp that summer. Nearby a large party of pale skins camped. Some wore blue soldier cloth, and they spoke a new tongue known to very few of the Rees.

"These new people call themselves Americans, Ne' hyo," Iron Wolf told his father. "They want to speak to us and give us presents."

"I fear them," Cloud Dancer said.

"They have good guns," Iron Wolf said, nodding in agreement.

"That's not what I fear," the old man said, gazing at the hairy-faced men by the river and their smooth-cheeked chief. "It's that box!"

Now Iron Wolf turned his attention to a pair of

241

slender men. They sat beside a large chest, touching sticks to yellow-white skins. Pictures appeared, as did little scratches.

"They've taken Eagle's spirit," Iron Wolf gasped as he looked at one drawing. Worse, they were capturing the faces and the dress of the Rees.

"No!" Iron Wolf cried when one of them started to sketch him. "I won't have you hold my shade!"

The Rees rushed to intervene, and the pale skin stopped his work.

"Don't fear," a young Ree told Iron Wolf. "My father tells them Chiens won't allow it."

The two pale-skin chiefs now spoke greetings, which the Rees translated. These Americans were on a journey of discovery, and they wished to know what the western country was like. Many moons they had floated up Muddy River. They had walked across the Shining Mountains and seen the great lake where Sun dies at dusk. Now they wished to bring word to their white father of all his peoples.

One of the pale-skin chiefs took a shiny disk from a small sack and held it in the air.

"He offers it to your chief," the Ree youth explained. "As a present, pledging peace."

The pale-skin chief started to hand it to Cloud Dancer, but the Arrow-keeper stepped away, allowing the object to fall to the earth.

"Look, it's like Corn Hair's cross," Iron Wolf observed. "There's a shade upon it. It's powerful medicine, Ne' hyo."

"It will steal our hearts," Cloud Dancer warned.

"Tell them he's old, and he keeps the traditions of our fathers," Iron Wolf told the Rees. "His medicine is strong, and he has the far sight. He is forbidden to touch anything the pale people have made, though."

"Perhaps some other might take it, to insure peace with the white soldiers."

"White?" Iron Wolf asked, staring at the blue shirts.

"Pale people," the young Ree explained. "They think themselves white, and call us red. They are strange, but they bring good things to trade."

"We'll trade," Iron Wolf agreed. "But my father will avoid these whites. He's seen things."

"We've heard. He foretold the spotted sickness which took my mother and two brothers."

"Yes? And still you let them in your camp?"

"We're weak," the young Ree confessed. "We need the guns they bring to fight our enemies."

Iron Wolf nodded his understanding, and the People began making bargains with the Rees, and with the white soldiers, too. When the whites began visiting Cloud Dancer's camp, though, he insisted it was time to leave.

"There's great danger in those people," Cloud Dancer said again and again. "We've completed our trading with the Rees."

"But there's to be dancing," some of the young men argued. "I thought to trade for a wife."

243

"We must leave!" Cloud Dancer insisted.

The fire in the old man's eyes quieted the most reluctant member of the band, and the People packed up camp and headed south. Once again they wandered the plain toward Holy Mountain. Once again they had avoided the accursed pale skins.

But for how long? Cloud Dancer asked himself.

Chapter Twenty

Life on the plains was changing. Even the smaller rivers now witnessed canoe-paddling white men. Some of the old traders continued to approach the tribes with gifts and swap for hides. More and more the hairy faces hunted and trapped on their own, ignoring the objections of the tribes and using new long rifles to silence complaints.

Two summers after the pale-skin soldiers had encountered the People at the Ree village, big flat-roofed canoes journeyed up Muddy River. White men had come upon the plains to stay.

"Ne' hyo, we cannot keep to the old ways," Iron Wolf declared. "We must acquire these new weapons. Rifles, the Oglalas call them. They kill from far, and the Crows use them against us."

"And where will you get them?" Cloud Dancer asked.

"From the Muddy River people," Iron Wolf explained.

The Wolf gathered a great herd of ponies, and together with Fox Warriors from his own and the other bands took them north. He returned without the horses, for the Hidatsa people had traded two hundred rifles for the animals.

"Now our enemies will shrink before us!" Winter Lance boasted. "We'll kill many Crows."

"Ayyyy!" the other young men cried.

Their elders shared no such confidence. They knew the war path was littered with dead men of both sides.

"Once counting coup on the enemy was enough," Cloud Dancer lamented. "I hear warriors boasting of the way they will mutilate the Crows. Can hearts be so cruel and retain respect for Mother Earth and Father Sky?"

The war against the Crows continued, but gradually the two peoples moved their winter camps farther apart.

"We cannot expose the helpless ones to the enemy," Iron Wolf said.

Surely the Crows, too, feared for their families. Raiding horses continued to occupy the young men during the green-grass moons, but war parties rarely found each other.

Cloud Dancer celebrated his fiftieth summer by sponsoring the New Life Lodge. As the many bands gathered to renew the earth, Cloud Dancer visited Gray Wolf, who led the young Foxes in the Windpipe camp. Gray Wolf's three small daughters welcomed their grandfather, and Raven's Wing delighted in showering the girls with gifts.

"A woman with only sons longs to show a grandchild woman's road," she explained.

When the Oglalas joined the People to hunt Bull Buffalo, Little Sky and his Oglala wife, Snow

Woman, introduced their firstborn, Sky Dreamer. The infant was reluctant to leave his mother's arms, but Raven's Wing coaxed him onto her lap with a bit of polished black flint.

"There are many rifles now among the People," Little Sky observed. "Ne' hyo, do you still fear these new things?"

"Now more than ever," Cloud Dancer answered. "My dreams fill with the cries of Bull Buffalo and Beaver. The white men promise great wealth for their hides, and the People kill what they don't need to keep hunger away. Already there are rivers where Beaver swims no longer. Can you forget what Sweet Medicine foretold? Once the pale people come, Bull Buffalo will not live long."

"Bull Buffalo blackens the prairie," Little Sky argued. "There are places a man can walk on the backs of them three days and never fall earthward."

"It won't last," Cloud Dancer warned again. But no one had ears to hear such words. And in truth, with so much family gathered around, Cloud Dancer devoted himself to sharing the remembered tales of old Gray Wolf and Touches the Sky and set aside thoughts of tomorrow.

By late summer, the bands had dispersed to hunt, and Cloud Dancer found himself alternately making the buffalo prayers and performing healing cures for those young men thrown from horses or otherwise injured. Sometimes he gazed off at the hunters and remembered the day he set off southward after Horse.

Memories. That was all that was left to a man grown old. Young men rode after buffalo or raided horses.

"I envy them," White Horse confessed. "And you. To help with the prayers and cures gives a man purpose. My sons have grown tall. I think I've lived too long."

Cloud Dancer nodded. He often thought that himself. But when Wolf Boy and little Two Feathers rested beside him near the fire, listening to the old stories, a glow spread within the old man.

"Nam shim', tell us again of Sweet Medicine's journey to Noahvose," Wolf Boy would plead.

"Yes, Grandfather," Two Feathers would echo. "Or tell us of catching Horse."

The admiring eyes of the boys melted Cloud Dancer's weariness and brought him new vitality.

Autumn brought new trouble from the Crows. A young chief had raised a war party and led them eastward to raid horses. This man, who carried a lance decorated with the hair of his enemies, was called Many Scalps. He rode a large brown horse with a white crown on its head, and he was utterly fearless.

"I've seen him, Ne' hyo," Iron Wolf told Cloud Dancer upon the return of the buffalo hunters. "He's not like other men. He hurries into the fight, singing and urging his enemies to strike. Our rifle balls can't find him. He turns them with his scalp lance."

"Is such a thing possible, Nam shim'?" Wolf Boy asked, leaning against his grandfather's side and staring up with probing eyes.

"Mahuts is not the only medicine power," Cloud Dancer answered. "But perhaps it's uncertainty in the hearts of our warriors that makes them miss."

"We'll soon know," Iron Wolf said. "Painted Robe and the Bowstrings are following him. They hope to attack the Crow camp."

"Did they make the proper prayers?" Cloud Dancer asked. "I saw no pipe carried. They should have consulted Mahuts."

Iron Wolf nodded soberly.

"No one questioned Painted Robe," Iron Wolf explained. "He's led many successful raids."

"Find White Horse," Cloud Dancer advised. "The Robe is his brother-in-law. Maybe he knows what we don't."

"I'll do it, Ne' hyo."

Iron Wolf gave Wolf Boy a reassuring nod before leaving. But neither the boy nor his grandfather was fooled by the gesture. Concern spread through the camp like prairie fire, and men readied their weapons. Women began making food bundles, and boys set out to collect horses.

This whirlwind of activity had scarcely begun when Iron Wolf and White Horse approached the Arrow Lodge. The Horse motioned Cloud Dancer aside, and the two of them walked off together.

"I know your heart is troubled, Brother," White Horse said, "but Painted Robe is a skilled raider. He always undertakes the proper preparations. I would consult Mahuts, but he has his own power, learned in the Suhtai camp long ago."

"But you'll ride to his aid anyway," Cloud Dancer said, gazing about him at the excited camp.

"He'll need help with the Crow ponies," White Horse said, laughing. "I'll bring you a good one."

"We've known each other too many summers to hide much. You worry."

"He's the brother of my dead wife," White Horse pointed out. "He was just a boy when he first visited my lodge. My own brothers died long ago, when we were boys."

"We should smoke and make prayers."

"We will when I return," White Horse promised.

"A man shouldn't ride to battle alone," Cloud Dancer objected. "We two have often fought side by side."

"This I'll do alone," White Horse said, sadly gripping his brother's wrists. "You should smoke and seek a dream, though. The People will want your vision."

"You should wait."

"Ah, I'm old, Brother. There's no time left to me."

Cloud Dancer nodded gravely as his brother, the companion of his youthful adventures, left the camp.

"Ne' hyo, should I follow?" Iron Wolf asked.

"The others will bring him back," Cloud Dancer explained. "Better we make prayers. Mahuts will tell us what to do."

"Yes, Ne' hyo," Iron Wolf said, obediently falling in behind his father.

250

* * *

Even without consulting the Arrows, Cloud Dancer knew White Horse wouldn't return. Death was written in the Horse's eyes, and once there it never left. Dancing Bear, the Fox chief, had witnessed both fights. He told of it in the council.

"Brothers, the Crows have a demon for a war chief," the Bear explained. "This lance-carrier led ten young men against Painted Robe's twenty. Yet there was no fear in the eyes of the Crows. They withstood the Bowstring charge and fought back. Our rifles were useless. Many Scalps himself drove back our men. Then he turned on Painted Robe.

"The large horse with the white head may also be a demon, for it runs on the clouds. Many Scalps blocked Painted Robe's retreat, then knocked the Robe from his horse. I could see little after that, but the Crow lifted Painted Robe's hair and held it to the sky."

"And White Horse?" Cloud Dancer asked, steadying himself.

"White Horse appeared later. He had come upon the frightened Bowstrings and learned of the failed raid. He rode on alone to recover the Robe's body. Many Scalps stood waiting, and White Horse was knocked down by the Crow's first shot. He, too, was scalped. This is a sad day for the People," Dancing Bear said, moaning as he sat beside the fire. "Two famous fighters and three young men are dead. Who will lead us against this Crow chief now?"

251

"I will," Iron Wolf insisted. "But this time we will make preparations. The Arrows will be consulted, and we will paint ourselves. My uncle's body should be returned to the People. And the Crows must be punished."

"Ayyyy!" the other men cried.

"I will carry a pipe to Mahuts," Iron Wolf added. "And then I will send one among the fighters. Prepare yourselves, brothers. We have a hard fight ahead."

Cloud Dancer drank in these words, and his heart ached from their news. His brother was dead. Painted Robe, too. Now Iron Wolf had vowed to lead the young men against this powerful Crow.

Wolf Boy and Two Feathers learned of their father's decision, and the small ones waited anxiously beside the Arrow Lodge. Cloud Dancer sent them to their mother.

"Grandfather, we can help make the medicine prayers," Wolf Boy pleaded.

"It's better you help Yellow Robe Woman ready food," Cloud Dancer answered. "Your father and I will need solitude."

Indeed, the Dancer even sent Raven's Wing off for a time. Father and son then sat alone in the Arrow Lodge, watching the flames eat willow logs. Cloud Dancer finally lit the pipe, and they smoked. When the Dancer asked Mahuts to offer counsel, the Arrows seemed to turn solemn as they twisted on their string.

"Is it a bad sign?" Iron Wolf asked.

"I must seek the answer in a dream," Cloud Dancer replied. "You'll wait until it comes."

"The Crows may escape, Ne' hyo."

"You'll wait," Cloud Dancer insisted. "My dreams will answer your questions."

Two days and two nights Cloud Dancer fasted and bled himself, hurrying a vision. It came slowly, then engulfed him in its clarity.

There were two scenes. In one Iron Wolf was a white-haired old man who walked slowly a ridge, surrounded by many sons. In the second, he was no older than now. Painted brightly and carrying an ancient bow, he fired a stone-tipped arrow into the heart of the Crow lance-carrier. Then he waited while the other Crows swarmed over him and brought his death.

"Nothing lives long," Iron Wolf's death chant sang out.

When Cloud Dancer awoke, feverish and cold at the same time, Raven's Wing brought him food and drink. She wrapped a heavy elk robe around his trembling shoulders and searched with questioning eyes for an answer to an unspoken question.

"It's not decided," he whispered. "Bring him to me."

Iron Wolf arrived a few moments later, and after adding a few logs to the fire, Raven's Wing left. She knew instinctively here was a moment for solemn words, words best reserved for men.

"You may live a long and honorable life," Cloud Dancer began. "Many sons may call you Ne' hyo, and you may teach them the ways of our people. This will not happen if you lead the young men against Many Scalps."

"No?" Iron Wolf asked.

"I saw two things, Naha'," Cloud Dancer spoke. The words chilled him, and he fought off a shiver. "The second vision showed you striking down this Crow with a stone-point arrow, as we used in the time before the pale skins brought iron onto the plains. Many Scalps can turn rifle balls, but he holds no power against the ancient weapons."

"But there must be more, Ne' hyo."

"The other Crows then charged," Cloud Dancer said. "You might have fought them, too, but you sang your death chant instead. I believe your sacrifice is what gave power to the arrow."

"I'm required to give up my life to kill this Crow?"

"I believe it to be that way, Naha'. I could be wrong."

"No, I've seen this vision myself," Iron Wolf said, forcing a smile onto his face. "Wolf told me long ago I would have a choice. I could follow Raven and learn the mysteries, as you have done. Or I could take Wolf's trail. My life then would be short, but I would win honor."

"Is that a good trade, Naha', giving up your life for a remembered moment?"

"You brought Horse to the People," Iron Wolf reminded his father. "If you were faced with the choice to do that one thing and be remembered, would you choose the long road instead, knowing you would only be bones at the end? Isn't a man put in the world to do something?"

"You have small sons," Cloud Dancer said. "A wife."

"My sons will grow tall, as I have, under your watchful eye. Long ago I asked you to tend them. They are at home at your side. They know your lodge already. It's a hard thing, leaving them behind. They're my heart, Ne' hyo. But it's a harder thing I ask of you."

"Yes?"

"To see them raised. And to let me find this death."

"If I could make it so, I would go instead," Cloud Dancer said, motioning his son closer. "Man Above, you make this road a hard one!"

"Have heart, Ne' hyo," Iron Wolf cried, clasping his father's hand. "Give me to this fate, even as you give up my ghost when I'm gone."

"My son, the grandfathers will sing of this death."

"Make my sons strong, Ne' hyo. Give them iron hearts to bear their struggles."

Iron Wolf rose slowly, and Cloud Dancer escorted the young man to the door of the lodge. Raven's Wing waited there, and she embraced her son.

"You won't see me again on this side," Iron Wolf whispered.

"I know," she told him. "But you will live on in your sons."

He managed a faint smile before leaving.

Cloud Dancer and Iron Wolf made the dawn prayers together the next morning. Afterward they swam

255

with the other young men and announced Iron Wolf would face Many Scalps in single combat.

Many voices howled objections, especially when Iron Wolf took only a bow and one stone-pointed arrow with him. But the Wolf's eyes silenced them.

Cloud Dancer had painted his son's face and chest with blue thunderbolts. He had added the ancient symbols reserved to those embarking on suicide charges. Iron Wolf took along his Fox lance and the thong he intended to use when he staked himself to the earth.

"He is the greatest of us all," the Foxes sang as they accompanied their lance-bearer toward the Crow camp.

Cloud Dancer himself followed with other warriors. Red Deer, the daughter of White Horse, came along with Yellow Robe Woman. They would tend the bodies and make the mourning preparations.

"Nothing lives long," Iron Wolf sang as he started down the ridge leading to the thin line of Crow riders. "Only Earth and Mountain."

There was a smile on the Wolf's face. In the distance, his brother creatures howled their approval.

It was, indeed, a remembered fight. Many Scalps stood in the center of the Crows, waving the bloody scalps of the recently slain warrior chiefs as he whipped his companions into a frenzy. The Crows quieted when they saw their enemy was but a solitary young man. Iron Wolf had yet to see his thirtieth summer — would never see it. His trim figure and ritual paint stirred neither fear nor anger in the hearts of the Crows. He shouted no taunts, made no motions of contempt. When he stopped a stone's throw away, they cheered him.

It was Many Scalps who first saw the bow. Even then he was not alarmed. The first trace of fear came when he recognized the stone tip on the arrow.

"No!" the Crow chief cried as he tried to kick his horse into motion. He had riders on each side, though, and before the big horse could shake itself free of them, Iron Wolf had raised his bow and fired the single arrow into Many Scalps' cold heart.

"Ayyyy!" the Fox Warriors shouted as the Crow chief fell.

The young Crows, amazed by this sudden disaster, whipped their horses into motion and started toward Iron Wolf. The Wolf had dismounted and staked himself in place. He made no effort to deflect the blows rained down on him by the enraged Crows. Instead he sang again, "Nothing lives long. Only. . . ."

The last words died on his lips.

Now the Foxes made their charge. The Crows, intent on killing Iron Wolf, were unable to escape his avengers. One after another the Crows were surrounded and cut down.

As the Foxes raised their triumphant howl, Cloud Dancer turned to comfort Yellow Robe Woman. She wasn't there, though. In the confusion she had joined the charging Foxes. Now she lay beside her slain husband, a lance protruding from her left side.

Red Deer Woman raised a mourning trill. Cloud Dancer cursed himself for not seeing this, too. Then

257

he started the long ride down to where his son lay.

Three days of mourning seemed inadequate. Cloud Dancer had again led the mourning prayers, but even they weren't enough. He had placed Iron Wolf and Yellow Robe Woman together on a nearby ridge, overlooking the place where Many Scalps' bones would become dust. White Horse was nearby, too.

"I feel so alone," Cloud Dancer told Raven's Wing afterward.

"You're not alone," she argued. "And you're needed," she added, pointing to where Wolf Boy and Two Feathers stood, gazing upon the burial scaffolds of their parents.

"We're old to start such a task," Cloud Dancer lamented. "But Man Above will give us strength to see it done right."

"Yes," she agreed. "Now go to them, Husband. Hold them close as you once held their father."

"I will," he vowed, hoping the day would never come when he set those boys in a high place. On that day Cloud Dancer would have lived too long.

Chapter Twenty-one

Cloud Dancer stood with a stern-faced grandson on each side while the People stripped Iron Wolf's lodge of its possessions.

"Our mother treasured those robes," Wolf Boy complained. "We should have taken them to the Arrow Lodge."

"No, you must walk away from everything," Cloud Dancer argued. "The shades of your parents must begin their climb up Hanging Road. To hold them close to you would be wrong. These first days their voices will be loud in your memory, calling you to hold them here. But you can't do that. Your lives are here, on this side. They have gone on."

The boys nodded, though their eyes betrayed confusion. Even so, they asked no questions. It wasn't until later, when they rested in the Arrow Lodge on thick buffalo robes, that their torment became visible. Wolf Boy thrashed about, whimpering like a whipped pup. Two Feathers rolled over against Cloud Dancer and clung to the old man's side.

"Nisha, I'm here," Cloud Dancer assured the child.

"Nam shim'," Two Feathers said, rubbing his eyes, "why did Ne' hyo leave us?"

"Wolf called him away," Cloud Dancer said, wondering if a child of seven summers could understand what swept a beloved father away.

"And my mother?" Wolf Boy asked, crawling over.

"I don't know," Cloud Dancer confessed. "Who can understand the great mysteries? She loved him and couldn't bear seeing him hurt. Or maybe she thought he needed company on Hanging Road."

"If I'd been older, I would have saved him," Wolf Boy boasted.

"It was his choice," Cloud Dancer said, gazing deeply into their troubled faces. "As it was that you should grow tall here, where your grandmother and I might see to your needs."

"You won't climb Hanging Road and leave us, too?" Wolf Boy asked, trembling at the notion.

"My road is hard and long, but it remains here, on this side," Cloud Dancer assured them. "Before I begin that other climb, you will both know all I have to teach."

They huddled close, and the old man warmed to their touch. In that way what began as an obligation became a comfort. Great trials faced the People in the years that followed, and the young ones served daily to remind their grandfather that life struggled on in spite of every difficulty.

"Our son has made us a great gift," Raven's Wing observed the day Wolf Boy killed his first buffalo. "Their need has made us young."

But Cloud Dancer didn't feel young. No, the winters were cruel hard now, and even summer failed to warm him as it once had. He had difficulty riding long distances, and often others made the buffalo prayers. He had passed on his knowledge of the New Life Lodge to others, and many knew the healing cures. As to the Arrow knowledge, he held that close to his heart and waited for one of the boys to become curious.

The same summer Wolf Boy celebrated his first buffalo coup, he joined the Foxes on a horse raid. He was young, passing just his fourteenth summer, but there were others younger.

"I go to hold the men's horses," Wolf Boy had explained to his grandfather. Cloud Dancer knew otherwise, but it was not his way to hold back a boy.

"Be brave, and carry this," the old man urged, passing on an elk-tooth charm. "Make the dawn prayers and respect your elders."

"Yes, Nam shim'," Wolf Boy promised.

It might have been true that he went along to hold the raiders' horses, but once on the plains, he became an equal. When the others became confused, Wolf Boy located tracks and led the band to horses. The others expected a Crow camp nearby; but these animals were wild, and it required great skill to maneuver a rawhide loop over their necks and bring them to camp.

Wolf Boy displayed a rare talent for the trick, and the others suspected here was a true grandson of the man who first brought Horse to the People. He was his father's son as well, for three times wolves were seen near the night camps. The young man had dreams, too, and twice he warned his companions away from danger.

When the Foxes returned from their journey and showed off the fine horses they had captured, their elders offered a feast in celebration. There, with the council fire blazing high, many tales of

Wolf Boy's exploits were shared.

"My grandson is a boy no longer," old Cloud Dancer said, rising to speak. "He's done many miraculous deeds, and it's time he should take the name I've long held for him. Two Feathers, bring three good horses to give away in honor of your brother. He's won a good name."

"What name?" Wolf Boy cried.

"The one your father won for you when he attached stone tips to his arrow," the old man explained. "Stone Wolf."

"Ayyyy!" the young Foxes exclaimed. "It's a brave-heart name."

Later, though, Stone Wolf questioned it.

"I always imagined I would carry my father's name," the young man said. "Even if they called me Young Iron Wolf, I would not mind."

"Had your father lived, his name would have changed," Cloud Dancer argued. "I called him Iron Wolf because he was strong. The name came in a dream. But I didn't understand. The white man's iron was not so strong as we supposed. No, it was the old stone points, like those on Mahuts, that carried the medicine to bring Many Scalps' death. There's the power, Nisha. This is the name your father won in death. You will carry it in life."

"Nam shim', there's much I still don't understand," Stone Wolf confessed. "I've passed years at your side. Together we've made the dawn prayers. I've helped with medicine cures. I have dreams, but they're not always clear to me."

"Some never are," Cloud Dancer replied.

"I thought I should be a great fighter, like Ne' hyo, but that won't be. Show me how to walk the sacred path, Nam shim'. Teach me the medicine trail."

"It's a hard road," Cloud Dancer said for what seemed a hundred-times-a-hundred times. "You'll give up much."

"Did you chose it? No, Man Above decides which path a man takes. I know I must follow yours."

"Then, stay with me a little longer, Nisha," Cloud Dancer declared. "It's time I pass on the Arrow knowledge. You and your brother must both have it, for I'm growing old, and it's not wise it should pass only to a single young man."

"Two Feathers and I have shared everything," Stone Wolf said, laughing. "Can this be any different?"

"Then, go and find him. It's time we should begin."

"Yes, Nam shim'," Stone Wolf agreed. "It's time."

Two additional years Stone Wolf resided in the Arrow Lodge. By then Two Feathers, too, had killed Bull Buffalo and won a name. Younger Wolf, he was called, and while some might have complained he would forever walk in Stone Wolf's shadow, that didn't seem to matter to Younger Wolf.

"The time will come when our paths take their separate directions," Younger Wolf predicted. "But even then we share a bond forged by pain and suffering. We are of one blood and one heart. To walk the earth as Stone Wolf's brother honors me."

Soon others were to think so, too.

Even as a boy, Stone Wolf's dreams had held power.

When, as a young man of eighteen summers, he was invited to join a band of Elk Warriors on a raid against the Crows, he reluctantly agreed.

"There's terrible danger for us in that far country," Stone Wolf argued. "I'll go, but you should listen to my warnings and turn back if the danger becomes too great."

Two Claws, the son of old Corn Planter, now led the young Elks. He had taken up the pipe and would lead the raid.

"We desire honor and horses, not death," Two Claws said. "Nothing you've said changes our intentions."

"Good," Stone Wolf answered. His only other demand was that Younger Wolf should come along.

"He can help you find the enemy," Two Claws said. "He rides well, and I myself have a scar given me while wrestling that boy near Porcupine Creek."

Two Claws and Stone Wolf then took the pipe to the Arrow Lodge and sought Mahuts's advice. After offering Cloud Dancer the gift of a fine spotted pony and three buffalo hides, Two Claws told of the proposed raid.

Cloud Dancer lit the pipe, and the men smoked. When Two Claws posed his question, Mahuts, too, predicted danger.

"This is a bad time to fight Crows," Cloud Dancer explained. "They use Coyote's tricks to fool us."

"Stone Wolf can warn against Crow traps," Two Claws argued. "Winter was hard. Many horses starved, and the young men need new mounts. Where should we go but into Crow country."

"Be wary, Nisha," Cloud Dancer advised. "Keep your brother safe."

Stone Wolf promised to do so. Still, once the raiding party departed camp, they were all filled with the same high spirits. Leaving their familiar hunting grounds and setting off westward into the mountains where the Crows often camped, the young men grew more cautious. Stone Wolf often rode ahead, seeking sign of horses and examining the country for signs of Crow scouts.

At last he discovered a small band of horses guarded by three young Crows. The Crows, in turn, spied Stone Wolf. Two turned to charge after him while the third rode off to find help.

"Man Above, lend this horse wings," Stone Wolf prayed as he galloped along. The Crows continued the chase for a time. Then, when Stone Wolf neared his companions, the Crows turned back toward the horse herd.

"You found horses," Two Claws observed as Stone Wolf reined his pony and fought to regain his composure.

"Yes," Stone Wolf answered. "And great danger."

"How many?" the other young men asked.

"Thirty, forty ponies," Stone Wolf muttered. "Many Crows. A rider went for help. There could be hundreds."

"With such a small herd?" Two Claws asked. "No, they're a small band. We'll fight them and take the horses. We'll win great honor."

"You promised to listen to me," Stone Wolf complained. "Have you heard nothing? Every Crow in these mountains will fall upon us!"

"How many are here?" Two Claws asked. "Do you know? Of course not. Even a small child knows a large band would own many hundreds of horses. Thirty? More likely you found a hunting party."

That appeared logical to the others, but Stone Wolf trusted his instincts. He couldn't explain his feelings, but he did know the enemy was near, and in great numbers, too.

"We'll take their horses and count coup," Two Claws vowed.

"I pray it's so," Stone Wolf said, frowning. "But I see it otherwise. My brother and I are returning. You will get them killed, Two Claws, if you raid these horses. Consider it well. Honor? Who will know what happened if you all die?"

"We won't," Two Claws grumbled. "But it's for you boys to go back to your old toothless grandfather. He has cause to fear the Crows, for they killed his son. My family chooses to kill its enemies instead."

Stone Wolf shuddered with anger, and Younger Wolf fumed. But the brothers turned homeward, leaving Two Claws and the Elks to meet their fate.

They rode slowly, for Stone Wolf's horse was tired already. And after crossing a ridge, they made a camp of sorts in a small cave and rested. If they had ridden farther, no one might ever have known what happened to the Elks. As it was, a young man called Runs his Ponies reached the cave as well. His horse collapsed when he halted, and Stone Wolf raced out to learn what had happened.

"Two Claws is dead," Runs his Ponies explained. "All

the others. It was a trap, as you warned. Our band was cut off and forced atop a small hill. Hundreds of Crows waited below. At dusk they charged. Many fell, but the survivors ran down our people."

"How did you escape?" Younger Wolf asked.

"I, Little Eagle, perhaps another or two were split off by the Crows. They thought to kill us, but my horse was too fast."

"Then, others may be alive?" Stone Wolf asked.

"That's my hope."

"Two Claws may escape, too," Stone Wolf suggested.

"I saw Two Claws fall," Runs his Ponies insisted. "He was with my brother, Curly Tail. The Crows killed them."

"We have sad news to carry home," Stone Wolf muttered. "Some will blame us for living. Others will say I should have foreseen it and stopped Two Claws."

"No one who knew him would believe anyone could stop him," Runs his Ponies disagreed. "They fought bravely and died. It's what a warrior asks."

Stone Wolf couldn't agree. Death needed some purpose. To be trapped by Crows and wiped out made no sense.

Two Claws was not the only one to fall victim to Crow cunning that summer. Soon thereafter a rider appeared carrying a pipe.

"We seek to avenge One-eyed Antelope," the young man, who was called Bull Hump, explained. When no one responded, Bull Hump went on.

"The Antelope was a fierce fighter," Bull Hump ex-

267

plained. "He and a party of Bowstrings set out to raid the Crows. They soon came upon a single Crow scout. Quickly they whipped their ponies and chased this Crow up a hillside. One-eyed Antelope had a rifle, and he shot the Crow dead.

"This Crow was a decoy, though. No sooner did he fall than Crows swept down on the Bowstrings like locusts. Our people fought with great courage, but were forced back to the top of a ridge. There, surrounded, the Bowstrings continued the fight. One after another fell. The Crows tried to get closer, but each time one charged, One-eyed Antelope leaped up, aimed his rifle, and shot the Crow dead.

"Four times the Antelope struck down a Crow. Then, with no ammunition remaining, he threw down his gun and took out a knife. The others did likewise, and the Bowstrings fell upon the Crows, fighting fiercely until killed."

"How many fell?" Cloud Dancer asked.

"It's said there were thirty that died on the hill and two others below. Only one survived, and he only lived because he had gone to scout the enemy. Hearing the battle, he hurried to aid his friends. It wasn't possible. A thousand Crows had gathered to kill the Bowstrings."

"Bring your pipe," Cloud Dancer said, waving the rider toward the Arrow Lodge. "Younger Wolf, see to his horse. We'll eat and smoke and consider this matter. A thousand Crows did this? Never before have so many fought us at once."

"Never before," Bull Hump agreed.

They entered the Arrow Lodge together. Later, Winter Lance, the Elk chief, and Night Hawk, who led the

Foxes, joined them. Raven's Wing offered food, and the chiefs spoke informally. It was later, after Bull Hump promised appropriate presents, that Cloud Dancer lit the pipe.

"Mahuts, these Crows kill our people," Bull Hump explained.

"Fifty of our young men are dead," Winter Lance added.

"Mahuts knows," Cloud Dancer said, examining the sacred Arrows. Their flint tips showed specks of blood, and a great uneasiness settled over the lodge.

"We must collect the People," Night Hawk said, "but not to raid Crows. The Arrows must be renewed."

"Yes," Cloud Dancer agreed. "It's too late in the year to do it now, though. We must await summer's rebirth."

"So long?" Bull Hump asked.

"Mahuts can only be restored if all the rituals are observed," Cloud Dancer explained. "It must be next summer. To lead a war party now, with the medicine broken, would be to invite even greater calamities."

"Return to your band," Night Hawk urged. "We'll send word to the others. Next summer we'll gather and renew the Arrows. Then we can have a council of the forty-four chiefs and decide how to punish the Crows."

"Warn of the danger, too," Cloud Dancer said, gazing uneasily at the dancing flames. "Beware of strangers who might bring sickness. Guard against raids."

"I'll send my own sons," Night Hawk vowed. "My nephews. And if our people are spared more death, I pledge to make the New Life Lodge."

"I, too," Winter Lance added.

The messengers left that next dawn to spread the

word of One-eyed Antelope's death and to warn of worse peril yet to come.

"Mahuts is powerless to protect us," the People cried. "Winter's certain to be hard."

It was, too. Game was scarce, and bellies were empty. Sickness ravaged the Hill People, and a small band of Windpipe People were killed by white men near Bear Lodge.

Fevers struck the Poor People, too, and Cloud Dancer kept busy administering cures and making prayers.

"Man Above, all that we have comes from you," the Dancer said as he made the dawn prayers on a cold winter morning. "Here among the People there is terrible hardship. Children are hungry. Others are sick. We cure what we can, but many are sick at heart. No herb tea or medicine powder can restore faith. Help us be strong. Give us heart."

Afterward Cloud Dancer summoned Stone Wolf and Younger Wolf.

"Come, stay with us," he pleaded. "Your grandmother is weak with exhaustion. I need help with the curing."

In truth that was only one reason for having the young men near. Whenever possible, Cloud Dancer repeated the Arrow rituals. Over and over they spoke of the renewal ceremony until finally Stone Wolf satisfied his grandfather.

"It's important he knows you can carry on," Raven's Wing explained. "He's grown old. He worries what will happen when he's gone."

"He'll live years yet," Stone Wolf argued.

"Next summer will be my sixtieth to walk the world," Cloud Dancer said, shivering from the bite of a gusty wind. "How can I be certain to last. If I die, it is only another old man climbing Hanging Road. But if the Arrow medicine is lost, the People die also."

"It won't, Nam shim'," Stone Wolf pledged.

In spite of the hard-face winds and snows deeper than any in memory, Cloud Dancer survived. But three days after the first thaw Raven's Wing began the long sleep.

"We'll build the scaffold, Nam shim'," Younger Wolf said, gripping the old man's trembling hands.

"And make the prayers?" Cloud Dancer asked.

"We know what to do," Stone Wolf declared. "You've taught us well."

"It's good to have strong hearts to carry on," the Dancer declared. "For my own grows weak. Soon we renew the Arrows. And afterward, we'll fight the Crows."

"We?" Stone Wolf asked.

"Yes," the old man answered. "My dreams have told me Mahuts must lead the way. This will be a remembered fight."

The young men nodded gravely as they set about their duties. There was time for fighting Crows later. Now they had mourning obligations.

Chapter Twenty-two

When summer came, all the People gathered to renew Mahuts. The Windpipe People, whose women sat with their feet to the left, were there. Nearby spread the camp circle of the Scabby band. The Pelt Men, Hill People, and Eat with Lakotas camped beyond them. Nearer the Poor People camped the Undershot band, those who made the Deer Lodge dance. The Suhtai, too, had come, along with the largest of the bands, called Eaters. Finally those who lay on their sides, the Mah sih' ko ta, arrived to spread their small circle among the People.

"It's good," Cloud Dancer declared. "All the ten bands are here. Now we can begin."

That first day, as always, was devoted to making offerings. Night Hawk, the Fox chief, had agreed to sponsor the renewal, and he provided many fine presents to the Arrows. These were placed inside the Arrow Lodge beside the sacred bundle. The Arrow Lodge itself was next made ready. Here old Cloud Dancer, with his grandsons at his sides, oversaw the preparations.

"It's for you to do," he told the young men. "It's necessary you practice your new knowledge."

Stone Wolf nodded gravely. He understood.

Cloud Dancer would soon pass on his burdens.

That next day, when the sacred bundle was un-wrapped, Stone Wolf made the prayers and examined the Arrows. Younger Wolf, in turn, promised to replace the feathers and clean the stone points. Stone Wolf and Night Hawk looked on approvingly. The actual work was carried out on the third day.

It was on the third day also that each family rededi-cated itself to the People. This was done by presenting a marked willow tally stick. The sticks were stacked beside a ceremonial altar, which was flanked by two small fires burning sage and cedar. Stone Wolf carefully held each tally stick over the fires, allowing the sweet smoke to en-gulf the sticks and provide blessings for every family.

Younger Wolf now replaced Mahuts's feathers and glazed the shafts. He reattached the cleansed flint tips with fresh deer sinew and submitted them to his grand-father's critical eye.

"You've done well, Nisha," the old man observed.

Elsewhere the medicine men prayed and fasted in an effort to renew their individual power. Young men en-hanced the protection of bear-claw and elk-tooth charms. A great sense of well-being descended over the ten camps. The sick cast off their ill humors and greeted the day with restored health.

On the fourth day, the ceremony concluded when the Arrows were exposed to the sun. Night Hawk brought a forked stick into the Arrow Lodge, and Stone Wolf af-fixed the Arrows, two pointing skyward to enlist the aid of Man Above and two pointing down to bring bounty and prosperity to the earth.

Night Hawk emerged from the Arrow Lodge, wailing as he brought Mahuts out into the light. The Arrows were set up outside. Then Night Hawk returned to the Arrow Lodge and brought their skin covering, which was set beneath them.

While the Arrows were exposed, all women in the camp were forbidden to leave their lodges. Boys brought forth additional presents while Stone Wolf and Night Hawk carried the offerings inside the Arrow Lodge outside. All males, from the smallest child to the oldest grandfather, now came forth to receive the blessing of Mahuts.

The long parade stretched from one end of the camps to the other. The younger ones averted their eyes from the Arrows, for Mahuts put off a blinding glow when exposed to the sun. The elders paused to offer brief prayers and enlist good fortune in their coming struggles.

Once all the men had passed Mahuts, the Arrow Lodge was broken down and raised again over the Arrows. In addition to the usual two medicine coverings, a third and larger one was now erected. Now there would be room for all the chiefs and medicine men. Meanwhile, in the place where the Arrow Lodge had stood before, a sweat lodge was built.

At dusk the medicine men assembled in the enlarged lodge to conduct the final rituals. Here they sang the four sacred songs Man Above had taught Sweet Medicine. After each song, one of the great prophecies was spoken. Finally, as dawn approached, the participants went to the sweat lodge, where the ritual bath cleansed them of all impurity and allowed them to safely resume their lives.

The offerings, meanwhile, had been taken off into the hills, and the great lodge was broken down. As for the Arrows, they were returned to their fox skin and placed in the care of Cloud Dancer once more.

After a day of rest and feasting, Night Hawk brought new offerings to Mahuts. Tail feathers of eagles, fine buffalo hides, fox pelts, and bear claws were carried by two young nephews. The Hawk had wrapped himself in a buffalo robe, taking care that the hair side should be out toward the light. Wailing and mourning, he made his way through the camp until he stood before Cloud Dancer.

"Here is a pipe, old friend," Night Hawk said, placing it on the earth before the Arrow-keeper. The nephews set down the presents. As was proper, Cloud Dancer took the pipe in his left hand and placed the palm of his right hand on the ground.

Quickly criers raced through the camps to inform the warriors. Soon the scattered Fox Warriors assembled around a tall council fire and sang brave-heart songs. Old victories were recounted, and young men were brought into the society.

Elsewhere the Elks and Bowstrings gathered in like manner. Cries for vengeance rose high. The Crazy Dogs and Red Shields added their voices to the war cry as well. For Cloud Dancer let it be known that Mahuts would go forth against the Crows. The Arrows would lend their blinding magic to this fight. Only a great victory could follow!

A thousand warriors moved out ahead of the assembled camps toward the country of the Crows. Men sang the remembered chants and whipped up their courage. Young men dreamed of counting coup and winning honor. The boys who came along to watch the horses whispered to each other of boasts made by brothers and cousins.

"I, too, will one day fight the Crows," they were heard to say.

Cloud Dancer saw it all. More than that, he envisioned the promised outcome of the raid. In a dream he had witnessed a great Crow camp of many lodges falling through the air. Below, waiting to accept this present, walked Wolf and Fox, Elk and Dog. There was a red shield there, and a bowstring, too. Nearby the chiefs danced and mourned those killed in the battle.

When the Dancer had told Night Hawk of the promised success, he had also warned that the young men must be patient.

"Keep them in control," Cloud Dancer warned. Before, when Mahuts set out to blind the enemy, young men had rushed ahead, spoiling the magic. Few remembered that time now. It was necessary the young men understood.

"It will be hard," Night Hawk confessed. "The young ones are eager."

"If they go ahead, many will die," Cloud Dancer declared. "Tell them to remember the blinding fire that touched their eyes. This is the magic we will turn on the enemy."

Before reaching the Crow camps, Cloud Dancer received a second vision. This time he saw a band of Crows attack the People. Using their Coyote medicine, the Crows had eluded the People's scouts and approached their camps. There, near the river along which the People camped, a single man walked. The Crows leaped out and killed this man, but now they were seen.

A war cry was raised, and men mounted horses and chased the intruders. The Crows lost heart and tried to escape. Two were caught and run down. The others were able to get away.

All this soon happened, but Cloud Dancer quieted the excited warrior chiefs.

"We'll mourn this dead man and make prayers," the Dancer explained. "Then we'll ride against the Crows."

"We must send out scouts," Night Hawk urged.

"Yes, but tell them not to go far," Cloud Dancer replied. "Mahuts will lead us to the enemy."

"And what if the Crows attack our camps?"

"My grandsons and I will make medicine," Cloud Dancer promised. "We'll make this place invisible to Crow eyes."

Others, especially the Crazy Dogs and Bowstrings, argued the Crows would flee when they learned of the gathering of enemies, but the old ones recounted Cloud Dancer's many dreams.

"He's a man of power," they said. "Trust him to make strong medicine. Mahuts leads our warriors. We can't fail."

Once the mourning ritual was completed, and the burial scaffold of the slain man was raised on a neighboring ridge, Cloud Dancer again summoned the chiefs.

"Gather the warriors," the old man instructed. "Now we will strike the enemy!"

Warrior songs again filled the night air. The People were certain of success. An Oglala camp now merged with the People, and these Lakotas agreed to join the fight.

As promised, the thousand warriors rode south after making the dawn prayers. Crow parties had also set out, but Cloud Dancer's medicine was strong. The Crows

277

failed to find the helpless ones. Instead it was the Fox and Elk scouts who discovered the Crow village.

Younger Wolf was among these young men, and he brought the news to his grandfather.

"Nam shim', the Crows camp on Horse Creek," Younger Wolf exclaimed. "There are more of them than we could count. Many women and young ones. Thousands of horses! Few men to guard the camp."

"Ayyyy!" the warriors howled. "Now we'll punish the enemy!".

"They are close," Cloud Dancer observed. "But it's late, and our horses have had a hard ride. We'll make the surround and wait for dawn. Then we'll strike."

Night Hawk and other chiefs agreed, and the leaders of the young men kept close watch over their companions. No one wished some foolish one to hurry the attack. Many were eager to count their first coup, and others hungered to avenge relatives killed in the previous summer. Three young men started toward the Crow village, but each was caught and quirted mercilessly by his companions.

"Are you a child to disobey your leaders!" the chiefs growled. "Be patient and you will have your chance."

It came at dawn. Cloud Dancer and the chiefs stood together, making the morning prayers. Then the Arrowkeeper brought out the sacred bundle and removed the two man Arrows. Younger Wolf brought over a lance painted black and red, and to this Cloud Dancer securely tied the twin Arrows.

"Ride ahead of the others, Nisha," Cloud Dancer instructed Younger Wolf. "Use their magic to blind the enemy. Guard them closely," the Dancer admonished the others. "The heart of the People leads the way, but it must not suffer insult!"

The chiefs nodded quietly. Cloud Dancer then made the final prayers and invoked the power of Mahuts. The sun finally broke the horizon, and a great blinding light flooded the Crow camps.

"Ayyyy!" Night Hawk cried. "Foxes, strike the enemy!"

Younger Wolf galloped ahead, and the Foxes surged after him. Elsewhere the Elks and Bowstrings struck. The other societies lent their strength, as did the Oglalas. Soon Crow lodges collapsed. The women and children cried out as they fled the vengeful enemies. The old men and boys who had stayed behind formed a line and fought the charging enemy, but their eyes saw only white light, and their arrows were driven, harmless, into the earth. Mahuts led the People. Victory was assured.

The battle was a great slaughter. Small circles of Crows resisted, but the struggle was unequal. Boys, armed only with hunting bows, tried to protect their mothers and sisters. Grandfathers, too old to walk without sticks, sang their death chants and flayed helplessly at the relentless attackers.

By mid-morning, the women were driven to the edge of Horse Creek like so many ponies. With them were two hundred small children. A second surround was made on the far side of the encampment. Here stood the horses and their young guards. Those who cast aside their weapons were taken captive. Only the older ones, boys of fourteen summers and more, were killed. Some of these fought hard and won the People's respect.

"He should have lived longer," Night Hawk observed as he stood beside one brave Crow. "But he had started up man's road, and there was nothing to do but grant him a quick death."

The victorious warriors soon began tearing down the Crow lodges and taking all manner of belongings. Good elk robes and buffalo hides were tied on captured horses. Many good kettles, some guns, strong bows, and hundreds of arrows were distributed. Lastly the horses themselves were meted out, along with the captives. Young men without wives picked out Crow girls, but afterward many remained. Old men adopted some as daughters. Others became second wives. Where possible, the children were kept with their mothers. If both parents were dead, the little ones were welcomed by men who had lost children to sickness. Scarcely a family failed to acquire some new relation.

The old women were a worry, though. They would only be a burden, and few wished to go anyway.

"Kill us!" one old grandmother pleaded. "You've slain my husband and stolen my daughters. Kill me!"

The words were translated, and Cloud Dancer forbid it. These people had come under the protection of the People, and it would bring misfortune to kill them.

"Have you sons, Grandmother?" Night Hawk asked. A Crow girl who knew the People's language translated, and the old woman answered that she had given birth to three sons. The youngest lay dead beside Horse Creek. The others had left to attack the big enemy camp to the north.

"These sons will return," Cloud Dancer declared. "Wait for them. Or go north and find them."

"I'm old and can't see," another grandmother pleaded. "Leave my granddaughter with me. I need her eyes."

"Find the little one," Night Hawk instructed. "She will stay with this ancient woman."

And so the People were generous with their vanquished enemies. The captives received good treatment, and soon the fear and confusion of the little ones gave way to gratitude and acceptance.

Cloud Dancer and Stone Wolf, after carefully returning the man Arrows to the medicine bundle, occupied themselves tending the many wounded fighters. Elsewhere, the few among the People who were killed were covered in buffalo hides and tied onto horses.

"It's a good day, Nam shim'," Stone Wolf observed.

"Yes," Cloud Dancer agreed.

Even the Bowstrings, whose blood was up for their murdered brothers, took pity upon the defeated Crows. Only a few of the slain were scalped, and even those weren't badly cut up. A few of the braver fighters were covered with blankets, and most all were left their clothing.

"This will be a fight long remembered," Younger Wolf declared later as he led the way northward away from the ruined Crow camp.

"Long remembered," Stone Wolf agreed, gazing at the handsome young woman riding along behind him.

"My brother's found a wife," Younger Wolf whispered to his grandfather. "Soon I'll have nephews."

"Or nieces perhaps," Cloud Dancer suggested. "Our family has been too long without girls."

"Gray Wolf had three," Younger Wolf argued. "Before the first son came, too. Little Sky has an Oglala daughter, too."

"I seldom see these," Cloud Dancer grumbled.

"Maybe I'll take one of these Crows, too," Younger Wolf said, grinning. "One of the tall ones with many children."

"You'd find her quarrelsome," Stone Wolf complained. "And she would compare you to her first husband. Better to take a maiden, Brother. Find a pretty one like Star Eyes."

"Is that her name?" Cloud Dancer asked.

"She speaks little," Stone Wolf answered, "but the others call her that."

"Yes, I see the way her eyes sparkle," Younger Wolf noted. "It's a good name. But will she make a proper wife?"

"I'll teach her to be one, Brother."

"You should at least teach her our language."

"Maybe she would make a better wife if she remained silent," Night Hawk said, riding by and grinning at the girl. She managed a shy smile in reply, and Cloud Dancer groaned. An immodest wife was the worst sort of curse!

She's young, he told himself. *She'll learn.* He fervently hoped so.

All the People mourned the few slain warriors and observed the required three days of prayer and sympathy. Then, after the dead were put up on scaffolds, a great feast was made. Young warriors received names, and many betrothals were made. There was much intermarriage among the different bands. Moreover, countless young men took in Crow women and adopted children.

During all this time little effort was made to guard the captured ones. A woman or child wishing to flee would find the chance in time, and it was thought better to make the journey short for them. Surprisingly few departed, though, and most were women with grown sons surviving among the Crow war parties.

Star Eyes, who began to recover from the shock of her ordeal, warmed to Stone Wolf, and the young man announced he would take her as his wife.

"We must make a feast, Nam shim'," Younger Wolf announced. "I'm to have a sister!"

Cloud Dancer sighed. He wished Stone Wolf had sought some advice, or asked Mahuts. There was something unsettling about this slender girl with the creamy brown skin. Raven's Wing, too, had been pretty, but her words always came from the heart. Star Eyes occupied herself demanding presents, insisting on the best horse to ride, and disdaining woman's work.

"The Crows pamper their women," Stone Wolf complained. "But Star Eyes will learn our ways."

"Haven't you wondered why she was still untouched?" Cloud Dancer asked. "Who was her father? She has the bearing of a chief's daughter. You could find it hard to stand tall in her eyes."

"She's won my heart, Nam shim'," Stone Wolf explained. "I know I should have sought a Suhtai woman maybe, someone who practices the healing arts. I know, too, I must find an old woman to help with the cooking and washing Star Eyes disdains. But if you've taught me anything, it's that a man can only follow his own path, and mine leads to her heart."

"I see that, Nisha," Cloud Dancer said, gripping the young man's shoulder. "And I wish you only happiness."

Chapter Twenty-three

Stone Wolf's wedding feast provided his grandfather with a chance to summon the many relations. Little Sky and his Oglala wife, Snow Woman, came, bringing their five little ones. Gray Wolf and Red Bead Woman came as well. Their daughters were now approaching womanhood, and Cloud Dancer welcomed their company. Gray Wolf had five sons, the oldest just eight, and none of them had passed much time with their grandfather. True, the Windpipes had their camp circle close; but an Arrowkeeper was often occupied, and boys were never long idle themselves.

Hairy Mane, long absent from his uncle's lodge, arrived as well. For many summers now he had ridden with the Oglalas, having taken a Lakota wife. Now this woman was dead, and the Mane had returned to the People.

"I, too, have chosen a Crow woman," Hairy Mane explained. She, of course, was not so young as Star Eyes, and she brought into her new husband's lodge two young sons. "I've heard Stone Wolf seeks an older woman to help his young Crow wife," Hairy Mane added. "My Oglala wife had a sister who has looked after my older sons. She's a good woman; but my new wife quarrels with her, and I must rid myself of one or the other."

"I'll talk to Stone Wolf," Cloud Dancer promised.

"She's called Red Willow Woman," the Mane said, turning to point her out. "She has no brother to go to, and her father's dead. She would go to her son, but the young man took a Nakota wife and lives in the far north country. She's old to make such a journey alone, and my sons are too young to take her."

"Yes, it's a long way to go," Cloud Dancer agreed. "I'll ask Stone Wolf."

That waited a time, though. First, Cloud Dancer had the feast to oversee. Younger Wolf made the giveaway, for he was rich with belongings after the Crow battle. Afterward the Poor People danced and sang and wished the newly marrieds health and prosperity.

"May they have many strong sons!" Night Hawk shouted.

"The People are stronger already," Gray Wolf declared. "It's good grandsons of Iron Wolf will walk the earth."

It was the next afternoon before Cloud Dancer found a chance to speak with Stone Wolf about Red Willow Woman. The new husband was occupied with other young Fox Warriors, recounting brave deeds and boasting of future coups. Cloud Dancer's arrival silenced the talk.

"Nam shim'?" Stone Wolf asked. "You need me?"

"My brother's son has come for the feast," Cloud Dancer explained. "He has with him a sister of his dead wife who has no place to go. You might speak with her. If she's suitable, you could ask her into your lodge. She's not so old she can't work hard, and she's too plain to upset even a young Crow wife. Come and meet her."

"Go," the others urged. "This pretty wife you've chosen will starve you before winter. See if the old one can cook."

It turned out Red Willow Woman could do much more

than cook. She had a talent for working hides, was tireless attending to camp duties, and knew many Oglala cures, too. In addition to looking after Stone Wolf and Star Eyes, the Oglala roasted meat for Cloud Dancer and Younger Wolf. She mended and washed and helped with the curing chants when otherwise idle.

Red Willow Woman also undertook the molding of Star Eyes into a wife. Great progress was made on the Crow girl's language skills, but Star Eyes neglected the more useful lessons in cooking, washing, and mending.

"She expects me to do these things, too," Star Eyes complained to Stone Wolf. "She fashions herself your wife and me a slave!"

"No, she seeks to teach you our ways," Stone Wolf argued.

"They're not *my* ways, Husband!"

"It's only what is expected of a woman of the People," Stone Wolf answered.

"I was born Crow," Star Eyes objected.

"Don't Crow women work? All I've seen have rough hands and worn knees. None of these others neglect their obligations!"

"Is that how you pass your time, looking at other women? Most men ride off to gather horses or hunt buffalo."

"I, too, hunt," he answered. "I'm already rich with horses. My obligations are to Cloud Dancer. I help with the rituals and practice the medicine cures."

"Women's work," she muttered.

"Ah? And I was thinking Crow women knew no work."

"She must leave or I will!" Star Eyes stormed.

Stone Wolf's anger rose, but he restrained himself. Another man might have struck out, but he knew such conduct by a medicine man wasn't allowed. Instead he left the lodge and sought out his grandfather.

"I've made a mistake, Nam shim'," Stone Wolf confessed. "My wife is good only for quarreling. Now she insists Red Willow Woman leave."

"Maybe it's best," Cloud Dancer admitted. "Those two women cackle at each other like jays fighting over a cottonwood. It's wrong to have such lack of harmony near Mahuts."

"What will I do, Nam shim'?"

"Nothing, Nisha," the old man said, laughing to himself. "Anyone can see this Crow girl owns your heart. I'll invite Red Willow Woman into my lodge. She will help with the medicine cures and attend the woman's duties. Younger Wolf and I won't eat everything, either. We'll always have some meat put aside for you."

"What will Star Eyes eat?" Stone Wolf asked.

"Nothing if she won't cook," Cloud Dancer said with a grin. "There are many ways to teach a reluctant wife, Nisha. Hunger is the best one."

Indeed, with no one to attend to the household labors, Stone Wolf's lodge became a place to avoid. No one visited there, for to do so was to invite hunger. The hides and even the lodgeskins needed attention. Sometimes Star Eyes forgot to bring water, and rarely was a root to be seen.

"I'm hungry," Star Eyes would complain.

"I brought a buffalo shoulder," Stone Wolf answered.

"It's not cooked. There's no fire!"

"I shot the buffalo, Wife. The rest is for you to attend."

"You're hungry, too," Star Eyes pointed out.

"Yes, but I am welcome in the Arrow Lodge," he replied. "Red Willow Woman won't offer you a slice of hump roast."

Star Eyes gazed sourly at her husband, but thereafter she joined the other women at the river each morning. When they went to gather roots or plums, she followed. And in time she learned to roast meat, fry bread, and boil tubers.

Red Willow Woman provided even better news that winter.

"Star Eyes grows fat," the Oglala woman observed. "It's not from her cooking, so there must be a child growing inside her."

"So, she has some talents, Nam shim'," Younger Wolf said, laughing.

"This is no matter to be taken lightly," the old man barked. "She has no family here. We must speak to her."

"No, that's for me to do," Red Willow Woman argued. "She doesn't like me, but we are acquainted. She's less likely to share her troubles with strangers."

"That's true," Cloud Dancer agreed. "When will you speak to her?"

"Tomorrow when we walk to the river," she explained. "You must talk to Stone Wolf when you go to make the morning prayers. Maybe some Crow woman will come and ease her burdens."

"Maybe," Cloud Dancer muttered. No true woman of the People would expect such aid. But aunts and mothers commonly provided help, didn't they? He recalled well old Otter Woman.

That winter the bands dispersed over the country south and west of Holy Mountain. There was good timber and good game there, so Cloud Dancer expected it to be a time of peace. But before the first snows fell, his dreams clouded with foreboding. He saw many birds nesting in the pines. First they appeared to be harmless swallows, but they quickly transformed themselves into eagles. Swooping down, they tore at the People with their talons and carried off the young.

When Cloud Dancer awoke, he found Younger Wolf at his side.

"Nam shim', your sleep is troubled," the young man observed. "Are we in danger?"

"Yes," the old man admitted.

"Who brings us harm?"

"I don't know, Nisha. But I will smoke and study the matter. Often a dream is a puzzle at first, but I've learned patience. Everything becomes clear in time."

Cloud Dancer did more than ponder his dream, though. That next day he sent word to the warrior chiefs to be wary of traps.

"Remember the Bowstrings," he warned. "Crows may hunger to avenge their dead. Be ready."

Messengers carried the warning to other bands as well. The Foxes sent scouts out onto the plains in search of raiding parties, and the Elks kept watch over the camp by night.

By winter nothing had come of the expected trouble. Many forgot the warnings. Others were too busy hunting to give thought to raiding Crows. Harsh winds and heavy snows made scouting the southern country impossible, and soon the People took to their lodges and prepared for the hard-face moons.

By spring the People had grown careless. Many women, Star Eyes among them, were busy with newborn children. Men climbed the hills to seek dreams or bring fresh meat into the camp.

"You said yourself some dreams are never understood," Stone Wolf told Cloud Dancer. "Cast these fears from your mind and help me seek a name for my daughter."

"It's for you to do, Nisha," the old man said. "My duty is to safeguard the People from peril."

And so while Stone Wolf gave away horses in honor of the child he named Dawn Dancer, his grandfather was again plagued by the terrifying dream. This time the swallows seemed smaller, though. And the claws of the eagle were sharper.

Again Cloud Dancer summoned the warrior chiefs. Once more the messengers rode out to the other bands. But most of the young warriors ignored the old man.

"Who can say what an old one like that sees?" Spotted Horse, oldest son of Hairy Mane, asked the young Crazy Dogs.

"He knows things," young Low Dog, leader of the young men, answered. "My father and his father learned to heed Cloud Dancer. His are the far-seeing eyes."

"He's seen nothing," Pony Foot, Spotted Horse's young brother, argued. "He only has dreams."

"And what would you know of dreams?" Low Dog replied. "Only now do you pluck your first chin hairs! A boy of fifteen summers shouldn't judge an Arrow-keeper."

The Crazy Dogs and all others in the camp were startled by a sudden cry. A boy ran over from the horse herd, shouting and waving toward a nearby hill. A solitary rider raced back and forth there, yelling or moaning or crying. It was hard to tell which. The Crazy bogs were nearest to him, and they started gathering their horses.

"There's a man on that hill, shouting!" a young woman yelled as she ran into camp with some wood she was gathering.

"No, he's mourning," another complained.

"You're wrong," a third, a young girl captured from the Crows, explained. "I know those words. He sings a warrior song!"

"Crows!" the cry rose.

Cloud Dancer rushed out of his lodge to have a look. Even now the Crazy Dogs were preparing to set out.

"Stop!" Cloud Dancer cried. "Don't you see? My dream has come to life. There is a Crow, pretending to be helpless. You would rush out and count a coup on him. It's a trick. Others are hidden behind that hill, and they'll kill you. Wait for the other warriors. We can go together. There will be too many of us."

"Listen!" Low Dog shouted. "Wait for the others."

But some young men have ears only for their own words. That was the way that morning Spotted Horse and his three brothers were the first to mount their horses. Hairy Mane, seeing them, urged his three nephews to restrain the young men. These cousins were Crazy Dogs, too, and they joined Spotted Horse. Five other Crazy Dogs went along as well, making twelve in all.

"I'll be first!" Pony Foot screamed as he whipped his horse up the hill. He waved a painted lance in his right hand and prepared to strike the Crow. The others hurried along on either side, their cries blending into a single war whoop that echoed across the plain.

"They ride into terrible danger!" Cloud Dancer said as he tried to collect the other men. "Younger Wolf, where is my horse?"

"Stay, Nam shim'," Stone Wolf pleaded when Younger Wolf arrived with the ponies.

"I must go," the Dancer said. "We must save the young men. Your cousins are among them!"

"Follow the Crazy Dogs," Hairy Mane said as he mounted. "Kill the Crows!"

"Wait!" Low Dog shouted. "Are we, too, to rush into a trap. Let the others come along. We must all go together."

"Hurry!" Hairy Mane urged.

Most did, but a few had trouble with their horses. Finally all the men were mounted, and they set out together after the twelve foolish ones.

Cloud Dancer had seen sixty winters, but he and Horse had been brothers since the time he had first spied the Kiowa herd so many summers before. He led the way, and only Stone Wolf and Low Dog could keep astride. Hairy Mane was close behind, for a father's concern drove him to exertion.

At first Cloud Dancer was confused by what he saw. The Crow was fleeing, but his horse seemed to race away and then pull up, seemingly lame. The twelve young Crazy Dogs would close with him, and suddenly the Crow would elude them.

"Uncle, you were wrong to fear for them," Hairy Mane said, easing his pace. "They'll soon have this Crow!"

But even as the words left his mouth, Hairy Mane saw the first concealed Crow emerge from his hiding place. First twenty, then twenty more appeared. A hundred Crows swarmed across the hill, encircling the young Dog Warriors.

For a time dust swallowed that hillside. Cloud Dancer's heart ached. Why had they ignored his warning? Why hadn't they listened?

Low Dog waved the other Crazy Dogs to his left and formed a wedge. Stone Wolf collected the Foxes and charged the right. Hairy Mane alone galloped toward the center, waving a rifle and screaming furiously.

What followed was mostly confusion. Dust choked that hill, and it was difficult to see much past the next horse. The Crows turned and met the People's attack, and there was some hard fighting for a time. Stone Wolf cut down one man, and Younger Wolf drove two from his brother's flank. Cloud Dancer clouted a Crow boy across the forehead, but the boy managed to hang on to his horse as the animal raced away.

Low Dog's party killed five as they scattered the Crows and chased them southward. As for Hairy Mane, his arms and thighs were marked by ten hard blows, but he remained atop his horse, shouting insults at the fleeing enemy. Only when the dust began to settle did he spy Spotted Horse standing with two cousins and his smallest brother, Willow Bark Boy, in the center of a circle of bodies.

"Naha'!" Hairy Mane cried, forcing a final effort from his bloodied horse.

"Ne' hyo!" Willow Bark Boy answered, limping toward his father.

It was Low Dog who first raised the mourning wail. For among the twelve rash young men, those four alone survived.

Cloud Dancer climbed down and pulled a young Crow from what remained of Pony Foot. A hatchet had severed an ear and cut halfway through the boy's neck. The ax remained in the hand of his attacker, who had received a lance thrust through the belly.

Hairy Mane located his other son, the latest in the family to carry the name Corn Boy. This Corn Boy had yet to see thirteen summers, and he didn't belong on that hillside any more than did Willow Bark Boy. One had been luckier, though. Corn Boy lay in the dust, stripped bare, with his scalplock cut away. His father lifted the small figure onto one shoulder and started toward a riderless horse.

"This was my brother," Low Dog said, moaning as he knelt beside an older boy who had likewise been scalped.

Others pulled the slain young Crazy Dogs free of the enemy corpses and set them atop horses for the long ride back to their families.

"I was wrong," Spotted Horse muttered, turning toward his father.

"No," Low Dog cried. "You were lucky. You can learn from your mistake. These others are dead."

"Ayyyy!" others screamed angrily.

"Ne' hyo, let me carry him," Spotted Horse pleaded as he reached out for his brother's limp body.

"Bring your cousins," Hairy Mane barked. "When the mourning is over, you must ride to the Oglala camp and tell their mother."

"Ne' hyo?" the Horse cried. "Why me?"

"Because I lack the strength," Hairy Mane explained. "And because when a man leads others, he becomes responsible for them."

"Yes," Low Dog agreed. "That burden forces a man to act wisely. And to listen to those who walk the medicine trail as Cloud Dancer does."

For an instant Spotted Horse glanced at the old Arrowkeeper. Only that long. He couldn't bear the fire that pain and sorrow had kindled in the old man's eyes any longer.

Once the dead were collected, the men led their weary horses back to the camp. From a distant ridge Crows shouted defiantly.

"Crows, hear me!" Low Dog answered. "Come and gather your dead before our women find them. Come and fight our camp dogs! And if you tire of living, meet me here in the open, without your Coyote tricks. Murderers of my brother! Ride far from here. Hurry from his ghost! Soon he will rest on the other side, and I will come hunting!"

Low Dog took up the mourning song, and it soon spread among the others. Long before they returned to the camp, they heard the high-pitched trill of the women answering.

"Nothing lives long," Hairy Mane whispered the next day when he helped Spotted Horse rest the second of the young cousins on a scaffold. The four young relations lay there, wrapped in buffalo hides and surrounded by their weapons. Nearby the other four slain Crazy Dogs rested in like manner.

"Nothing lives long," Willow Bark Boy said as he leaned on a forked stick. His maimed left leg was wrapped in deerhide, but it would never entirely heal.

"Nothing lives long," Cloud Dancer whispered as he affixed a pony's tail to each scaffold. A boy killed in battle should ride Hanging Road.

"Only the earth and the mountains," Stone Wolf said.

I wonder if they're glad of it, Cloud Dancer thought as he eyed his distraught nephew. To grow old, after all, was to know death like an old friend. And to accept sadness as one accepts winter.

As he turned away from the burial hill, he saw the ugly red scar on Stone Wolf's neck, another reminder of the hard fight. It brought back Touches the Sky's prophecy of so long ago.

I knew he would be the one to lift my burden, Uncle, Cloud Dancer thought. *Soon Mahuts must be given over again. Yes, soon.*

Chapter Twenty-four

The loss of so many relations turned Hairy Mane bitter, and he left the camp of the Poor People to take his Crow wife and family back to the Oglalas. It saddened Cloud Dancer to see his nephew and the grandsons of White Horse leave, but there was too much sadness for them there.

"We, too, should flee their ghosts," Stone Wolf argued. And so the Poor People turned north and followed Bull Buffalo into the holy country of the Black Mountains.

More and more this country was coming into the hands of the Lakotas. Oglala and Sicangu bands often joined in buffalo hunts. Arapahoes, too, formed circles nearby. More and more families intermarried between these tribes, and it wasn't unusual to hear all three tongues spoken around a council fire.

Along Muddy River other words were spoken. The old French traders, called red white men by some, were seen less and less. Cloud Dancer had avoided them, especially the black robes with their silver cross medicine, but he respected them for their courage. He even found sadness when Little Sky sent word the Freneau Trading

Post had been burned by the Rees and Corn Hair killed.

Now blueshirt soldiers arrived to scout the country. These white men brought along thunder guns that hurt the ears. Suhtai hunters had witnessed one of these weapons fired from a soldier boat that had knocked down a tree!

"They bring many presents, these white men," Night Hawk explained. "For buffalo robes and beaver pelts, they give us beads that shine in the sun, iron axes and knives, good rifles and much powder to make the hunt successful. The Crows have all these things, as do our other enemies. We must trade for them, too."

"Have you forgotten Sweet Medicine's warnings?" Cloud Dancer cried.

"How long have you spoken this same objection, old friend?" Night Hawk asked. "The whites are here. We must make them our brothers, as we have brought the Lakotas into our family. We seem different, but we are all men after all."

"These whites walk the world with heavy feet," Cloud Dancer complained. "Everywhere they mark their passage. They put up walls and call them forts. They kill off the game and make the land barren. Even Bull Buffalo will not outlast them."

"I've watched from the tall hills," Night Hawk argued. "This summer the plains are black with buffalo. Not even thunder guns could kill them all."

"These whites will find a way," Cloud Dancer said sadly. "Have you seen their hungry eyes? A man gives them a buffalo robe, and they ask for another. They ask to make camp on Muddy River, and soon they are building lodges. The Mandans welcomed them, and what has become of that people? Dead of the spotted sickness!"

But no words would hold back those eager to trade with the white men. Tall hairy-faced Americans now crossed the plains on horseback or paddled up the many rivers in long canoes. Wearing buckskins and hide caps, they offered a pipe and spoke softly.

"Don't be fooled by them, Nisha," Cloud Dancer warned Stone Wolf. "They seek to own the earth, the air, even the sky."

"No one can own Mother Earth," Stone Wolf said, laughing at the foolish notion. "The air? The sky? It's not possible."

"You judge only what you know," Cloud Dancer said. "I speak with the power of dreams."

"Tell me what you see, Nam shim'," Stone Wolf pleaded.

"If I told all, you would share this old man's despair. A young heart must have hope."

"Yes," Stone Wolf agreed. "Look in the eyes of my daughter and find that hope. Listen to the laughter of the little ones when we make the morning swim. It's life you hear, Nam shim'. So long as there's life, there must be hope."

It was a warming thought, even for an old man.

When it came time to gather the bands and make the New Life Lodge again, both Stone Wolf and Younger Wolf declared their intention to hang from the pole.

"Our father suffered when he had not yet earned a name," Stone Wolf explained. "Perhaps we can

298

bring better times to the People."

"Perhaps," Cloud Dancer agreed. Clearly it would draw the young men closer to Man Above and raise their stature among the People.

Indeed, it did just that. And afterward, when Younger Wolf led the buffalo hunt, even Red Willow Woman found cause to smile.

"These grandsons make you proud," she observed.

"They're my heart," Cloud Dancer confessed.

"I've known great pain since the death of my sister's sons," Red Willow Woman added. "I may have grandsons, too, but I will never see them."

"Stone Wolf would take you north," Cloud Dancer said, lifting her face in his hands. "Is that what you want?"

"I'd only be a burden to them," she whispered. "I'm needed here."

"Yes, you are."

Two years of prosperity followed the grandsons' suffering in New Life Lodge. Crow raiders came and were beaten off. The People met great success on their hunts and horse raids. Children were born, grew tall, and made the ten bands strong.

No birth was as welcome as that of Stone Wolf's son. This child, who was called Arrow Dancer by his father, drove off the worst chills of winter from old Cloud Dancer's bones.

"Our family continues to grow," the Arrow-keeper boasted as he cradled the child. Already Dawn Dancer was hopelessly pampered by her uncle and great-grandfather. Red Willow Woman always had some sweet put aside for the girl, and now here was a boy to be equally and shamelessly spoiled.

The birth of the children seemed also to gentle their mother. Star Eyes lost none of her beauty, but she complained less and accomplished more.

"She'll prove to be a good wife," Stone Wolf announced. "She was young when she came to us. There was no time for her to ready herself for woman's road."

Red Willow Woman, who saw the little ones had warm clothes and soft moccasins, complained the Crow girl still had no sense.

Two more years passed, and matters grew no better.

"She's too free with her advice, and far too generous with her attentions," the Oglala woman grumbled. "How often have I seen her walking river road with some young man!"

"I'll talk to her," Cloud Dancer promised.

"Better she had relatives to do that. She has no ears for our words, old man. Speak to Stone Wolf. Warn him."

But Stone Wolf seldom heeded such complaints, either. His eyes saw much, but the young man was snowblind where his wife was concerned.

If for no other reason than to separate Star Eyes from her many young admirers, Cloud Dancer suggested a journey eastward to visit Gray Wolf.

"I have grandsons among the Windpipes who can share the hunt with their cousins," Cloud Dancer suggested. "The granddaughters will take husbands this summer."

"Maybe," Stone Wolf agreed. "We'll see them when we gather to make the New Life Lodge."

"Yes, but I hunger to visit now, Nisha. Later the boys will be busy with preparations for the hunt, and we'll be occupied with the rituals."

"We'll go, Nam shim'," Stone Wolf agreed. "It's certain to be a hard journey with the little ones, though."

"Give them over to Red Willow Woman," Cloud Dancer suggested. "She hungers to tend them, and it will give you and Star Eyes time to share."

Stone Wolf eyed his grandfather with suspicion. Then his lips formed a smile, and he hurried to tell Star Eyes the news.

She feigned enthusiasm for the journey, but Cloud Dancer recognized the cold scowl she sent his way. She shared in the work of breaking down the lodges, though, and she entertained the children with Crow songs on the long journey to where the Windpipes made their camps well to the east.

If not for that journey, Cloud Dancer might never have learned of the peacemakers. The Windpipes knew all about them, and their chiefs rejoiced that the Arrows were on hand to be consulted.

"A bluecoat soldier chief meets with the many peoples who walk this country," Little Moon explained. "He offers presents, and he pledges peace."

"These things he gives us," Cloud Dancer said, considering it. "What does he ask?"

"That we touch the pen to his peace paper," High-backed Wolf said. "These white men have good tobacco, and they are generous with gifts."

"I know their hearts, these strangers," Cloud Dancer said sourly. "Remember what Sweet Medicine predicted. You must take nothing from these people."

"All the People trade freely with them," Little Moon argued. "We give nothing away to the white men. We promised only peace."

"I've dreamed of these treaty papers," the Arrow-keeper said, frowning heavily. "The man who touches them gives up his shade to be used by these white enemies. You don't know the Coyote tricks the white man can use. For him paper scratches speak louder than hearts. We are rooted deep in Mother Earth. He drifts on the wind, friendless and alone."

"Come and speak to them yourself, Cloud Dancer," High-backed Wolf suggested. "Hear their words and read their eyes. I know an honorable man when I face him. This star chief, Atkinson, has a good and generous heart. He asks how he might help us."

"I don't trust him or any of these strangers," Cloud Dancer declared.

"We know this, Ne' hyo," Gray Wolf said, joining the discussion. "You keep the old ways. Once it made sense to keep out the whites, but now there are too many of them. It's best we have them on our side."

"Ask the Arrows," Stone Wolf advised. "Counsel with Mahuts. Then we can speak again, Nam shim'."

"Yes, Ne' hyo," Gray Wolf agreed. "Maybe we will go meet with this star chief of the blue soldiers then."

"Maybe," Cloud Dancer answered.

It was Little Moon who brought a pipe. The other Windpipe chiefs followed him inside the Arrow Lodge, and they smoked and talked with Cloud Dancer a long time. The Dancer consulted Mahuts, and the Arrows turned violently.

"They hear our voices raised and worry the People no

longer know harmony," Cloud Dancer explained. "Also they don't trust this star chief."

"They advise us to refuse the presents?" Little Moon cried in disappointment.

"They urge us to practice patience," Cloud Dancer answered. "And to use wisdom as we remember the old warnings. I will do as Gray Wolf suggests. I will go and talk to this white soldier chief."

The chiefs howled their approval. But Cloud Dancer ached with despair.

"Nam shim', what's wrong?" Stone Wolf asked.

"I go to look upon the face of the ones who will murder Bull Buffalo," the old man explained. "I would rather face a thousand Crows than these whites and their tricks. Crows I understand. You can fight them with honor or kill them, depending on their nature. But these strange people with the pale skins are a puzzle. I fear them."

When the four chiefs left to meet with the soldiers, Cloud Dancer went along. Stone Wolf remained to tend the Arrows. Younger Wolf accompanied his grandfather.

The whites had built a small village at Teton River, but their white box lodges formed no circles. They made lines instead which began nowhere and had no destination.

The chief, General Atkinson, greeted his visitors warmly. He spoke through a trader, who interpreted.

"Star Chief is glad you come," the trader translated. "He brings the treaty paper and asks you touch the pen."

"What does the paper say?" Cloud Dancer asked.

"Only what he told you before," the trader explained.

303

"That Great White Father salutes the Chien People and promises them prosperity."

"Who is he to promise this?" Cloud Dancer asked the others.

"Great White Father is chief of all the blue soldiers," Little Moon said, waving at the star chief's men. "He rules over great villages."

The general spoke again, and the trader laughed.

"Star Chief says perhaps I've said the wrong things," the trader explained. "The words on the treaty paper say Great Father recognizes the Chien, and the Chien recognize him."

"We don't know him," Little Moon said, his eyes betraying confusion. "What does this mean, to recognize?"

The trader exchanged words with the general, who shook his head from side to side and spoke a few heated words.

"Star Chief says you appear fearful," the trader said. "I tell him everyone knows the Chien fear nobody. They are famous fighters. This paper speaks of respect. That is what it says. Great Father respects you. He'll look after your needs."

"Are we children to need such attention?" Cloud Dancer asked. "Is it a father you promise or a woman to nurse us? We need neither. I say turn away from this paper."

"Star Chief brings many presents," the trader insisted. Soldiers carried tins of tobacco and strings of shiny beads to a table and spread them for the People to look at.

"All this is ours if we touch the pen?" Little Moon asked.

Again the general spoke, and the trader answered.

"These things are yours now," the trader said. "You don't sign unless your heart's in it. Star Chief's offering his friendship. Would you turn away and make him an enemy?"

"This is a matter of importance," Cloud Dancer said. "See how this chief of the whites grows impatient? Turn away now, brothers. Send messengers to the other bands. Only the forty-four can speak for all the People."

"We speak only for ourselves," Little Moon argued. He then accepted the star chief's pen and touched it to the paper. High-backed Wolf, Buffalo Head, and One Who Talks Against the Others did the same. All took presents and shared the white soldiers' food.

"Star Chief asks if the old chief will sign, too," the trader said, extending the pen toward Cloud Dancer.

The Arrow-keeper stepped back, avoiding the pen as if it had been a deadly lance.

"My grandfather is no chief," Younger Wolf explained. "He's a man of strong belief, of medicine power. Others have ignored him and suffered for it. I fear you, too, will see the wisdom in his arguments."

"We should go," Cloud Dancer told Younger Wolf.

"Yes, we go now, Nam shim'. You have grandchildren to visit. They'll want stories, the younger ones. Maybe we'll ride out and find the Oglalas, too. Little Sky would welcome you."

"Yes, that would be good," Cloud Dancer agreed. But his words had no enthusiasm.

When they returned to the Windpipe camp, they found Stone Wolf anxiously waiting.

"I, too, have had a dream," Stone Wolf explained. "I

305

saw darkness over Holy Mountain. Bull Buffalo sang his death chant, and the clouds performed the mourning ritual. Nam shim', what's happened?"

"Nothing," the old man said, nodding gravely. "But soon I must make a long journey. We'll speak of it, Nisha, you and your brother. Now I go to sit with the young ones. I would hear their laughter and feel their touch. Tonight we'll smoke. Tomorrow we'll talk."

Stone Wolf agreed without understanding.

As he said, Cloud Dancer entertained the young ones with many remembered stories. He listened to the older boys tell of their ponies and the buffalo hunt they would soon begin. He met the granddaughters' husbands and held Prairie Fire's young son.

"Help him grow strong in the true manner," Cloud Dancer told Gray Wolf. "Soon I go to climb Hanging Road, Naha'. There I join your grandfather and mother, old Touches the Sky and Iron Wolf."

"Ne' hyo, you're young yet," Gray Wolf objected.

"Sixty-five summers I've walked this country," he said, feeling the weight of those years pounding on his chest. "I remember when we grew corn beside the great river. Then Chippewas drove us from that place. I myself brought Horse to the People, and that, too, changed us. We moved far on Horse's back, and now we dwell in the shadow of Noahvose, Holy Mountain.

"When the Lakotas came, we moved again. We fought the Crows for a new country, and many good men died. Soon, though, there will be no more places to move. The world grows smaller, Naha', and darkness approaches. Sweet Medicine foretold of the day we would lose our way. He said to turn away from the pale people, and he was right. Their iron tools and thunder guns bring us death. With shiny beads and false promises, they steal our hearts."

"We've endured change before," Gray Wolf replied. "Is it so unthinkable that we will survive the whites, too?"

"Survive as what?" Cloud Dancer asked. It was that unanswered question that plagued him as he entered the Arrow Lodge that night and lit a pipe. Neither Mahuts nor sacred smoke would lift his spirits. Not even Arrow Dancer's touch or his faint words brought warmth.

"Nam shim'?" Stone Wolf asked.

"Tomorrow we talk," Cloud Dancer explained. "This night I will dream. And remember."

Chapter Twenty-five

That night the heavens were still and calm. The stars rained down bright lights upon Mother Earth, and the hunters beyond the Windpipe camp remarked at the strange touch to the air.

Inside the Arrow Lodge an old man dreamed. Once more he danced across the clouds with Buffalo and Horse. He sang the brave-heart songs and remembered the boy who had long ago been introduced to the mysteries of life.

When dawn arrived, Cloud Dancer, as he had done for more than half a century, dressed and walked out past the village to greet the morning sun. Stone Wolf came along, as did Younger Wolf and the male children of Gray Wolf.

"Nam shim', why do you raise your arms?" Running Antelope, who had now passed his thirteenth winter on the plains and would soon go with the other young men to hunt Bull Buffalo, inquired.

"I invoke the powers of the sky," the old man explained.

"And the song?" Running Antelope asked.

"It comes from the Suhtai, my wife's people," Cloud Dancer answered. "It celebrates life."

The younger ones, too, had questions, but the Dancer only smiled.

"Your father will speak to you of all these things," he assured the children.

"Won't you?" Running Antelope asked.

"My time is short here," the old man said, sighing. "Sit with me awhile and let me etch your faces in my memory. My eyes aren't so good anymore."

The boys crowded close, and Cloud Dancer brought each one close in turn. For the smallest he whispered prayers and counseled wisdom. The old man produced an elk charm for Running Antelope and tied it behind the young man's ear.

"This is the last one I will ever make," Cloud Dancer said. "When your brothers come to be tall, send them to Stone Wolf, their cousin. He'll know the medicine chants that give the best protection."

"Nam shim', why do you talk as if to leave us?" the Antelope wondered. "Among our people there's great feasting. The blue soldiers have promised us peace. Many new things have been brought into camp. Won't you come with me and see them?"

"No, my path leads me elsewhere. Yours is just beginning. Be strong, Nisha, and always put foremost the welfare of the People."

"Ne' hyo, too, urges that," the boy said, grinning.

Cloud Dancer embraced them each. He had great difficulty pulling away from the younger ones, for their arms gripped tightly, and the need inside the old man's heart for their affection was great.

"Come," he finally said. "We must join the men at the river."

The older boys hurried to the bank and stripped. The younger ones hung back.

"Come, even you," Cloud Dancer said, waving Raven Boy, the youngest at six, along. "It's right a boy shares a swim with his old grandfather."

The Windpipe men, who might have objected another time, saw the dimness in an old man's eyes and kept silent. They knew, as did Cloud Dancer, that good memories could warm a man on the coldest winter nights.

Cloud Dancer left the youngsters to Gray Wolf's attention after a short while. He himself instructed the horses be collected. Soon they would tear down the lodges and pack up for the long journey south and west.

"Now's the time to talk," he told Stone Wolf.

Younger Wolf waited outside while his brother and grandfather stepped inside the Arrow Lodge and sat beside Mahuts.

"A long time now you've known this day would come, Nisha," Cloud Dancer began. "Soon I will give up my pain and embark on the long sleep. I go willingly, knowing you are here to accept my burden."

So saying, the old man lifted the sacred bundle in his arms and passed it into the care of his grandson.

"Nam shim', I'll keep the Arrows safe," Stone Wolf promised.

"You know what I can teach you," Cloud Dancer said, choking with emotion. "You've practiced the medicine cures, and you know the rituals. Now hear my warning, even as Touches the Sky gave me his. The

310

People can prosper only so long as Mahuts knows harmony. Difficult times approach. You will know trials and struggles, both from within and without.

"I see many enemies tormenting our people. I see clouds of blue soldiers coming to rub our names from the children's memory. But the greatest danger to the People, and to Mahuts, comes if the Arrows are abused."

"Nam shim'?" Stone Wolf cried. "You know me. I will not dishonor your trust. I will keep them well."

"You will come to face a terrible challenge, here," Cloud Dancer said, touching the young man's heart. "You'll know grief and loss. You'll hunger to kill. An Arrow-keeper must always hold the well-being of the People foremost in his heart, though. You must put yourself above worldly matters."

"I don't understand."

"You will, Nisha. You now take up my burden. Keep Red Willow Woman with you. She can help with the women's cures."

"I have a wife, Nam shim'," Stone Wolf declared.

The old man didn't answer. Instead he chanted a solemn prayer and gazed a final time at Mahuts.

"This lodge is now yours," Cloud Dancer declared. "I take but a few belongings with me."

"You're going away?"

"I must find my rest on Holy Mountain, where the bones of Touches the Sky rest. Where Sweet Medicine first received Mahuts from Man Above. There I start the long walk up Hanging Road."

"You can't go alone, Nam shim'!"

"Younger Wolf will guide me," Cloud Dancer said, resting a weary arm on Stone Wolf's shoulder.

311

"It's a small favor to grant an old man. You, Nisha, have made the greater gift. My burden is lifted. Ayyyy! You're Arrow-keeper now!"

Cloud Dancer left the Arrow Lodge and shouted the news to each of the cardinal directions. Then he sat for a time with Dawn Dancer, shared a story with Arrow Dancer, and bid farewell to the three grown granddaughters.

Finally he led Younger Wolf aside.

"I wondered if you had farewell words for me, Nam shim'," the young man said, resting his head on the old man's shoulder as he once did as a boy. "The others say you're going away."

"I must visit Noahvose, Holy Mountain," Cloud Dancer explained.

"It's a long journey, Nam shim'. You can't go alone."

"The one who takes me will have a long ride back, across dangerous country."

"I'm a Fox," Younger Wolf declared. "Give me the hard things to do. They are mine."

"I want your company, young one," the Dancer explained. "You can go freely, leaving no obligations behind you. Your mind will be clear and your ears eager to hear my words."

"Yes, Nam shim'."

"Gather four good horses, Nisha. Find two others to carry our robes and weapons. The rest are Stone Wolf's."

"He's a rich man," Younger Wolf noted. There was a trace of hurt in his eyes, but it quickly passed. "But I will share this adventure with you. If I walk naked from Holy Mountain, I would be a richer man still."

Younger Wolf's smile was contagious, and Cloud

312

Dancer's grim gaze brightened.

"Wait for me, Nam shim'," the young man said. "I go to make the preparations."

By the time Younger Wolf had packed up the needed belongings and made ready the horses, a crowd had gathered. Word had spread the old Arrow-keeper was leaving. Mahuts had been passed. The Windpipes now saluted the old man who had given so much of himself for the benefit of the People.

"Ayyyy!" the warriors shouted. Young men sang going-to-battle songs. Then the women took up a mourning trill, and tears began to fall.

"I've lived a long time," Cloud Dancer told them. "Willingly I go to the end of my path. I leave you to keep the sacred ceremonies. Remember Sweet Medicine's prophecies. Live long, my children. Be strong!"

So saying, Cloud Dancer mounted his waiting horse and followed Younger Wolf from the camp. Theirs was a long journey barely begun.

Even so, the days passed all too quickly. Cloud Dancer had sixty-five summers of memories to share. There were sacred medicine charms to explain and warnings to issue.

"Why give these things to me?" Younger Wolf finally asked. "My brother will keep the Arrows. People will come to him for the cures."

"These are for the grandsons," Cloud Dancer explained. "They hold power to turn the white man's aim. Later, you will know better how to use them. I will whisper in your dreams, and you will tell the young ones."

"Nam shim', already I grow lonely," Younger Wolf cried.

"Be patient. You will know sadness and isolation on your long journey back to the People. This will prepare you for the disappointment life will bring. But later, when the winters seem longer and the years shorten, you'll know both fame and great contentment."

On and on they talked as they rode. Younger Wolf shared his young man's doubts. Cloud Dancer spoke with the certainty of old age as he quieted his grandson's concerns. Finally they arrived at the base of Noahvose, Holy Mountain.

"We're here," Cloud Dancer declared. "My journey nears its end."

Cloud Dancer kept four camps on Holy Mountain. Each dawn, after making the morning prayers, he moved farther up the slope. Finally, when they reached the summit, he lit a pipe and smoked with Younger Wolf.

"Here, where the wind could sweep the dust of his bones across the holy country, I put Touches the Sky," the old man explained. "Tonight, when we are finished with my prayers, you will construct a scaffold here. Put me on it at dawn, when you make the morning prayers."

"Still alive?" Younger Wolf cried in disbelief.

"No, Nisha, I will begin the long sleep this very night. As you put my bones high up, my feet will already have started the long walk up Hanging Road."

"No, Nam shim'," Younger Wolf said, embracing the old man. "You're strong yet."

"No, Nisha, I'm tired. My burden's been great. I long to be at rest."

"I'll kill your horses. You'll ride at least."

"Yes, it will be good to have their company," Cloud

314

Dancer agreed.

"The man who brought Horse to the People should have it so."

"Yes," Cloud Dancer agreed, smiling. "Now, I set my pipe aside. It's time to show you the holy places."

Cloud Dancer tapped the burned ashes from the bowl and returned the pipe to its fox-skin cover. He then led Younger Wolf across Noahvose to a deep cave.

"Here Sweet Medicine was given his vision," Cloud Dancer explained. "Here Man Above bestowed Mahuts on the People. When you are older, some young man may ask you which was the place. Even as my uncle showed me, you will reveal it to him."

"This young man, who will he be?" Younger Wolf asked.

"Who can say? Nephew. Cousin. Grandson. You will know when he asks."

"And if no one asks?"

"Then it will be time for this old story to fade from the People's memory, Nisha. That will be a sad day. I'm happy I won't see it. I hope you don't."

They sat in the cave, and Cloud Dancer recounted the well-known story of Sweet Medicine's exile. They spoke again the four prophecies, and Younger Wolf shared his own varied visions.

"I'll always remember this time, Nam shim'," Younger Wolf promised when darkness finally draped the mountain with its thick cloak, and they returned to the summit. "I'll share these stories that they may be remembered."

"Tell only the young ones," Cloud Dancer urged. "Only they have the ears and eyes to recognize truth."

"I'll make a fire now. And prepare food."

"Yes," Cloud Dancer said softly. "As I prepare for my journey."

Later, after eating, Younger Wolf erected the scaffold. It was dark, but the night sky was illuminated by a fat moon, and the stars danced overhead in great numbers. After finishing the burial platform, Younger Wolf joined his grandfather beside the fire. As they warmed their hands, Cloud Dancer pointed out the many creatures formed by star groups. As he did, Younger Wolf recounted their stories.

"It's a heavy burden I've brought your brother," Cloud Dancer finally said. "I know you will help him as you can. When his feet turn from the medicine trail, try to guide him back. He has great power, Stone Wolf. Power comes from suffering, though, and he will know pain. Help him to see the joy that's there, Nisha."

"I will," Younger Wolf promised.

"When I'm gone, place my pipe and bow with me. Tie the tails of my ponies near my feet."

"Yes, Nam shim'. I know what to do."

"You alone will mourn for me. It's a hard thing, making the sad songs alone. You should have others to support your heartache. The spirits will be close, though, and they will visit your dreams and give you courage.

"Already I've given away most of my medicine. There is this single thing remaining. It's for you, and for the son who will one day follow you."

Now Cloud Dancer took from around his neck a rawhide thong. Tied to it was a hard black stone on which was etched a wolf's head.

"This is the greatest medicine I own now," the old man

explained. "I should perhaps have passed it to your father, to keep him safe. Now I give it to his son. Long ago Wolf spoke to me, Nisha. I have kept his image close that I might find courage when it was needed. Maybe Wolf will ease your sadness as you make the burial songs here in this distant place."

"Thank you, Ne' hyo," Younger Wolf said, taking the charm and gripping Cloud Dancer's wrinkled old hands.

"Ne' hyo?" the old one asked. "Father?"

"Truly you've been the one to give me birth, to show me the way. Sleep well, knowing I will see all these things done. My word is stone, and it will be kept."

"I know," Cloud Dancer said, bringing the young man near.

As the fire burned low, the skies overhead exploded with falling stars. Long white streaks painted the sky, and Younger Wolf gazed up in amazement.

Cloud Dancer saw nothing. He rested in the comfort of his thick robes, dreaming of Raven's Wing and the good days of their youth. He saw again Horse for the first time. And he watched Iron Wolf hang from the pole.

A great peace settled over him, and his shade departed the wrinkled skin and brittle bones below. Again he danced upon the clouds, singing buffalo songs and flying with Eagle and Hawk.

"Ah," he whispered, seeing the ponies waiting below where Hanging Road started the long climb into the heavens. "It's time for this last ride." And so the shade departed.

Younger Wolf set his grandfather on the scaffold as instructed. The young man cried and sang and tore his clothes.

"Nam shim', I never dreamed the pain would be so great!" Younger Wolf cried.

The Wolf continued the mourning songs, letting his sadness pour out of him. He knew to speak Cloud Dancer's name was to hold his ghost captive, to keep the shade earthbound.

Nam shim' was weary, Younger Wolf told himself. *He's earned this rest.*

The required three days came and went. Each night when Younger Wolf took to his bed a wonderful contentment grew inside him. His dreams flooded with remembered stories. The final night Wolf came.

"There's much to do," Wolf told him. "Be brave. Return to the People and seek your destiny."

Younger Wolf awoke with dawn. He walked to the top of Holy Mountain, passed the burial scaffold, and stared at the first golden trace of a new day.

"Man Above, thank you for new life," he chanted as he bared himself. "Thank you for the young ones who will make the People strong and for the old ones who led the way. Make our hearts pure, and keep our feet on the sacred path."

Sun bathed him in its warming light, and he cast aside his mourning gloom. He was young, and all the world spread out before him. Here was a beginning, not an end. He finished the dawn prayers and dressed himself. Then he packed his belongings and mounted his pony.

"I return to the People!" Younger Wolf howled. "Wolf, speed me homeward!"